JOY

Also by Jonathan Lee

Who is Mr Satoshi?

Jonathan Lee

JOY

WILLIAM HEINEMANN: LONDON

Published by William Heinemann 2012

2 4 6 8 10 9 7 5 3 1

First published in Great Britain in 2012 by
William Heinemann
Random House, 20 Vauxhall Bridge Road,
London SW1V 2SA

www.randomhouse.co.uk

Addresses for companies within The Random House Group Limited can be found at:
www.randomhouse.co.uk/offices.htm

The Random House Group Limited Reg. No. 954009

A CIP catalogue record for this book
is available from the British Library

ISBN 9780434020423

The Random House Group Limited supports The Forest Stewardship Council (FSC®), the leading international forest certification organisation. Our books carrying the FSC label are printed on FSC® certified paper. FSC is the only forest certification scheme endorsed by the leading environmental organisations, including Greenpeace. Our paper procurement policy can be found at:
www.randomhouse.co.uk/environment

Typeset in Perpetua by Palimpsest Book Production Limited,
Falkirk, Stirlingshire
Printed and bound by CPI Group
(UK) Ltd, Croydon, CR0 4YY

For Amy

‘Happiness is the light on the water. The water is cold and dark and deep.’

William Maxwell

Act One

DREAM LOGIC

. . . Do bats eat cats? . . .

Lewis Carroll, *Alice's Adventures in Wonderland*

1 a.m.

WHY IS the door ajar? The front door should not be ajar. 1 a.m. in Angel, fatigue buzzing in Joy's brain like a trapped fly, and the door is ajar. At a certain stage in your life every single thing gets complex.

She checks her BlackBerry. Nothing new. Not since she checked it in the taxi seconds ago. No email or voicemail or text message from Dennis to explain why the door isn't closed. As the black cab that delivered her here purrs out of earshot she runs a fingertip along the teeth of her house key, the house key which is now surplus to requirements, and feels sharp little judgements scissor through her thoughts: irresponsible – unsafe – did this once before – left it open when he went to bed – went to bed with late-night toast – Egyptian cotton and he snacks on toast! A tingling, achey sense of irritation takes over, a state which is exacerbated by the very next thing she notices: a pavement-laid present from Zorro, her neighbours' manifestly incontinent cocker spaniel, a halo of mocking moonlight round its rim.

Lately Joy's been making an effort to suppress expletives but she feels a few floating up her throat now, heat rising to her ears and eyes and lifting a hint of perfume from her skin. 'You're too hard on people,' her father used to say, and she's been working on that, being less hard on others and herself, has resolved to pass her last day alive in a wraithlike serene state wearing her most implausible heels and treating strangers to generous wide smiles, but now the door has been left ajar, one hour into this final Friday it is noticeably ajar (*wide open*, almost – yawning, *gaping*), and the Atkinsons are unacquainted with the term 'pooper scooper', and the air outside her home is a doggy fog of faecal stink, a stink made cheaply sweet by floral tones from her own perfume, and a deep frown is forming on her forehead which even the wispy silken fringe above and always-shining eyes below cannot make unserious.

She swallows down a *shit* and a *prick*, settles for muttering *tit* under her breath. Calling your husband a tit, watching the word become a tiny vanishing cloud in the January air – it's surprisingly soothing, actually. Already feeling a bit better, standing here. Less woozy. Less of the week's frustrations, its toast crumbs, clinging to her skin. After a period in the office like the one just gone – an absurdly stretched series of meetings flecked with stress and caffeine; sixteen hours of painstaking discussions about food law and what you're allowed to inject into chicken breasts; of not-so-furtive glances at her own breasts by men sporting splayed B cups under clammy jaundiced shirts – it feels like a fitting and blessedly succinct coda to her Thursday: *Tit*.

An animal is passing between parked cars, reddish in the sombre glow of street lamps. Above these street lamps Victorian rooftops wear aerials and a hook of moon hangs in darkness. She keeps her head tilted upward, acknowledging the fact she'll never see the moon again, determined to appreciate its abstract elegance, then hears the soft spinning of wheels – a bike light illuminating the fox's face – and reaches out for the doorknob, tired of lingering in the street, the leather of her handbag flirting with her skirt as she enters the deeper gloom of her home. Her objective for the coming hours? To avoid over-thinking, to execute her plan with methodical calm, a quality her employer, naively deaf to the inevitable acronym, recognises as a Tier 2 Soft Skill called Conscientious Office Conduct ('You need more COC,' say Joy's colleagues, 'the partners love COC'), but somehow it is not –

Cre-aack.

The sound – what is it? – makes her pause.

There is silence as the moment gathers itself in and then, again, *cre-aack*. Somewhere between a creak and a crack and it – wait – was that different?

Yes.

Different.

Punctuating the *cre-aacks* she hears a noise that carries more air, a . . . *woo-wooh*? Almost like the backing vocals on that Stones track, the one Peter likes, 'Sympathy for the Whatsit' – *woo-wooh* – 'Devil'. Odd. Frightening. Only she and Dennis use this front door; the bedsit above their split-level property has its own entrance. She hears nothing from up there, never does hear a thing. This weird mix of two sounds is coming from *her* kitchen, *her* lounge.

Cre-aack.

Woo-wooh.

Probably nothing . . . unless . . . probably nothing . . .

She slips off her shoes and begins to move, in slow motion, down the hall. The air, even with the front door open, is syrupy with central heating. Flushed, afraid, she acquires a highly inflamed sense of everything ahead of her: the dust-green rug, the shadowy walls, the balled fuzz under the radiator. It makes no sense to be scared. *Cre-aack*. So what if a psychopathic burglar jumps out and takes her life? He'd be saving her the trouble of taking it herself. *Woo-wooh*. But if he hurt her, only hurt her . . .

Hesitates. Thinks about turning back. Wake the Atkinsons up? Return with Zorro?

Then, in the midst of this hesitation, a surge of self-hate: come *on*; the approaching hours are about courage; the Atkinsons are *Latin teachers*; Zorro's only frightening feature is his bum.

One step, two steps, three. Beyond the kitchen doorway now so the sounds are coming, must be coming, from the lounge. She pauses again. Focuses. Calls out Dennis's name. It arrives as a thin rasp, a match flare in vast darkness. She considers unplugging the lamp. Make it a weapon. Where is her tennis racket? Her tennis racket is normally under the table which holds the lamp that in the absence of the tennis racket may be the best weapon she almost has to hand.

Cre-aack.

If she survives this encounter with the intruder, but nonetheless finds he has stolen her tennis racket, then she will miss her lunchtime tennis game.

Woo-wooh.

Which would be far from ideal, since it was due to be the final tennis game she would ever play, and with finality comes ceremony, and although Joy is on the whole an authentic and unpretentious person the trappings of tradition – the precedents, preambles, kind regards and chauffeured cars that constitute a career in law – have made ceremony a part of who she is. And she is Joy, still Joy, despite her doubts of late – the niggling sense that she's in the wrong skin, that even her feelings are borrowed or false.

With adrenalin blundering through her body she finds her attention snagging on the puzzlingly banal question of whether, if the burglar takes her racket (but not her life), she should cancel tennis with Christine, should instead do a final gym workout with her personal trainer at the office, but she had hoped to be in the company of a friend and she doesn't want in any way to disappoint a friend who has been as good to her as Chri—

—*A-AACK.*

Louder now, and the volume brings unexpected clarity, the two sounds less tangled than before, and Joy thinks, Joy concentrates on the present problem, and finds it funny, really quite funny, that one sound should seem so breathily human and the other more like a piece of furniture sort of creaking and – could it be –

She feels, somewhere in her fear-fogged brain, the silent glide of a fresh idea.

WOO-WOOH.

The noises. The noises are. The noises are surely something to do with Dennis's new fitness thing.

She exhales. *Jesus.* All well. *Christ.* Ever since he took his sabbatical from the university, Dennis – safe, dependable Dennis – has been spraining muscles in front of fitness DVDs, sipping drinks that have the consistency of wet cement. Older men. They should come with a health warning. He was young enough when she married him, but no one explained that the gap would seem somehow to grow, that for men past forty every year is a dog year bringing flatulence, paranoia, regular naps and vigorous barking up the wrong tree.

CRE-AACK.

Joy has formed the mental picture now: he will be doing some kind of ridiculous late-night breathy I-don't-look-forty-five *woo-wooh*-ing midlife-crisis tricep dip with his heels digging into the costly carpet and his weight leaning back on the *cre-acking* Jacobsen sofa and she can live with this scenario, she can tolerate it, for it is a scenario that does not involve her going to the trouble of unplugging the lamp and murdering a burglar hours before Hanger's attempt to present her with partnership, ask her to sign the papers, try to take from her a capital contribution, tie up her finances, make the business of dying as tricky as the business of living has, with relentless quiet persuasive force, proved itself to be. She wants to go as planned, in the afternoon, on the anniversary of the day her life most fully fell apart – with the least fuss possible, with hardly any fuss at all.

In the tempered darkness of the hallway a memory starts to flicker. Sees herself, and her nephew, in a tent. A tent pitched in the middle of the dining room in her previous home, hastily assembled on the carpet in the hope it would make the child's bottom lip wobble less. He was missing his parents, wasn't he; camping with friends in the South of France. As both babysitter and tent-pitcher she found she had a lot to learn. Designed to be a free-standing structure, it nonetheless needed improvised guy lines to remain in place – lengths of string tied to bookcases and table legs which went periodically slack as, excited by the torch beam

Joy rolled around the sloped walls, the child unsettled the fibreglass frame. 'Auntie Joy can I perform the torch?' he said . . . those words or words like them . . . a curious precision to his question. His role as a tiny god controlling light and dark made him giggle for a while but soon, growing bored, he asked for more cereal . . .

Motionless amid the continuing *cre-aacks* and *woo-woohs*, exchanging stares with a pair of discarded glasses on a console table, her own fear has segued into boredom. Nothing more dreadful than discomfort awaits her, the aggravation of debating unlocked doors and early-hours exercise. The cycle of fault-finding and grumbling is loathsome yet habitual, somewhere safe she can snuggle into. It's the same with Dennis's exercises, she supposes. He is doing them before bed because they whittle the day down to a manageable scale and shape. And there are worse habits, if she's honest. Take the guys at work, guys who'll probably sneer when she's gone (Couldn't cope! Too much pressure!). Guys like Peter, who likes to end each day gazing in that mirror by the burly Coke machine, his self-regard so intense you can almost *hear* it sometimes, a waveband fizz, a twiddle of excited static. At least Dennis doesn't do mirror-love, is merely trying – in a vaguely manly fashion – to keep fit.

As verdicts go, 'tit' was perhaps a little harsh.

Except that. This is strange. As she leans her head forward and relaxes her posture, to squint past the glasses and the table edge, into the submarine light of the lounge, something new comes into view. A scrap of material on the carpet, its colour muffled by shadow. And is it – are those – *knickers*?

Peter

If you walk down the same corridor for a hundred months, hearing the sound of tapped keys and sipped tea, you know something about what it is to feel safe. Even a man of my vision and experience would be forgiven for seeing the office as a sanctuary, a place where the wider world was both abbreviated and improved. Beautiful women. Pleasant furnishings. A range of enjoyable biscuits. Yes: Hanger, Slyde & Stein was – until last Friday – a kind of paradise. And I'll tell you the really troubling thing: when it all goes wrong, when colleagues start to do horrific things to each other and themselves, their appearance remains the same. As people become monsters, they grow no horns or extra eyes. No. They stay perfumed in pencil skirts.

What's that?

Oh, I see. Skirts, suits, kilts – I was making no distinction. I met my wife here, and more to the point Joy, so it's not as if I have anything against the firm's female contingent. Have you heard anything about Joy, by the way? About her condition?

Naturally. Say no more. I'm no stranger to confidentiality. Although, to let you in on a trade secret, at Hanger's confidentiality is considered against the public interest. Law firms are networks of people who want to digest every tiny private detail. The appetite for humiliation, for the finer points of a disgrace or discomfort, is particularly great. In 2008 a camera-phone clip was circulated of Nigel Beast dozing off at the Annual Partners' Dinner. His head bobbed over candlelit petits fours and in an instant his famously frenzied nasal hairs, full of the kinks and curls of gift ribbon, caught a naked flame. Like a firework, people said. Like a Catherine wheel. Your average bystander is pretty loose with their imagery, but you get the idea. Nigel Beast's charred button nose was the talk of the office for nearly a year. Committing an embarrassing act at Hanger's meant Doing A Beast right up until spring '09, when a woman in Real Estate was discovered naked, in the ladies' fourth-floor lavatories, allowing a gym-built reprographics assistant to snort coke off her clitoris. Nobody is amused by what happened to Joy, of course. That's not what I'm saying. But the incident is still public property. It is Beastgate, but with more blood; Clitgate, but with less blow. Good employees, like good citizens, are curious. They will talk it over. They will get their story straight.

I must admit, I was a little intrigued to meet you. You see all these American programmes – do you have a chaise longue, at least, in your normal office? – but you don't expect your firm to bolster its occupational health function like this. In the spirit of enquiry, I thought I'd be the first to come and say hello. Ease you in with someone senior and sane. I'm afraid Friday has left some employees, and of course Dennis, two snacks short of the full picnic.

Dennis.

No one's told you about Dennis?

They may have! They *may have*. You really are taking this privacy stuff seriously, aren't you?

For the avoidance of doubt, he's Joy's husband. The sort of boarding-school toff who belongs in Parliament, though in fact he's housed in another fossilised institution: academia. He was here when the incident happened, and – wink twice if I'm right – the firm has made your services available to him as well as us? They called him in yesterday to impart that news, and afterwards, stirring coffee in the kitchen pod, he cornered me with one of his monologue moans about the CCTV footage doing the rounds. I tried to explain to him that it's only natural people will be curious. Did she jump? Did she fall? Will she wake? I told him, these are all valid questions.

You're not sure they're valid, or you're not sure they should be asked?

But of course. Everything in life depends on your perspective. Even the most niche activities – using vegetables to sodomise a loved one, for example – depend on your perspective. But does unremitting relativism advance the argument? Does it get us any closer to understanding why the curt courgette, the prim parsnip, might be considered arousing?

Well, no, he didn't take my comment well. There was this tense little pause in which I fancied I could hear Damon Turner from Finance burping. Damon has a way of adopting a wide-set posture when he feels one coming, making it a kind of performance. But I ignored the quality of both the foreground pause and the background belch and continued in my attempts to explain to Dennis how a big law firm operates. This is one of my abilities, you see: effective expression under pressure. I sit in the Disputes team, but my specialism is on the insolvency side. Do you know any insolvency lawyers, at all?

No. I thought not. But, if you did, you'd know that we tend to live on the brink. I get involved just as companies are going under. Board members are panicking about the present, shredding the past and shielding their behinds from future claims. My job is to drill down into pressure, risk and the reservoirs of lies in which true testimony lurks. There's an addictive creativity to deceit – if you doctor one detail you'll alter the adjoining – so the reservoirs can be pretty deep, and interconnected.

When I got back to my room after the awkward exchange with Dennis, the lovely Jess, my trainee, was absent. That left me free to unzip Peter the Great and hang him under the desk. He likes to get some air, plus it helps me relax. One thing about sharing your office with a hottie: you can't always completely relax. When I'm on my own, and a little excitable, it's fun to see how many elastic bands I can hang off the big man. Personal best? One hundred and twenty-nine. The thick type from the third-floor cupboard, naturally. The other somewhat amusing thing is to hang bull clips from your ear lobes, but you can only really do that after five, when the secretarial bay has emptied.

Tiny Tony O turned up at my door. There's no public-school irony in his name. He's an official midget. In addition he is possibly gay and definitely Asian – an HR wet dream. He delivered one of his little interrogations, but I won't trouble you with it. I can see you're the type that's easily shocked and, anyway, that's not what we're here to talk about, is it?

Whatever I would *find helpful*? My word, you do have a strange turn of phrase. I think I'm going to call you Doctor Odd. Does that strike you as a satisfactory nickname? Doctor Odd?

Well I doubt Doctor Who was either, but the name still stuck. Here's roughly how it went. You'll have to excuse me, voices aren't my strongest suit.

Oi oi, Tony said, did I miss her? Shitty shitty bang bang, must have missed her. Was looking for the Jessmeister and all I get is you. Doing some work for me on the nuclear project, the one where the plant got security guards from the care home. Things are getting uggggg-ly. Keen for the Fox after work? I heard Sutcliffe's had the heave-ho. You didn't hear that from me. He hasn't heard yet. Who knew they'd sack more Seniors even with the good Joy Stephens in a coma? Man I miss those teeth around the place. Nothing better in life than a set of perfect teeth. You know they're getting some junior barristers in on secondment? Last thing we need is those wankstains in their wigs and shawls. I really need a holiday but I can't see how it's going to work with this nuclear thing exploding. My stomach, man, swear to God the canteen food's getting worse, the sausages, those sausages, tried to tell me it's firm policy to serve them medium rare! You've probably heard about Kennedy. You must have heard. Which reminds me, he reckons he's next in line. Personally I can't see Mental Brian letting him go while the tobacco thing's still smoking. God, Kennedy's a bell end. Un-be-lievable. I've got to admit, Peter, that tie works well with the shirt. If I don't get some time off soon *I'm* going to throw myself from some place tall. The fact is Jessmeister's a flirt and you're a married man. Have you heard anything about me, you know, my future?

I stayed silent.

Anyway, Tony said, how's it hanging?

An ironic question, Doctor Odd, if you consider what I had going on under the table.

Not bad, I said. Busy?

Intensively so, he said. By which he meant *I hope to avoid the next round of redundancies.*

Me too, I said. Bent over on Project Poultry, completely shafted. By which I meant *My discomfort is palpably sexual, my superiors want and desire me, I have a job for life.*

Then things got really tricksy. He asked how my wife, Christine, is coping. She and Joy are close friends, you see. We all started here together. The three of us were one happy family, until Friday. Happy in the dysfunctional way familiar to most families. And the thing that really irritated me with the questioning which followed was the implication that . . . Anyway, that's the sort of thing Tiny Tony said. An impressionist sketch, if you will. Luckily he got bored of quizzing me and took himself over to the secretarial bay, to watch Olivia Sullivan filling the colour Laserjet with paper. Everywhere you go there are girls leaning, bending, kneeling, crouching. If they let you out of this makeshift therapy room you should have a wander round. In every cubicle and stairwell, every kitchen pod and corner office, you'll see magnificent nipple-shadows through tight white shirts. As I said, it's a kind of paradise, until it's not.

Well, what I mean is this. Ever since what happened last Friday, it's become clear that a lot of people around here have something to hide. Particularly that Asian chap from the gym, and Barbara, and even Dennis – people who *may have* been asked if they'd like to partake in these . . . what would you call them?

Chats! Ha! I like you more and more, I really do, your humour is positively postmodern.

My point is that the three of them, if you watch the CCTV closely, are the first to move towards Joy's body. It has only been about two seconds since we heard her bones crack on the marble, but already they're weaving through the crowd to get close. And on the shaky black-and-white footage their heads are already down, as if they are not just afraid but ashamed.

Me? I was moving too, I suppose, champagne glass in hand. I was feeling very strange. I hadn't seen it coming. This was the day she was to make partner at Hanger, Slyde & Stein. Strong-willed, successful and modestly wealthy, arguably the most talented and attractive woman in the Disputes team. On a stone floor, no signs of life.

In the days since it happened I've heard people say that, even before the fall, there was a blankness in Joy's face. They say the thud was like a bass drum in their brains. They say her features looked vague and undefined. And they say she seemed like a broken chair, lying there: designer furniture for a cleaner to clear.

They make this stuff up, of course. But the more they put the experience into words, the more elaborate the shared memory becomes. This is a problem with Londoners, don't you think? We talk so much shit just to get along! We can't bear for our fears to recur in isolation, so we get together, we discuss. We endlessly analyse that unspoken something in her eyes as she addressed the crowd, the unfocused pain or purpose in the pupils – the fear of a wasted existence, or the thought of what to have for tea. Unceasing interpretation. Murmured consensus. Sonorous stories. No offence, but I find that kind of care-and-share psychological masturbation incredibly tedious. And that's coming from a man who is really rather fond of –

Do I think it was a suicide attempt? Personally, you mean?

I know for a fact she was working past midnight the night before. She had, in truth, been doing those hours for several weeks. She was overworked, but then we all are. So her personal life must have played a part. Sometimes when you come home from a day's hard slog it's a little thing at home – the sleeping pills are finished, the milk is off – that sends you lurching into some dark corner of yourself. It's a point I've thought about, naturally. The question of what happened when Joy finally got home in the early hours of that Friday. Something the police and press will do, I suppose. Try and reconstruct that last day from the beginning, right through to the 5 p.m. fall.

Is that clock right?

Really?

I've got to attend a Senior Associate Forum on how to bring more women into the partnership. Ones who aren't comatose, presumably. It's part of a diversity initiative.

No, I said *diversity*. The firm's new word for Shit We're All Men.

You're like my trainee, Doctor Odd. A non-stop note-taker. Except you appear to prefer loose-leaf. Personally, I'd worry about the pages getting muddled. I'm terribly keen on structure, you see.

Where do you stand on elastic bands?

1.10 a.m.

'WELL THIS must look bad, Joy-Joy. Not that I, well, I do to a degree – yes – admittedly this must look bad.'

Dennis says this standing, hands on hips, head slanted to see her.

'I mean to say, I recognise this is, somewhat, a departure from the norm.'

He says this naked, except for the socks on his feet, and the condom growing slack on his penis.

'She turned up, by she I mean, ha, this very lady still crouching . . . and we were just having an innocent drink to pass the time (it would have passed anyway, of course, goes without saying, gin and tonic and lime), but you'll excuse my imprecision in situations such as . . . and you'll see I have somewhat accidentally –'

'Tripped dick first into her vagina?'

His Adam's apple bounces to accommodate a swallow. 'You have a way with – always did – words, but what I was going to say is that we –'

Bastard. Not listening to this bastard. Standing there explaining with his buttocks clenched. Pouchy-buttocked bastard with his girl in the living room. Nubile girl on all fours on the Jacobsen – the Jacobsen! – shiny hair dangling down like the leaves of some nice thing, tree, nice young sun-soaked birch tree, and her buttocks all firm, faultless, poised beneath the bastard's pelvis and that yuk Jesus black banana thing lodged inside her and him still trying to explain as the condom yawns – harassed, wrinkled, ready for retirement.

'You are um,' he continues, 'staring at this lady's . . . rear, Joy-Joy, sorry, sorry, shouldn't keep using our real . . . Rude to stare, and all that, ha ha.'

Joy knows that all objects of desire look vile when the appetite's not right – oysters are gloopy hellish things when what you want is cake – but she's always considered dildos to be, from all angles, repulsive. The girl's litheness makes this one seem particularly sinister: a torture instrument, or the oversized valve on an inflatable doll. He's not into doll-sex yet, but interrupting an affair with plastic and air would be preferable to this distinctly human betrayal. She has never been a slave to the conventional rules of relationships, but witnessing this, the final phase of their dissolution, is making the furniture twitch and gleam to the cadence of her own pulse.

'Um, darling? Perhaps you could throw those knickers over and this girl can, perhaps, move from this position and cover her bottom?'

'I was comparing it to your bottom,' she says, adrenalin flowing into aggression. 'Looking fat, of late.'

'Fat?'

'Piggy,' she says.

'Right,' he says.

'A series of fleshy sacks.'

'Ha! Even with the workouts, you're saying.'

'Mini-buttocks and maxi-buttocks.'

'Hm.'

'Chinchilla-like.'

'Chinchilla, right, as in the –'

'Pet. Fleshy. Overgrown. Grey.'

'Yes. Yes I see. Comparing your husband to a crepuscular rodent, that's . . . I'm *sorry*,' he says.

The apology, modest though it is, satiates some of her hunger for a brawl. Objects are beginning to lose their liquid glint; settledness is returning to the room. Does she want to end five years of marriage with a fight? She's fond of him like you're fond of a well-worn dress – after the shimmer and tease have gone, it is fully yours, hem-stain and all, making up in familiarity what it lacks in fun – but now he goes and spoils even that, starts breaking the rules, makes her feel stupid, stupid for not linking the *cre-ack*ing and *woo-wooh*-ing to their secret Thursday-night habit, the ritual which while shameful is supposed to be (crucially) shared.

Still patiently poised on all fours, the dildoed guest breaks her silence. Her words come in the lulling voice of a pro who could do this in her sleep and occasionally probably does: 'Would you like to settle up now, guys, or is this part of the game?' In one smooth movement that stretches the skin across her ribs she unplugs the dildo to the tune of a disturbing slurp and takes a seat, knees together and feet apart, arms mirroring this coyness so the four thin limbs make a letter X.

'Darling,' Dennis says, ignoring the interruption, 'fancy a G and T, perhaps, as a peace offering, darling? We have chopped limes and ice over there.'

'On the Noguchi coffee table. Thank you for that. Thanks. You were supposed to cancel her, Dennis. Awful day, you know, hectic. I thought you were a burglar and then . . . I thought it was your exercise routine.'

'Well, in a way –'

'Don't.'

'It *is* Thursday night, you know. This is our night, Joy-Joy.'

'And if one of us wants to cancel?'

There is a pause, his eyes catch the melting ice, and as if softened by this sight his voice returns quieter than before. 'That's the rule. I know that's the rule. And I did try to cancel, once I knew you had all that stuff going on with your case. But I didn't get round to it this afternoon, Joy-Joy, I was distracted when you called to tell me, I met this amazingly well-known author on the train, you see, and buoyed by that the ideas were bobbing up furiously, *furiously*, the white heat of creation, it really was, just like when I'm going at the weights and an extra pocket of energy bursts inside my vein and I'm superhuman, super-Dennis, and then the agency said she was already on her way, and she turned up at the usual time, and –'

'Just get dressed,' she says wearily, and then, afflicted by etiquette, shifts her sightline to the girl. 'We're not normally like this.' Her words are met with a simple shrug, a gesture which, coming so soon after Dennis's wordy bid for vindication, seems like an act of astonishing expressive economy. His idle, spiralling style of speech was one of the quirks which once made him charmingly different, an old-school academic in a London full of one-dimensional professionals, dull polished types with cello voices and cello tans. His hesitation, like his floppy hair, made him human. But after nearly five years of marriage, with every eccentricity painstakingly examined, her husband seems – in tonight's light – less Hugh Grant and more village idiot.

The hired help is out the door with a purse full of fifties when the village idiot finally reappears. In the regularly revamped kitchen, amid the tomato-red fridge-freezer, the yellow-and-green check of the tablecloth, the still life of Valencian oranges hanging where the family snaps once were, he alone has no colour. His appearance of late is a source of irritation but also admiration – irritation at the lack of effort, and admiration for his indifference to flawlessness.

'Bed, darling?' he asks, nervously scratching a patch of stubble.

'No.'

'G and T?'

'That tonic stops me sleeping. As I've explained.'

'Wine?'

'. . . OK.'

'And may I enquire which of the delightful –'

'Red.'

Expensive wine, expensive fridge-freezer, expensive call girls. When, exactly, did they become such avid consumers? In her delicate freighted state the whole house feels like an erroneous impulse purchase, yet another mistake weighing heavy on her brain.

As he pours the Merlot she thinks about telling him. She has lain awake for so many weeks thinking how she might tell him. None of the imagined scenarios featured call girls, sex toys or arguments over chopped limes. They tended towards scented candles, fine food and classical music. She has even gone so far as to construct a fitting mental playlist, taking care to avoid morbid chords, *Psycho*-style screeches, violin bows quivering on the bridge. She wants to tell him, firmer than before, that she hasn't felt right for the last few years. Mornings begin with a sick dwindling deep inside. The route to the bathroom is an assault course littered with ghosts. The face that meets her in the mirror is less a face than a random arrangement of regrets – the nose that received an adulterous kiss, the eyes that have let so much slip from sight – and her lips have started to wrinkle and loosen as if in a dark daily fairy tale they're getting poisoned by the things they touch. With replenishing balm and special gloss she smoothes them down for the day ahead; can, through the effort of smiling, get them taut as the sheets on the guest-room bed. But by each evening they are loose once more, downturned. She wanted to tell him this one night, explain that her suicide would be a rational, muted thing, truer to her temperament than the lurching flash of normal life, but she has run out of time and, anyway, she knows what he would say. *Bullshit, Joy, you can't grant yourself a neat, aesthetic end. You won't be able to pat yourself on the back afterwards. You can't perfect death like it's a room in need of redecoration, or a memorandum in need of redrafting. You'll make* The Lawyer, *not* The Times. *Shakespeare isn't around to write a play about your last day. History won't miss you, but I will, and that's selfish.* He wouldn't put it so succinctly, but that's the gist of what he'd say.

'Drink some, Joy-Joy,' Dennis urges. He is wearing an expression that is childish, stubborn – and handsome, actually. 'It'll relax you, and really, really I am sorry about the girl.'

'She was very young.'

'Nonsense. Twenties, but no younger, no younger than others we've had here. Is it corked? It can make you ill if it's corked, I read today, did you know that, that it could actually make you *ill*?'

She shrugs, and finds that shrugging is less potent, somehow, when you're the one doing it.

'I'm sorry about the heat, boiler still on the blink, had the front door open to cool the place down and then forgot about it, the door, I suppose.'

'I'm tired,' she says, head tipping towards his chest.

'You work too hard,' he says, spreading his arms.

'Other women in the office have children to look after. They're lawyers *and* mothers.'

'Yes, well, granted, but I bet, if I was a betting man I'd bet, that they are either bad lawyers or bad mothers.'

'And what would that involve?' she asks, withdrawing from his sweater and the nest he's built around it. 'To be a bad mother?'

'Joy-Joy, come on, you work too hard.'

She works too hard. She has exhausted herself. She never questions Dennis's reluctance, of late, to have one-on-one sex with her. She never questions her own willingness to let his fantasies, kick-started at some seedy party they attended years ago, intrude on her sense of self-esteem. Before his sabbatical, he sometimes complained that the university campus carried a palpable smell of death, the scent of literary theorists deconstructing his favourite books, and it must be the same with her. She is thirty-three but scarcely there; he can smell the death in her hair; he needs someone who can bring life to their bedroom. She used to think traumas killed you off with the rudeness of pure force, a nail to the brain, but now she views her remembered failures as a degenerative disease, a slow tilting into shadow and cold. The dusky scent of death must account for the way Dennis rolls over instantly, feigns uninterrupted sleep, 'feigns' because she wakes each morning to find a clotted Kleenex on his side of the bed, and it is no big deal, she says to herself, both of the morning tissues and the Thursday girls, no big deal. Yet she has become sensitive to the tremors in the mattress. They feel, more and more, like the ground itself is shaking.

'Did you close the door on your way in, Joy-Joy? I'd better go and – why don't I? – I think I'd better go and close the door.'

She listens to his footsteps, and the hinge-creak, and wonders how young that girl was, and looks at her watch, and is reminded that Friday has already engulfed her, and when the latch goes and the first gulp of Merlot leaves her lips dry she turns to the sink and vomits.

Being sick on red wine: there are few things worse in the world. It makes you convulse, afterwards, with self-disgust.

Dennis

Now, Doctor, it all depends on whether you have the time, but the point at which I'd like to begin is the day before my wife's accident, and it involves some seeming irrelevancies, and to be honest I do sometimes mix the salient with the irrelevant (I often say to my students that they should interpret my speech as if it incorporates the footnotes and parentheses of which I'm so textually fond), but should you have the time it (what I propose to say about the Thursday) might be useful background to what happened to Joy-Joy on the Friday and, indeed, what is happening to me, to my own mind, on an ongoing basis, don't you agree?

Too kind, and I thank you, because yes, I think I will, I think I *will* have one. They may work their lawyers hard, but the facilities and refreshments are quite something, no?

So. Three times I've travelled in a first-class carriage. The first time, nothing happened,[1] whereas on the second occasion I found myself sitting next to (provided you erase the

[1] Not literally, of course – there's always *something* happening – but I mean to say nothing of particular significance occurred such as to warrant the time of a busy young expert in matters of the mind.

centre aisle from your mental floorplan) ex-Conservative Party leader William Hague. He'd recently returned to the backbenches,[2] and after silently weighing up possible conversational openers and intellectual entry points for two-thirds of the London to York journey, I finally spoke up.

Nice cap, I said. Baseball, is it?

Thanks, he said, peering over his newspaper. It is.

Now I can see what you're thinking, Doctor, and you're right, quite right, I did indeed want to ask him (William Hague) how it could be that only months after resigning as Conservative Party leader he was entirely alone on a train to York, no security guards or trusted circle of advisers, a briefcase on his knees that was not red and barely looked lockable, but – here is the issue – it was obvious from his taciturn response to my comment on the hat (the baseball cap) that he was still sore about the Labour landslide (2001), and for that reason, and moreover the scowl on his little bald face, I held back and, for the remaining portion of the voyage, pretended to sleep.

The third time I sat in first class, I was directly opposite a very famous female author. This was last Thursday, the day before my wife had her fall, hours before she came back from work and found the front door open and me inside with . . . well, hold your horses Dennis, first things – usually – first.

Now I trust you completely, it goes without saying that I do, and I see no conflict of interest, as my wife would say, none at all, in you having a fiduciary medic–patient type

[2] This was before his Foreign Secretary days in the well-spoken Clegg–Cameron government.

relationship with me on the one hand and on the other proverbial hand having a pay-my-bills type relationship with the esteemed legal eagles in whose branches we are currently nested, but, at the same time, I have always been careful not to betray any confidences, it has been a rule of my adult life to avoid betrayal, so I am going to call the famous literary author Beverley Badger. That is not a real name.[3] But despite it not being her real name you may find, if you are very clever, that the *nom de plume* I have created for said author gives, via an approximate anagram, a clue as to her most famous female character, and thereby – in a roundabout fashion – to her (i.e. the famous literary author's) true identity. That, I'm afraid, is the only clue you're getting.

Jolly good, very sensible, write that down in the old doctorly handwriting!

Not a . . . ?

But perhaps a PhD sort of thing?

Right, I see, I see, so your proper title would be, even though it makes you sound a little like a moustachioed member of local government . . . ?

Understood, Counsellor. Now my two previous first-class adventures were funded by the university, but not on this occasion. Even if a 240-mile round trip to watch a friend-slash-rival delivering a lecture to his postgrads were an expensible item under the university's English Literature

[3] By which I mean it is not *her* (the famous literary author's) real name. Clearly it could be *someone*'s real name, that someone being unrelated to the anecdote now in progress and having parents who must have had – yes – a couple of drinks on the night they named her.

Department Expenses Policy 2011 (sub-section: Travel; sub-sub-section: Rail; para 2(b)), which strictly it is probably not,[4] I have by virtue of my long-term sabbatical from the position of Senior Lecturer forsaken all remunerative privileges enshrined in that document. On the day I met Beverley Badger (not her real name, remember) I therefore had in my possession an Advance Purchase Off-Peak Super Saver Return ticket with reserved *standard*-class seating. Had I not boarded the train at Bristol Temple Meads and found my reserved seat occupied, and had it not been occupied by a woman with a friendly open face holding a small screaming baby to her vaguely veiled breast, and had it not been a surprisingly packed train for that time of the day, and had the conductor not subsequently checked my ticket as I stood attempting to read my book squashed between the constantly swinging toilet door and the incrementally slideable window, and had he not felt sorry for me given I had paid for a reserved seat and was nonetheless standing, well then I may not have ended up in first opposite Ms Badger.

I suppose I may partly have picked the seat opposite her because, in addition to it (the seat) being vacant, she (Ms Badger) was attractive in that refined unthreatening way unique to ample women. Given the choice, everyone will sit among the best gene pool they possibly can, don't you think? My wife's mother is a New Yorker and, on the one occasion Joy-Joy and I went over there together, ostensibly so Joy-Joy could try and make contact after years of estrangement, but in the final analysis simply to drink alcohol and

[4] Though it depends, frankly, on your interpretation of the phrase *exclusively for the purposes of departmental business*.

eat cupcakes, the gene pool on the Continental Airlines Boeing 767 was positively disheartening, Counsellor, really it was. But anyhow it was only when I saw that this ample woman in the first-class carriage was using a pencil to scribble in her book, and that the front cover of the book bore the words Uncorrected Proof Copy, that I realised quite who she was, quite how well my powers of seat selection had served me, and, learning from my William Hague experience, engaged her in a discussion of her own work (not, e.g. – though she did not wear one – her hat).

After a nervous start we talked excitedly, practically uninterruptedly, for the next hour and forty-five minutes.[5] The discussion was marvellous. She told me many fascinating things about the publishing industry, all of which I data-inputted into my excellent memory in case I should be able later to recycle them and thereby impress-slash-engage-slash-attract a literary agent to represent my own in-progress work of prose.

I beg your pardon, Counsellor?

Ah, quite! Yes. Yes that's exactly what I was suggesting. Nail on the proverbial head. On this sabbatical of mine I've

[5] I say *practically* because, thirty to thirty-five minutes into the journey, there was a pause as we considered the offerings of the refreshments trolley which a toadish teenager wheeled down the aisle (not the aisle you erased from your mental floorplan for the William Hague story – that was a different train on a different route on a different date – but similar in width and most other significant aisle-like qualities) and Beverley ended up going for a bottle of still water which, despite its brand name, is not manufactured in the Scottish Highlands, whilst I opted for a black coffee, which following a period of reflection I did not drink, as it looked thick with cancer-causing compounds.

been working on a non-fiction book about Shakespeare, but not as academic a work as my previous efforts, published as they were by the university's own press. No, this book is going to bring Shakespeare to the people. It will be a completely unpretentious, thoroughly engaging, heavily commercial homage to the Bard.

It *does* sound interesting, doesn't it? I thank you kindly for your feedback. And whilst I wouldn't presume to guess at your own views on such matters, my personal feeling (and my wife would disagree, and I make a qualified exception for Ms Badger's opus) is that fiction these days always, sometimes, occasionally lacks a certain truth, no? Can fail to represent faithfully the way that, in real life, the absurd jostles with the serious, the dirty with the clean, the excessive with the spare, to create a disconcerting but amusing overtangled mess? Now of course with some kinds of fiction – novels told in the first person, say – everyone suspects they are reading disguised memoir. And with memoir, of course, everyone automatically suspects it's pure fiction. But when I suggest I have a preference for non-fiction, for the messy truth, it's not really memoir I'm talking about, indeed I've always found the very notion of memoir a touch egotistical – must be an arrogant literary form, don't you think, to have both the words me *and* moi in it? – no, when I talk about the delights of non-fiction I'm ruminating on biography, historical account, literary criticism. A work on Shakespeare which is meandering, populist and *true*: this is the thing to which I devote my days.

Is it difficult? To . . . concentrate, you mean?

Of course . . . I . . . just a little. The book has been rather on the backburner, in the last few days.

Nonsense! No, I'm fine, absolutely fine, thank you for your concern.

Well it is simply difficult, that's all, to get going with the book, when previously, as I tried to finish a sentence or a paragraph, there would be my wife calling on the phone, or having a box of kitchenware delivered to the door, or – late at night – rattling her keys in the lock. There were these external forces nagging at the walls of my concentration, generating a certain creative pressure within, a protective power to keep the world away, and now there is none of that, none at all, and I have all the time I could want to think about my book (or to consider the sell-by dates of particular products) and yet I find my sentences lying so flat on the page, crushed by the very qualities Lawrence saw as murderous to good free verse, showing *too much* finish, too much polish – no impulsive edginess, no insurgent naked throb, no lived experience poking through – and the half-heard rumours and refrigerated items that make up my days, these too seem to hold a certain settled loneliness I cannot explain.

For instance the rumour that my wife tried to commit suicide, Counsellor. I know my wife, I have been married to her for almost five years, and she may have had low points during her troublesome twenties, there was the business with her nephew as perhaps you've heard, but those (those difficulties) are all in the past now, and I believe she (my wife) had come to terms with prior mistakes and misfortunes, and quite frankly the suggestion, the suggestion that she wouldn't have left a note, that someone as meticulous and imaginative as her would not have left her husband a note, or that she would try and do it (the suicide) in such a public forum – in front of me and, what, two hundred colleagues? – quite ridiculous. Indeed I find the notion of suicide *essentially* ridiculous, frightening in its retrospective glitz, its sidestepping of death, its avoidance of the natural albeit chilling erosions of old age, its greedy grasping for the philosophical advantage, and what if you regretted it, what if Celan, Plath, Woolf, Hemingway, Gertler, Berryman, Pavese, Van Gogh, Rothko, Pollock regretted it all when the trigger clicked or the pills kicked in, as any sensible person surely would? No, not Joy-Joy; the suicide theory is ridiculous. But then, of course, it is only as ridiculous as some of the conspiracy theories.

Why would I mind expanding? It's not as if you are one of the lie-spreaders, Counsellor.

I'm thinking, for example, of the one (the conspiracy theory) involving her friend Christine. The suggestion that Christine, simply because she hasn't yet visited Joy in hospital, may have been involved with Friday's events, the events following my first-class journey with B. Badger. I find that to be tremendously unlikely. Whereas Christine's husband Peter, another Hanger employee, a bitter West Country bully who's tinkered hard with his accent and clothes while remaining ultimately uncouth, I will certainly be keeping a close eye on him, and if I get so much as a hint that he somehow . . . well, yes, I rule nothing out.

9.15 a.m.

THE OFFICES of Hanger, Slyde & Stein stand between two thinner glass towers: the Icarus Hotel on the left, and on the right a financial institution said to outsource its recruitment function to a Shoreditch model agency. The twenty-somethings from the financial institution, all skinny ties and left-swerving hair, like to lunch at the pan-Asian restaurant in the Icarus. The restaurant is called Pacific Lust. It is full of tight-skirted staff and fortune cookies that contain advice like *The secret to getting ahead is getting started*.

Joy is tired. As she walks through the courtyard she takes a glance around her. It will be a relief to see it no more, this place so lavishly landscaped that it appears as a pixelated version of itself. A strange, simple relief. Like unleashing a yawn. She yawns. She decides that Dennis should ditch Shakespeare and write about the underrated art of yawning – the elastic release, the wash of air. That bespectacled American whose novel six people gave her for Christmas (six times 500-odd pages made him the most prolific author on her shelves, she calculated), he'd managed to capture the varied banality of everyday life, the different shades of boredom at home and at work, the freedom which comes from the yawn itself. Why can't Dennis turn his hand to a project like that? *Yawn: a Great American Novel*. She'd buy it in a flash, but Dennis won't write it; he's rarely great, never American, and too often on the wrong side of yawns to feel comfortable trumpeting their virtues. There is also his distrust of modern fiction, a strangely tireless scepticism she considers while circling the firm's award-winning Japanese water garden, its six bamboo fountains and staggered granite stepping stones. She worries about him. An unpaid sabbatical seems so out of character. People like Peter love taking chances – risk is their religion – but not Dennis, never Dennis, his fear of failure is total, like baldness, or a purge. He must be unhappy. Her unhappiness must be making him unhappy. It's what every book and song and film is about: happiness and unhappiness. He could write about that, she supposes, though there's probably not much more to say on the subject.

When she first walked through this courtyard ten years ago (a decade! how has it happened?) she decided, actually *decided*, that she would either love the job or loathe it. She has always avoided at all costs the grey decisionless centre ground on which so many build their lives, the sorts of people who waste your time with *I don't knows* and *Up to yous*. There are only so many *Up to yous* a life, let alone a conversation, can survive. Vehemence of feeling, colour, precarious energy – however flawed a person is she'll forgive them all sins if these traits show through. In the '87 election, she amused her parents by urging them to 'vote Thatcher – more lively than Kinnock'. And when old enough to cast her own vote, she opted for Blair because he seemed more memorable than Major. The thing she cannot stand is lack of vitality and when, as a graduate of Oxford PPE and a now defunct London law school, she arrived for the first day of her training contract, she renewed her Life Promise not to be passive, not to be dull. If Joy did fortune cookies, they'd say *Make it a miracle, make it a disaster, but for fuck's sake don't get stuck in the middle*. She realises this needs some work.

Her mother was very into sayings, Life Promises and joss sticks, but never prepared Joy for the complexity of everyday adulthood. No one did, actually. Was it unreasonable to expect a heads-up on issues such as the fact she might start work and find she loved it *and* loathed it, the precise state of fence-sitting flux she'd always wanted to avoid? It seemed obvious that workers would sometimes be riven by these contraries, but not that they could – as she now does – find them enshrined in every dotted i, every filed email, every late-night machine-made mocha. The biggest surprise of her career has been that no one else finds her ambivalent attitude to office life disturbing. Many, in fact, appear positively impressed by it. Joy cares and doesn't care, has – as her ten-year appraisal put it – the fierce, relaxed intelligence that engenders confidence and calm. She started in 2001 with forty-eight other trainees; she is one of only four in her intake still here. Joy, Clare, Christine, Peter. Clare Harris-Bowler's partnership potential evaporated when the firm's Head of Public Relations & Brand Strategy found her enjoying class-A sex in the fourth-floor ladies' loos (why didn't they lock the door? Why not the spacious privacy of the disabled toilet? Nobody knows). The woman now cruelly known as Coke-Cunt Clare, or Triple C in polite company, is unlikely to stick around after her bonus this June. Christine's primary goal is pregnancy, not partnership, and her husband Peter – well, he's as complicated as Joy. There is a loose electricity in his eyes, some wiring gone wrong, and she doesn't know which way he will go.

She walks through the revolving door and steps into one of six glass lifts. A flustered trainee carrying boxes marked CONFIDENTIAL is already inside. Without taking his hands off the cardboard he gives her a three-fingered wave and they float silently skywards. She wonders how long it will take to get Project Poultry in order, an irritatingly drawn-out libel case in which she acts for a huge frozen-food manufacturer suing a gang of pamphleteers. She will need to leave soon after lunch. She is not hanging around for the crap that comes after.

'See you later,' Joy says, exiting on the fourth floor.

'Oh,' Flustered says, doors closing on his words. 'I'll hopefully make it to your speech at five but I've a doctor's thing at –'

People, Joy has noticed, are a lot sicker than you imagine.

Here it is, her end of the corridor. She takes a breath and lingers in the doorway to her office and says to Alfredo and Barbara in loud ringing happy church-bell tones, 'Good morning!'

In moments like this she feels like a poorly paid actress in an advert for antidepressants. They look up with flummoxed expressions, but are nonetheless well versed in office theatre. Their smiles arrive. They return the greeting. They place emphasis on the *Good*. One of the Employment partners in Christine's team wanders by and he smiles too, a Gordon Brown lip-caught-on-gum kind of smile. The trouble with Gordon was he seemed too clever to be human. A whiff of robot fuel about him. At least you can imagine

Cameron winking at waitresses, or sticking cashews up his nose to make Samantha laugh.

Suddenly hungry, Joy walks onward to her desk. She sinks into her swivel chair. It squeaks. The chair has been getting creakier for the past six months, its slow demise into second-rateness dovetailing with that of the giant yucca in the corner, and now the creak is – yes – a squeak. If it's yours you shouldn't let it wither or whimper away, better to chuck it out completely, yet each day the Admin column of her doggedly updated To-do List becomes a catalogue of deferred decisions. The chair remains unoiled and the yucca stays tucked too far from the light. As she settles her handbag on the floor these minor tasks and all the unresolved jobs back home drip through her thoughts, soft droplets from an unfixed tap. Less and less of them are her concern.

Maybe she'll make time to go down to the river today. She used to make a point of getting some air down there each night, before catching her taxi home. A stroll through midnight drizzle along the Thames, it always seemed to relax her. Found it slackened her pulse to see how each passer-by on the Embankment looked tired, half vanished in their City clothes, a bland suaveness to their bodies, whereas distant tourists on the South Bank side stood out against the spent bulk of London's buildings – the Tate Modern, the National Theatre – seemed, in their choice of bright jackets and umbrellas, to want to master the place. There was something soothing about wandering beneath the twisted branches of plane trees, inclining and recovering in the breeze, about staring into those hesitant brackets of light the London Eye left on the water, starry around the edges from lit Lambeth windows . . . Yes, maybe later, a quick look at the Thames.

Samir

IT IS a fear bigger than heart attack. That is what they say in *Testomuscles Monthly*. Heart attack is only number four. Number three is bleeding nipples. A common effect of the friction between T-shirt and skin. Number two is to soil yourself in motion. Very bad. Very very bad. But it is not number one. No. The number-one fear London Marathon runners have is being defeated by someone in silly fancy dress. Homer Simpson. Michael Jackson. Giant panda. Something of this nature. Right there on the line in front of your family and friends.

Me? I do not worry about the panda pipping me at the post. Fancy dress is brilliant. Most people like a fancy-dressed person do you not think?

Yes. In the restaurant my father works in I once saw a bald man in a nappy. I believe from the message written on his forehead he was soon to be married. His expression was extremely serious as he ate his Jalfrezi. Sweaty red . . . Thoughtful . . . But he was dressed as a big baby and that meant every other customer gave him a smile. Something like a nappy can sort of pull the world towards you.

Runny . . . ?

Running! Yes. I am running the marathon in April. I am excited to finally do it. Afraid as well. But excited.

Afraid of the possibility of . . . the chance shall we say of number two.

I was thinking of the *Testomuscles Monthly* numbering! But you have understood. The distance and jolting upsets the body cycle. It is not uncommon to see a runner who has the backs of his legs . . . streaked. I do not expect to have supporters there on the day but I would rather strangers and the BBC did not see me in a streaked condition. Everything is on the cameras these days. Even Miss Stephens up on the thing. Viewing platform. Last Friday. Down in the staff gym we have a camera too and sometimes I need to stand on the weights bench to clean the lens. Father says privacy is a thing of the past. I think this accounts for his surveillance of Mrs Hasan in Flat 15.

Even without any physical jolting I have since Friday suffered from . . . They are small difficulties but it is necessary to develop tactics. The Astaire for example. Or the Full Bollywood. But in a marathon context these strategies will be less brilliant.

Oh the Astaire is a foot tap. During the movements. To help disguise unwanted noises. The wall between the basement bathroom and the staff gym – it is exclusively staff we deal with in the gym – is very fragile you see. An extremely nice bathroom. Very very clean. But the wall is fragile.

The Bollywood? That is for very desperate situations. You are a man of refinement. Of taste. I admire your jacket very much. I would not think you have much need for the Bollywood. Even I do not usually have much need for it.

But some things I did on Friday have put stress on my thoughts. My stomach . . .

Would you mind. Would it be rude. If I moved your cup slightly in this direction?

You are very kind. Thank you very much. And look how the sunlight shines on it now! Brilliant.

The biggest effect is on my work schedule. It cannot easily accommodate the additional toilet commitments. Miss Stephens would tolerate me having to step out for a few minutes during her session but some other fee-earners I train do not. I just joined the Facebook to try and . . . I joined and was looking at it when Miss Stephens came in that Friday for her session. Unprofessional I realise to be looking at such things not working. Less than brilliant. But the point I make is Miss Stephens was the type who did not mind. Came in and chatted to me. Did a very fast run. She is a very very determined lady. And kind. Kind and pretty everyone says. Often Jack would smile at her when she came in all nice and neat in her Lycra. Turn to me and whisper between his white Australian teeth What do you think of those legs Sam Man? He calls me Sam Man. And I would agree that they had a good shape. And he would say with something new going on in his eyes Gotta love those spacewoman tights mate. He calls them spacewoman tights. And whatever I said to him next was usually sort of lost.

I like Jack because he makes good choices. Good choices of words and good decisions like to have the alcohol-gel dispenser installed. Jack is not manager of the HS&S staff gym for nothing. Did you know he drives a motorbike?

Yes. I would too. Look at Miss Stephens's legs. Broken now. In plaster when I visited. No one had written on the casts as they did if you were popular at school. Friends. Girlfriends. People of that nature.

You mean . . . ?

No. I have not got one. I did have a meal with a Fitness First lady. Once. But it all went very wrong.

She asked what I thought of her outfit. I paused. Questions of this type are delicate. I tried to decline to answer. But she said Go on have a view. Therefore I told her the red shoes were brilliant . . . And she said Go on. And I said But perhaps clash a little with the pink skirt.

Very very bad idea. But I cannot lie at all. It is not in my nature.

She proceeded to make a number of observations about me. For example that I seem to blow my nose loudly and for prolonged periods. Which I do. To keep the airways clear. I hate the idea of eating without the airways clear. She gave me her verdict on these nasal habits but also my shirt my childhood and my face. In response to each of these observations I tried to put forward suggestions of skirt colours that might better suit her red shoes. An attempt to be helpful. Make the feedback what Jack calls constructive. The exchange ended with her saying very loudly If you like red so much have some of this. Which is when the house wine struck me. It was followed by a barrage of wholemeal rolls. As I exited she was attempting to launch breadsticks in the manner of javelins.

The worst thing. The worst thing was the disappointment from Jack. The next morning he said You've gotta show the woman who's boss mate. I explained she was definitely boss and I had shown this fairly clearly. He said I was way beyond help. Suggested I was better off avoiding sensitive ladies of this nature. Never date a raw prawn he said. Which provoked a very good discussion about sushi . . . I do not know if you know but Jack has brilliant knowledge of international cuisine. In Sylhet sushi was not on offer but I have had it once in London. I ate it with my hands but the waiters were kind. They did not laugh.

I watched a brilliant science-fiction film once. Everyone ate out of neat little boxes like Japanese people sometimes do. Compartments for all the different types of food. So the rice and meat did not touch. A brilliant idea. And people did not speak. They had microphones sewn near to their hearts and the beat of the heart told other people all they needed to know. Whether the person was excited or bored. Happy or sad. It made the communication simple but true. Every wall and floor was made of clear sparkling glass. That is probably the feature I like best about Hanger, Slyde & Stein. About working in the gym for the busy HS&S staff. The glass. And if you had those microphones at the marathon it would be a brilliant orchestra of drums do you not think? Thirty-six thousand hearts beating at the same time.

Although I suppose the fitter pulses would be slower.

Although even if they were not in time each heart would yes would sound at the finish line tired but very very happy do you think?

I find exercise makes you tired but happy. You feel sort of I want to say joined up afterwards. Less like a toy someone not concentrating has created. A bit there with too much glue. Another bit loose or lopsided . . .

I have been working on my triceps and quads and I am happy with the progress. Jack indicated recently that I have a chicken neck. This was a blow but I am working out a routine to correct the issue. It is not just about health it is also how do I say this about becoming someone who has an appearance pleasant enough to . . . to put people into a kind of tunnel.

Yes. So they smile. So they are interested in your words.

Apart from early morning and lunchtime barely any of the lawyers make it down to the gym so often it is only me. Behind the desk there is a lot of time to consider problems and the possible corrections. I have found an old issue of *Testomuscles Monthly* which contains isometric and head-harness routines under the heading Collar Girth Is What You Need. Quite simple exercises. For example it was suggesting you do this. If you perhaps copy what I am doing with my head here. Tilting it. A bit that way. Left. That is it. Very very good. All the way round. And then next –

Of course! My apologies. Sometimes I get carried . . . Anyway your neck appears very strong. I appreciate your time. Do not let me waste it.

Microphones on your heart! What was the name of that film? I think about it sometimes. There is no natural light in the basement we work in. Not like up here. You are down in your dreams and memories a lot. Very small scenes that dissolve or get interrupted. We were eating phuchka. Phuchka and fresh mango on huge cushions around the tiny television. All of us huddled watching this film. Me Mother Father and my older brothers. Mosquitoes humming in the distance. It was a brilliant night. Whole months before Father and I moved to England. Tower Hamlets to be precise.

Father used to love films. When he was a teacher in Sylhet and my mother was around. But now after he gets back from the restaurant he prefers watching sport. And Mrs Hasan. Through the window.

Do you know which film I mean?

Perhaps I am lucky. If people could hear my heart they would know I was hiding something. They would hear how fast it has been beating since Friday.

9.20 a.m.

AMONG THE usual pile of post on her desk is a stampless envelope containing a greeting card. The front of the card is a print of that famous seventies photograph of a blonde in tennis whites walking away from the camera, teasing her skirt up over bare buttocks. The thing that draws Joy's eye is the way the buttocks themselves have their own shy tan, as if the girl has, in her pre-photograph life, always (who wouldn't?) spent summers without pants. It's a detail that gives the image its own beautiful fakery, and gets her thinking again about last night's call girl. Her mind provides an unpleasant image of the girl on all fours, and from there Joy's thoughts tumble and roll into her relationship with Dennis, their unsatisfactory sex life, the sordid little routines you enter into as a means of pleasing others, of saying sorry . . .

With vigilant eyes she absorbs the message inside the card – *Congratulations again, darling Joyous. You'll make a very clever partner. Cheeky drink after I beat you at tennis, if you like* – and the three lower-case kisses that always trail Christine's signature 'C'. The word 'cheeky' is underlined, and like the surplus 'darling' Joy senses in this narrative touch a somewhat affected emphasis, as if Christine is, consciously or not, mimicking the flamboyant tone of one of their more eccentric colleagues at Hanger's. The handwriting, by contrast, is anything but flamboyant; uniform, small, devoid of the runaway passion which shows itself on a page (and in a life) as a kind of negligence. On their first day at Hanger's Joy and her future friend began chatting as they queued up to autograph a piece of paper headed 'Trainee Security Pass Registration'. Christine went first, and with 'Reid' sitting two rows above 'Stephens' in the surname grid the differences in penmanship were immediately apparent. Christine's scratchy straight lines made the gleams and curves of Joy's own strokes look both elaborate and impetuous. It was a baffling mystery how Christine, like so many of the other signatories, managed to stay within her allotted space. Joy's curlicues needed room to breathe and be beautiful; to scale them down would entail a sacrifice of style.

Staying still to minimise seat-squeaks Joy studies the card for a few more moments, flicking from buttocks to message, message to buttocks. After ten years of friendship Christine's thrifty characters still seem startlingly understated, but since that Hanger, Slyde & Stein induction day Joy has noticed in the author a skilfulness that does not translate into her text. As a tennis pair, Joy possesses the more shapely presence on court – the vulnerable beauty of her body; the glossy intelligent momentum; the embarrassing tendency, after exhausting stalemates in the depths of each set, to win every tie-breaker – and this winning charm seems to have been equally effective in the context of the office, where it is Joy who has garnered most professional praise. Yet in life, in real life, Christine's plainness seems to contain and even sustain a clinching prudence. Joy envies the functional manner in which her friend can shrug off bad days, weeks, years. If a bout of flu sinks her holiday, or a pigeon's liquid discharge ruins her best dress, she half smiles and says, Oh well. Her technique of unshowy indecision and rueful resignation – hair often only half straightened for morning meetings; non-committal notes of advice emailed with pre-emptive apologies – seems to leave her able to greet Fate's dizzier modulations with a passive grace. Like a building designed to withstand an earthquake, Christine bounces and sways minutely on impact before settling back down to the simple business of being. It is an undemanding brand of happiness, but it might explain why, among all the girls in their intake, it was Christine who managed to marry Peter. Joy's noticed that beautiful men, by dint of their inevitable arrogance, often prefer submissive women.

'Oh well,' she mutters, closing the card with a final insincere flick, wishing – as she so often wishes – that she meant exactly what she said. Must tell her about the mislaid racket; going to have to cancel that match. She picks up the phone, dials her friend's extension and hears Christine's voicemail kick in – *Hi, I'm not here to take your call right now, so . . . um . . . sorry about that* – which makes Joy laugh every time. Maybe she's in a meeting; will try her again in a bit.

'Somebody in a good mood!' Alfredo says, arriving through the door frame with Barbara close behind. 'Must mean promotion today and holiday tomorrow!'

'I suppose it must, Alfredo.'

'Remind me where you go? Maldive again?'

'I forget the coordinates. Somewhere exotic but intimate.'

'Ha ha! Keep them guessing, eh? Go wild! No BlackBerry reception! Throw caution out the window!'

Joy smiles. Alfredo is the firm's only male secretary, here

on a year's secondment from the Milan office. In furtherance of a favour owed to his Italian boss she's been helping to facilitate his integration into the Disputes team. As if to answer initial question marks over his sexuality, Alfredo's integration to date has involved him sleeping with no fewer than three female paralegals. Work-wise, he is supposed to be shadowing Barbara. But Barbara – who has the distinction of being the firm's oldest secretary, cheating retirement year after year – isn't keen on being shadowed, and neither are the other senior PAs. They can't work out why Joy doesn't have him sent back. They say Alfredo sits at his work station doodling all day. They say he has minimal proficiency in Word, Excel, Outlook and English. They also say, more interestingly, that he once appeared on the cover of *Dentists' Dreams*, a niche US publication aimed at the 18–30 second-tier medical role-play market, wearing only dental floss. And although they are very probably right on all counts, Joy doesn't care. Alfredo is *lively*.

'So who you have for the eleven o'clock handover meeting? Mental Brian?'

'And one other,' Joy says, seeing Barbara's angry, folded face over Alfredo's shoulder. 'To be confirmed. How is your day shaping up?'

'More training on the Visualise software trial. They tell me when I have quiet time I must think up data relevant to the office and represent, as practice.'

'Good, you can make it your thing. The firm is pushing for PAs to pick up skills like that. Text-saving diagrams, graphs and charts.'

Barbara finally loses patience and barges past Alfredo, her throat a bundle of cords unravelling. 'Lemme do my job,' she says, waving the walking stick she never seems to need. 'Go make some pasta swirls with your Etch A Sketch.'

'Thanks Barbara!' he says, backing out of the room. 'Fingers cross for this afternoon presentation, Joy!'

'You've got to get rid of the Italian,' Barbara confides for the sixth or seventh time this week. 'With the Italian around it's impossible to concentrate.'

But, left alone with Barbara, Joy finds the opposite to be true: her concentration drifts as soon as he is *not* around. She hears the odd word her secretary says but in the main is remembering her morning back at home, the sex they had, the sex which – for the first time since summer – was free of third-party involvement. She initiated it and, perhaps feeling some residual arousal from the call girl (why does she shy from the word 'prostitute'?), Dennis too seemed hungry and hurried.

'Won't you be late for work?'

'One day won't hurt.'

There is sex where his eyes are fixed on your eyes and you're told you are a wonderful person who makes excellent flapjacks – the kind of cosy lovemaking Joy's sister, when they still spoke, used to call Making Flapjack Sex – and then there is the Eating Flapjack Sex, where it's messy but you're hungry and greedy to finish each other and the talk is about cocks and cum and the buzz in your veins seems to be sourced from somewhere other than you. This morning's sex started as the bloodbuzz kind. She took delight in suspense, in feeling the orgasm slowly building into itself, a string inside her going tight, took delight in this even as the day ahead started slanting into her thoughts like a too-bright light. But, as with most anticipated ecstasies, the orgasm did not arrive as imagined. A brief shiver of pleasure, no more than that.

'Are you OK?' Dennis said in the dark.

As he dozed she piled papers on the dresser. He would think nothing of them until he heard the news and then he'd be grateful, she hoped, that their financial arrangements were all laid out and the address book was to hand.

She took a long shower slumped against the tiles. The damp curtain kept clinging to her skin like a pensioner in a Pac-a-Mac (her sister once accused her of being addicted to odd similes and metaphors; the whimsy of resemblance, escapades into untruth) and she thought about the way the inquests she'd looked up on the Internet ended with the coroner saying *She took her own life while the balance of her mind was disturbed*. When you studied the detail you found the woman had cancer, and her dad was a paedophile, and someone had set fire to her cat, and her husband had fucked half the women north of Watford. Was it really her, this woman, who was disturbed? The question had stayed with Joy as she got dressed and kissed Dennis goodbye and rode the escalator underground until, leaning into the windrush of the tunnel, waiting for the southbound train to come crashing through the dark, she saw a mother and child standing safely nearby, well behind the yellow line, and noticed the boy's proudly pinned *I'm Six* badge, and with the machine roar rising to an insane level, pitched to oblivion bliss, defined by its own derangement, a new thought came: so then, that's what six looks like.

'Are you listening?' says Barbara, banging the floor with her stick.

Barbara

WELL I'LL come to your point – I've got things to say on your point – but first lemme make *my* point: Alfredo does nothing all day and gets paid close to what I get paid. Now I'm sorry what I'm doing will cause him trouble, but does that seem fair to you? Does it? Have a shortbread and mull it over. They're free. I'll pass you a shortbread. Reach over and grab a shortbread for heaven's sake, you're closer than I am.

Pardon me?

Yes, yes, that's all very sensible and whatnot, but how easily can you compare qualifications in – let's say – *your* industry? Because yours is a strange role, isn't it? That's just how it seems to me. It seems to me the two things you do most of are listening to people and writing down the things they say. Now, some deaf souls excepted, we can all listen. And, some ethnic souls excepted, we can all write. If you want the truth, I've been pretty good at listening and writing for the best part of seventy years – if it's the still water you're after it's the blue cap not the pink – but I wouldn't think of setting myself up in business based on those two skills alone, would I? If I were you then personally, despite the exams, I would have become a proper doctor.

I said the *blue* top. Blue means blue. Although Alfredo would probably tell you blue was yellow and pink was whatschacall, *magenta*. Lemme tell you, he gets everything wrong. The other day he says to me, he says, Barbara, maybe you're right, but let me play devil's advocado. Advocado! It's none of my concern. I just sigh. I tell him I didn't know the devil was a vegetarian but that it makes perfect sense. But really, I mean really, I'm trying to help him by explaining London-office house style isn't the same as Milan-office house style – the margins and spacing are different, but also the letter templates – and he's mumbling on about the devil's five a day? Our boss is in a coma, her husband's gone crazy, the Halfwit Peter Carlisle's sliming around like nothing's happened, and Alfredo decides it's time to mumble out his pagan vegan values? It's not right. His team supervisor back in Milan – Mario, Luigi, Mussolini, whathaveyou – he also happens to be Alfredo's cousin, did you know that? Do you think that might help explain how he came to get a secondment to this office? He's pulling all these strings like a whatschacall, *puppeteer*, and claiming the same salary as someone – me – who next week will have been at the firm forty years. I sometimes think, I honestly do, I think to myself that if something happened, if he was sent back to Milan, if something unpredicted happened to make him leave, if someone took a step for the benefit of the majority, John Stuart Mill and whatnot – even PAs *read* – then the girls in my section, without Alfredo's assistance, would have less work to do, not more.

Hmm?

Do I see? Of course I see. Nothing wrong with my eyes. I have a proper doctor for my eyes.

Because he's a slippery little sponger, that's what I'm saying. He actually *generates* work for us. We have to check his things and correct and cover for him. And he repays us how? By taking overtime which is rightfully ours, is rightfully for those of us who have airfares or whathaveyou to save for – want to get to New York – spend a day or two with Jackie – can I? – damn right I can't. It's none of my concern but, even with Joy gone, I'm flat out. By rights if someone like the Halfwit Peter Carlisle needs secretarial cover then Alfredo should do it. But not even the Halfwit Peter Carlisle would put up with that. It's like the only English Alfredo knows is clichés and sayings. Useless. It's as if he's learnt English from a dodgy thesaurus.

Well that's just another word for *thesaurus*, isn't it?

You want to know what I think? Lemme tell you what I think. I think the world's got too clever. I'm not saying you want to be surrounded by the unschooled. Back in New York I got married to one of the unschooled. English girl in America – I should have attracted the refined! Nothing refined about my husband. He thought oregano was a Japanese art. Food was supposed to be his first love! When he died I had the girls round for biscuits and singing. I'm saying it seems to me that it's better not to be one of these highly striving reflective types. I've worked thirty-nine years here, forty next Monday, and I've seen a few. They're too intelligent to enjoy a meal or a walk. It's none of my concern.

Eat one, won't you? The Bulgarian says if you don't eat the biscuits they'll cut the quota next year. That's in no one's interest. I moved back to home turf because my sister Sarah married an Irish lawyer. I wanted to be close to her. She's gone, he's gone, but I've still got the job he fixed me here. The shortbread is one of the only things that hasn't gone and I'll be damned if I'm going to lose it without a fight.

Why are you looking so afraid? What's wrong with you?

And that's exactly it. How do you think Joy got herself so exhausted she fainted over those railings? We're all tired. Health and Safety manager got the axe – always support staff who get it, I don't have a view – but what about the partners giving her eighty hours of work each week? Now they'd say she could have asked for help. But don't they have a responsibility, knowing about her high-strivingness, not to leave her working all night on client notes and pitches and presentations and possible settlement agreements and press releases and disclosure thingies? If I on occasion have a difficulty, like maybe my eyesight's not what it was, a difficulty like I can't read the partner's mark-up so well, I ask Liz or one of the other girls for help. Used to, at least, before they got too busy covering up Alfredo's messings. But I'm not Joy, am I? I don't equate happiness with being a genius at every little thing.

If you want to be heard, you'd better speak up.

I don't know where you've been for the last five minutes, but we *are* talking about my feelings on the accident. As an alleged listener I thought you might be familiar with it, the concept of there being more than one way to tackle a topic.

Fine.

Fine.

Well she's gorgeous, as you'll have heard. Lovely face and figure. Her skin smooth and her hair silky blonde. It's not natural, the hair colour, but that's none of my concern. She has a very Manhattan sort of look to her.

She's half-American, did you know that? Half-Manhattan, anyway, which my cousin Jackie would tell you isn't quite the same thing. Joy grew up there till she was seven or eight. The one thing we've got in common, me and her: both of us spending time on that side of the pond, with our parents, in different decades. I was dragged there by parents with itchy feet. My parents had itchy feet before the phrase was invented! Must have been a lovely child. I have a daughter of my own, you know – high-flyer – and she was a lovely child. Being good-looking causes issues. I should know. You think I always had a face for radio and a stick to walk? I forgot to mention the tea. Also free, as you probably guessed. The tea's good. The coffee not so much. These solicitors have it so strong. But the real trouble comes from being good-looking *and* intelligent. I came back in '71 as a young widow. Michael had died in Vietnam. Straight away I moved up a class thanks to Fancy Irish and his connections. I met all these women who were too clever and pretty to be happy. I knew when I was lucky. I kept my limits in mind. Not them. Someone like Joy looks in the mirror, or at her grades, or curriculum whatschacall, or the queue of men around the block, and she gets used to this feeling that the whole world is just garnish on herself. And when she started to realise that wasn't true, that events weren't just parsley sprinkled round her plate, she felt she'd failed. Had this very detailed picture of success in her head, see. Once you've got that, you might as well give up on life. I'm not saying ignorance is bliss – I was married to Ignorance and it was about as close to bliss as a poke in the throat – but a certain unthinkingness when it comes to the overall architecture?

That has its benefits. Ask Alfredo. Have the last shortbread. Someone like Joy's got her own logic going on. I'll have that shortbread and if you call 5999 the pantry'll bring you more.

Helpful to drill . . . ?

Truth is, and no hurt intended, I find your approach to this occupational health business a little strange. Not a great deal but a little. I'm struggling to take what you say at face value. Your questions are open to several interpretations. They devalue the facts. Your aftershave, while we're on the subject, is borderline ridiculous. You spin the line about how you want to find out how I truly feel, but have you considered whether that particular approach will bring a smile to anyone's face – *anyone's* – given all that's happened? You remind me in a sense of Fancy Irish. He was always quoting bits of books to me. Your kind of height. Athletic. Adept at trampoline. Did it in the garden while reciting poetry. You know, as a party piece. Had a taste for dips. Just a preference but a strongish sort of one. Hummus, tzatziki, sour cream and chive. Couldn't get enough of them. Had a whatschacall, spring in his step. Lemme tell you, it was all very curious. You could be his twin, if you lost a few pounds.

Hmm?

Ha! Well, I can see you're obsessed with examples, so . . . give me a second . . .

How about this. Joy would get me to get Jackie to send this Manhattan face cream over. Cream Joy's mother always used on her when she was a girl, she said. A wealthy woman, Joy's mother. One of these types that never worked, from what I can gather. Actress. Exaggerator. It's by La Prairie and contains real platinum. Costs one thousand US for maybe a 1.5-ounce jar. A thousand dollars! For a face! It's none of my concern, but is it fair that after years of scrimping I'm still unable to buy a flight to visit my cousin Jackie, Jackie who I've only seen once since Michael died, her little family I've never met, and every quarter Joy can buy a face cream for the price of two air tickets? My church takes that in donations in maybe a year. Religion is out of fashion. Fashionable to disparage religious happiness. But why kick away our crutches? It's like Joy expected to find a tub of cream big enough to smooth out the whole world. Basically I organise her life, so – yes – I know how much she earns. Do you know? You probably know. Into six figures, plus a 10 to 20 per cent bonus, health care, income protection insurance, life assurance, the whole package. Yes. With that sort of money we could get a new crucifix and go electric with the lanterns. Joy could go back to New York whenever she wants. Doesn't, of course. The young these days have no respect for roots. I don't begrudge anyone anything, but is it the real world? Give a poor old man a fish and bread? He'll thank you and sleep content. Give one of this generation a fish and bread? They'll want a range of full-colour cookbooks and a non-stick pan.

We all know the things we want and the things we need, don't we? What I want is my section back how it was, and what I need is a flight to Newark or Kennedy. It's all connected. And so really Alfredo is none of my concern, but I'm not having it, which is why – between you and me – I've had no choice but to check his online workspace. The workspaces are public unless you make them private. Italians don't know what private is. Look at Berlusconi! I'm too busy to care. I've emailed myself the last few documents he's created. I'll bring the printouts next time, the ones I'm going to take to Debs. It's obvious he's doing no work. Joy took some liking to him, I don't know why. Maybe they had some kind of flirtation. It's none of my business. With her out of the picture for a while or forever, the Italian's protection racket is full of holes. It's not fair on me and the rest of the PAs. They might not mind but I do. I mind on their behalf. We're working all day and he's just making nonsense pictures – they're not even funny – on the Visualise software. He does that all day and then takes overtime! But enough. Enough of that. I need to ask you a . . . a personal question. Can I do that? Can I ask you a personal question?

One thing I really need an outside view on. Move that plate out the way and come close. Lean in a little more and listen. Come on, closer. I know these talks are about me doing the talking, but I ask this one thing of you, and one thing only. It's a theoretical, but an important one. So tell me. Tell me the truth. Tell me no lies. British Airways: would you trust them?

10.35 a.m.

HER FIRST bedroom in Britain had a window overlooking a pond. The pond was the best bit of the garden. In summer, with the lawn sprinkler sending out lazy spray in overlapping arcs, she and her sister would find frogs in the spangled grass, catch them with breathy giggles, hold them in quivering cupped palms and throw those frogs up into the sun, down into the splash, each daring the other to stand further back, throw further still, until the squelch of flesh on stone made Joy run to Mum. The pond was the last thing she saw as the curtains closed. It would stay with her in sleep, expanding outwards unstoppably, Joy dreaming the whole house was surrounded by water, full of dolphins and whales, always dipping and bobbing in the same places. You sensed their movements before they came, like inflections in a well-known voice.

She has found half an hour before her eleven o'clock handover meeting, so she has come here, to take one last look at the Thames, the stretch of river that once relaxed her. Mess is a thing she's always hated – she passes a woman hugging a baby who smells of, of . . . vanilla? – the horror of the frogs was not so much their death as the mess it left, and the whole point of the meeting, the pretence of going on holiday, is to enable Joy to leave things in good order. Today the river's glassy green surface holds one of those land–water vessels they dress up as ducks. Tourists, ducks, but no whales – not like five years ago, when the bottlenose got lost in London. Drifting in the wake of the mechanical duck is a thing that, if you squint, looks like a tennis ball or an apple, but is actually a swollen plastic bag. The Millennium Bridge is above, two joined hammocks hanging, Londoners swaying in nets.

Nets, tennis balls, Christine. Competitors and friends ever since starting as trainees, but it is a remembered day in 2005 that is the curious glue between them. Joy got three Wimbledon tickets from the pro at her club: Ladies semi-finals. Her five-year-old nephew was charged at full price, which seemed steep, but there was no choice but to take him along.

'Can I want a mini tennis ball, Auntie Joy?'

In the intimate pink of memory the child's questioning face is intense.

'Yes sweetie,' Joy replied, holding his hand on the walk down the hill.

'Offal please.'

And then she told Christine, didn't she, that he meant 'official'. His friend Alfie had an Official Wimbledon Tennis Ball Key Ring. Christine nodded; Joy remembers the motion of her complicated hat. It was supposed to supply the drama her features needed, but it looked a little sci-fi with her sharp ears either side.

'So, Joyous,' Christine said, probably then, probably on the hill. 'Is this Dennis chap a keeper?'

'Not sure there's enough.'

'He seems clever and charming.'

'That's a euphemism for old and average-looking.'

'It's a euphemism for what's-wrong-with-you,' said Christine, with the pouty smile that is her only form of firmness. 'And anyway, me and Peter, it may look perfect but punching above my weight has caused its own issues.'

Joy did not give the empty compliment protocol required – *it's Peter who's punching above his weight!* – for even then her life was overfull with lies, the big and the small all intertwined. Instead she said, 'What issues?'

'Oh, you've seen how it is in the office. I think he gets a lot of attention, and we married young. I worry his head will get turned. Do you see his head getting turned?'

She came up with a line by way of reply. 'Show me' – yes, this was it – 'Show me a man whose head doesn't turn, and I'll show you Stephen Hawking.'

With bad taste smothering the truth they passed giggling through the gates, found a food stall and a merchandise stall, bought strawberries and a key ring, circled Centre Court. Her nephew nibbled at the fruit delicately, sharing the neatness of his mother's features. It was day three of four in Joy's first full-time babysitting assignment – her sister would return from France tomorrow – and the prospect of handing him back filled her with grief and relief.

How lucky were they? Their seats were only three rows back, metres from the umpire's futuristic chair. All they needed was for the child, perched on a cushion that needed constant rearrangement, to settle down and enjoy the show.

'I thought the key ring would keep him busy,' Joy said,

might have said, over his head. 'But he seems to have wrapped it in tinfoil and put it in the cold bag.'

'Safest place, Joyous. He's a boy genius.'

'Can I want a fridge manet, Auntie Joy?'

'Sweetie, you've already had a toy, and you're thinking of *mag*net. Do you consider this normal,' she said with an upward glance, 'this obsession with products?'

'Oh yeah,' Christine said. 'My niece, she's massively into merchandising.'

Too quick for them, seeing hair dangling over the back of Row B, he tugged on the tighter of two pigtails.

'So sorry,' Joy said as the middle-aged victim revolved, 'he's very into hair.'

'If you can't control it,' the woman replied, 'you shouldn't bring it.'

And Joy, glancing at Christine to confirm that this meant war, pointed out that his particular area of interest was impossibly outdated hairstyles and the humourless women who wore them. Even the child looked pleased with the put-down, chuckling with a brilliantly exaggerated shoulder shake he'd seen somewhere. Despite the brutal weather, his small compact body was padded with layers of designer pastels, the idea being that the more clothes he had on, the more easily his appearance could be revised after inevitable accidents with food and drink. The three of them were, in this moment, their own empire: the boy on his cushion was king, they were his loyal subjects, and no one would dare invade their world.

'Ah, here she is, the Lovely One.'

Maria Sharapova stepped off the corner catwalk and into Wimbledon sunshine, fine-spun fingers raised to the crowd, racket pack swinging from an elegant shoulder. A suited man standing by the service-speed machine stopped whispering into his walkie-talkie. Hooded TV cameras swung towards her legs. The crowd made tiny transitional gasps and sighs.

'Bitch,' said Christine over the clapping.

'Utter bitch,' said Joy.

They looked for corroboration from the child, but he stared straight ahead, oblivious, in love with another woman.

If there were points for style, style and only style, Sharapova would have taken the first set. Instead, her fine ground strokes tensed in the tiebreak and – as the match reports have since corroborated – she gifted Venus a break when the second set had barely begun. The American looked powerful, focused, a sure thing for the final, and on that day Maria looked lovely but ineffectual, bending forward like a ballerina, twirling her racket, giving the ball a sensual pat, straightening her back. She sprang into the air with liquid grace, knickers flashing at the precise moment the ball slapped the tape, a strong sharp noise like flesh on flesh. The yellow orb shivered in mid-air for a charged second, then dropped on the server's side of the net.

'Another break point,' Christine said, then mumbled something about defending the title.

Joy's nephew interrupted. 'Can I go toilet, Auntie Joy?'

She ran fingers through the soft blonde quills of his hair, but otherwise ignored him. 'Sis says he's going through a false-alarm phase,' she explained to Christine, Little Miss Pigtail hushing them as a second serve looped and blurred. It landed deep, didn't it, but Maria's opponent saw it coming, had a gift of foresight Joy lacked that day, dispatching the ball with a brutal shovelled backhand.

'Toilet,' he said, louder than before, and as the crowd clattered its hands she became convinced of his need, told Christine they'd be back in a minute. The light was slimmer now, the sky cross-hatched by wet slate clouds. They ascended the cement staircase, a thin grey break in the patchwork of people, finding a path framed by exposed beams and posts.

Joy selected – always would select – a cubicle that was clean, its surfaces wiped and swept, helping the child unzip his flies.

After waiting a while, inventing some mental escapade to amuse herself, she said, 'I thought you needed the toilet.'

'Yes.'

'But not now.'

'Yes.'

Nothing came. She was in a toilet cubicle on her annual leave, staring at miniature Nikes, the criss-cross laces suncream-stained. Waving his hands under the tap, she gave the feeble wrists a sadistic squeeze.

Hands dry or nearly dry, they stepped back out into the corridor of concrete, and it was at this moment, definitely, now or a second later, that the rain came, heavy on eaves, thoughts of tennis bombed away. Joy heard distant seats flicking into upright positions. They were alone in their shelter, hidden by the curves and grades of the stadium's bowl, but not for long. A crocodile of giggling schoolgirls headed their way – tanned girls, pale girls in tight jeans, girls with wet ponytails that wagged in the eel-skin light, their voices ringing with boys' names, with celebrity news, insults and compliments they'd heard their parents use.

She picked up the child and heard his plea: 'Toilet please.'

'No way. We've just been, and you didn't need to go.'

'Now I'm very ready,' he said, eyes so close she could discern the blurs, swirls and shadows between the pupils and the whites.

There was by now a long unstable queue for the ladies' lavatory, a capricious line of sun hats and flip-flops and the occasional glittering cagoule. Joy carried the child to the back, the whorl of her ear tickled warm by his breath.

The stretch of queue behind them became longer and thinner, and the tract in front became short and fat. People sighed and looked at their watches. They tried to create the illusion of progress by taking small sidesteps, turning to one another to discuss the weather, stroking the dials of portable radios to tune in to predictions, warnings, odds. Joy looked down and saw the child jigging his leg, a sure sign he couldn't hold on much longer. She checked her BlackBerry, tenderly stroked the rollerball to keep up to speed. There were only seven or eight people ahead of them now. She flicked through two more emails, sighed when she saw she was wanted in the office tonight. Would he wet himself before their turn? Could the day get any worse? The feeling of something brushing against her ankle seemed to offer answers: it would be him, tugging for attention, about to tell her it was too late. But a glance down revealed the disturbance to be something else entirely: chocolate wrappers sparring with her shoe. She tilted her head right, then left. She swallowed, repeated the movements. The child was gone.

Joy did a clumsy pirouette on twisted knees, found herself facing the belt buckle of the person behind, a twenty-something guy in a pinstriped suit who must have been waiting with his wife or mother because otherwise he wouldn't be in the queue for the ladies, would he? She gave him an apologetic smile. She was not yet beyond self-consciousness.

'Sorry, the Rugrat seems to have given me the slip. Did you see him?'

She was worried by the tremor in her own voice; it alerted her to a panic she didn't know she felt.

The man said something like, 'No, I mean, I didn't even see . . .' but by now Joy was pacing up and down the line, crouching, looking through legs. The shower was softening and people heading back to the court made clicking noises with their tongues as she ducked at their feet. She felt a thickening of the spit in her mouth, strings of mucus whipping around the larynx as she took short shallow breaths, but still she thought this was a symptom of unreal anxiety. Easy, with fear wobbling your eyeballs, to overlook a small child. He wasn't an explorer. He liked colouring and eating and wrapping key rings in tinfoil. He wouldn't take himself far.

Not until Joy had skidded up and down the length of the queue twice, made herself tall, made herself small, did all sense of decorum leave her. She shouted the child's name, rearranging the rhythm, changing the pitch. A strange liquid heat crept up her spine. This was it, she was being punished: the childish violence with which she held his wrists too tight under the tap; her objection to the sickly squidgy language of preening mothers; the way that on day two, in the tent in the dining room, she gave him cereal for all three meals. She was tired, just tired! Shapes slinking into her field of vision; astonished faces appearing; mouths whispering in the rain.

What's this?

Tell me.

What's she doing?

Tell me why.

They spoke like children, confined to basic phrases. She turned away, ran into the toilet, banged the doors of cubicles, re-emerged bawling louder. She only had to keep him safe for four days. Her feet beat concrete, useless heels clipping her own grey shadow, taking her to sets of steps and gratings and fire escapes, vantage points from which she looked up, looked down, cursing passers-by. Four days. Four days! Didn't recognise this wild flailing version of herself. Didn't recognise the ground beneath her feet, strangely hard, the way it seemed to rise and fall.

Why; why; what's this why?

When she returned to the chocolate-bar litter for a third or was it fourth time the onlookers were waiting and they began to speak once more. A boy? they said. Child, missing, here? And Joy, suddenly sitting, her weight on one arm, veins pulsing, breathing with awful desperate effort, heard them fully for the first time.

'Gone,' she said, and her own vowel came out long, G*o*ne, a weird airy drone that seemed to expand and surround her. Tears came at the thought – he was gone – they came all at once like the shakes in her hands.

Soon a human circle had formed around her, growing wider, more volatile, with time. And then Christine finally arrived, looking embarrassed. She asked strangers questions as she was pulled into the middle, her voice flat and enquiring. Only when she saw Joy's crumpled figure did the hat come off.

Looking out at the river now, at the bridge strung across the Thames, Joy remembers Christine's mouth, opening and closing, miming some useless message. No words came but Joy could see in the slow, slow parting of the lips that Christine knew, had knowledge that for an instant could not be processed or expressed. A child had been lost. This was the simple, unspeakable truth. Lost; she'd lost him; he was lost.

For Joy it is the moment her friend's lips parted, the point at which the mouth filled with pink light, that comes back to her most often – a space, an instinctive blink, a soft little pause in the flow of her days and nights.

Peter

AROUND MY eyes? I'm not surprised. They're regularly considered to be among my Top Ten Physical Features but in the days since Joy tried to top herself I've barely had time to sleep or eat. Been too busy on Project Poultry. It's a hospital pass of the highest order. Granted, Joy's the one in hospital, but who's left clearing up the chicken shit? The Meat Musketeers have been on TV. Claim to have received a leaked document proving their statements about the company were true all along. Maybe you saw the coverage? Egg on their face, as the *Sun* put it. Manufacturer didn't give a cluck what went into your nuggets. Board accused of Fowl Play.

The share price has sunk through the floor. Jessica and I are left billing sixteen-hour days. Outside my practice specialism to begin with, more a favour than a career case, but now it looks like it might become an insolvency job after all. Mental Brian has declared himself happy for me to take the lead in Joy's continuing absence.

Here are the papers, he said yesterday. It's all I've got.

Lawyer-speak for It's off my desk! It's off my desk! It's off my fucking desk!

When he'd gone I raised my eyes up over the piles and piles of marbled-cardboard files and saw the lovely Jessica coming towards me, all shiny shoulders and mammoth eager eyes. I love the bright panelled light at Hanger's. It's more real than daylight, somehow, and people never seem as golden as they do here. With that pendant dancing on her collarbone she looked a bit like Joy used to when we first started, before a decade of late nights gave her beauty an edge of feasibility.

Hi Pete, Jess said, for I allow her to call me Pete. Sorry, got stuck in a big meeting with that partner who's got the cat with Aids.

Gray? I said.

No.

Harris?

Yeah, Harris, exactly. He's really nice, she said. He was asking for my views on stuff. Says he really values input from all strata of the team.

She will learn. She will learn to distrust those partners who encourage participation. She will learn that they recruited you for your three-dimensional character, free-thinking nature and abilities at team sports precisely so that they could spend subsequent years making you flat, subservient, and too busy to play. She will learn that the constant email surveys to assess employees' work/life balance are covertly linked to the redundancy consultation process, ensuring that those who feel overworked will soon have ample time to devote to their families. She will learn that every six months a Health and Safety officer will have you fill out a Workstation Assessment Form, and that if you remark in the Any Additional Comments box on your chronic all-nighter-induced back pain, screenburn or borderline blindness they will punish you by replacing your adjustable swivel chair with a catastrophically humiliating exercise ball. She will learn that everyone has a film-script idea or a promising design for a new kind of duck-down duvet, but that everyone ultimately lacks the energy to write the words or pluck the duck. She will learn that the senior PAs know a thing or two about fear, the small words and gestures that send terror bubbles bobbing through the blood (*He wants to see you now; I'll schedule the meeting for midnight*), and as such are some of the most revered professionals in the firm. She will learn, in addition, that when a piece of privileged and confidential information falls into your lap, e.g. re the long-term health of a superior's British shorthair, you store it up, hold it back from everyone, even from your magnificent mentor of a supervisor, and wait to trade the secret in an appropriate forum, for instance the annual Hanger, Slyde & Stein Christmas Party, hoping to receive in exchange some lascivious factual nugget about the sex life of your secretary.

I told Jessica she should have the confidence to wear more skirts. Then I got her to spend the next six hours producing a set of lever-arch files containing all available press clippings re the Project Poultry matter. This was in case the client's Head of Legal wanted a set of said files to impress his Marketing Director. The opposite transpired, alas, so when the files were finished and properly indexed I told her with a hint of regret (but not so much that it would compromise the hierarchy of our professional relations) that she was going to have to spend the evening dismantling the files and feeding the contents through the shredding machine.

You see, the client has, since the press leak, insisted that all its advisers amend their engagement letters to include an undertaking in relation to the production and destruction of non-essential hard-copy materials. Studying the look on her face, I sensed that I was making progress towards achieving the exact blend of unpleasantness and confidence that all women find irresistible.

In the end both Jess and I were here till three in the morning, hence the tired eyes today. I'll need to stay late again tonight. I always stay late, Doctor Odd, and what you need to appreciate is that a day in office life is too varied and rich to waste working. Productivity is for the night.

What does my wife think of what? The antisocial hours?

She works here too, don't forget. And anyway she's not around at the moment. Stomped off to her parents' house at the end of last week, and she's been stubbornly silent ever since. Sometimes she likes to have, and I'm quoting her here, *space to think*. I'm pretty sure some minor mix-up with her cousin Isabel is to blame. Isabel is in advertising. She exaggerates for a living. Just as a new brand of tampon is transfigured into a lifestyle choice for active mothers, so a friendly pat of encouragement or support from an interested in-law becomes, to the advertising executive, a serious attempt at intercourse. And I suppose Christine, through my voicemails, now knows about Joy's condition. Another reason she might want space to think.

Time to try a different line of communication. Just before catching the lift up here I took a reassuring glance in the gents' mirror, tightened my double Windsor, and phoned Mother.

Peter? she said. Peter, it's your mother.

There was no point in explaining to Mum that *I* called *her*, no point at all.

Now, Peter, she said, I'm sorry to bother you, God knows you've got your own troubles.

I told her patiently that I don't have any troubles, and then we got into this time-draining exchange about light bulbs, with her saying she has to change one for the first time since Dad took to bed, that these days he barely knows if he's alive or dead, but that he might nonetheless appreciate a visit and a bulb-change, and me asking if she needed bayonet or screw cap, and her saying she wasn't fussy either way. Mother's technique is to hold up a problem, ask for help, and then show complete disinterest in the solution.

I told her I'd try to drop round next weekend and then I cut quickly to the meat of the conversation, namely whether dear old Mum could give me the phone number for Christine's parents. My mother and my wife's mother are quite friendly, you see, liking nothing more than to exchange monologues re primetime soap series and my perfectly good marriage.

Mother ended the conversation by saying she'd try to find the torch and, following that, the address book. She hung up. I was left listening to the dial tone, the sort of sound that's simple but – within that simplicity – complex. Do you know what I'm getting at? Formless yet intricate, not unlike a nightmare. The sort of experience I have every time I bump into Dennis.

Indicating? He's a deeply hostile and unpredictable presence, that's what I'm indicating. Has some irrational grudge against me.

No, no reasons spring to mind. Although . . . Well, in

the spirit of full and frank disclosure, I *have* slept with his wife. As in, we had a bit of history before he turned up. But even if he knew about that bygone business, which he doesn't, would it be an excuse to treat me so aggressively? Everyone sleeps with everyone sooner or later. Has he not heard the one about monkeys, typewriters and his beloved *Hamlet*?

Me. Joy. My fine wife Christine. We all started as trainees together. It was . . . 2001, must have been. It was a great time. The time, perhaps, when I was happiest. Fifty of us sharp young things, picked from the country's best universities to work at Hanger, Slyde & Stein. Quite a few of our crop did non-law degrees. I was History. Joy was PPE. Christine, I'm embarrassed to say, was Geography. And the thing we had in common was that, approaching our finals, each of us suffered one of those Oh Fuck moments where you panic about your place in the world. So you go to the Careers Office and the big-pored buffoon behind the desk, who's never managed to find a career for himself, confirms what you've always suspected. For the middle classes, there are only six available professions: investment banking, accountancy, civil service, journalism, teaching and law. If you like money but can't do maths, that leaves law. We were fifty twenty-somethings who liked money but couldn't do maths, so we did law. If it didn't work out, so what? For me, getting a job here *meant* something, *announced* something. It said: Peter Carlisle hasn't spent a decade working his arse off in piss-poor Swindon state schools for nothing.

On the first day of the induction period, after the slapstick mimes of cheek-kissing, vice-like handshakes and insistent eye contact – the sort of public-school pantomime the rest of them had rehearsed in the womb – a hard core of around ten of us decamped to the pub. And we pretty much stayed in that pub for the next two years of our training contracts. For hundreds of hours at a time we were elsewhere, of course – proofreading into the early hours, making ourselves sick on too-strong coffee, becoming acquainted with palpitations and panic attacks. But, as the working days became increasingly open-ended and our non-law friends fell away, the Wig and Pen was the barracks to which we returned, waiting, tense and wild, BlackBerries at the ready, for our next call to war.

I started sleeping with Christine straight away. There were several other interesting girls in our intake, but none with whom I could speak so easily about the onset of Dad's dementia, or my plans for world domination. At expensive team-building dinners laid on by the firm we found our lives overlapped. There was the relative pauperdom of our backgrounds (for all we knew back then, broth, jus and foam were the new Stock, Aitken and Waterman); there was Oliver Stone's *Wall Street* being our favourite film. It didn't matter when it transpired that Christine considered the whole movie to be a critique of eighties capitalist culture – we were married by then – the point was it spoke to both of us. Our personalities kept chiming in these small ways. And because Joy was sexily aloof, it took longer for me to chime with her.

She was chatty on the first day of the induction, but some time thereafter must have read a dangerous little book about the rules for bedding men and decided, I suppose, to play hard-to-get. She didn't become part of the hard-core Wig and Pen club, and even when she did join us for Wednesday drinks, or Thursday drinks, or Friday drinks, she was attentive only to Christine or her other closeish girlfriends. On the very few occasions she submitted to being chatted up by David or Harry at the bar she seemed always to be standing like some exquisite flamingo, one foot slipped out of its expensive shoe, painted toes touching polished wood panels, a look of disinterested beauty about her. She was unthinkingly elegant. That's one of the reasons why, a few years later, when her nephew went missing, I could tell it had a profound effect on her. She was still elegant, but the elegance was so effortful all of a sudden, as if some part of her character had fallen out of place. At that time Joy started, increasingly, to resemble her sister, a woman I'd met once or twice and now saw on television, jumpy but tearless, jolting out words: Instinct tells us our son is alive; If you know anything please come forward; He'll be back for his birthday, we know he will. A policeman usually sat next to her, holding up an identikit picture of a suspect. The face looked like everyone and no one: chin of a TV presenter; hair every middle-aged man has; lips you've seen somewhere, on someone, probably.

A year into our training contracts, before all that mess with her nephew, just as we were realising that our chosen jobs represented a unique combination of mundanity and stress, a group of us went on holiday to Morocco. Who else were we going to go on holiday with? I was, by now, officially seeing Christine. Harry was dating Jennie. Mark was trying to get into Rachel's knickers. Joy only joined the attendee list at the last minute; David, stuck on some nightmare transaction, had to cancel.

Essaouira was hot, empty and windy. The men in robes

had frightening eyes. On the beach, sand blew into our ears; on the toilet, seafood blew out of our stomachs. There was something fraught and lonely about the whole expedition. The cocktail lounge in the hotel served no alcohol and in the early evenings, as doors in stone corridors slammed, us men sipped pathetic faux mojitos as we waited for the girls to get ready. Harry and Mark talked about skiing and shooting, two things I know nothing about. You have to be bourgeois from the beginning to get the full benefits. One by one the girls turned up. For some reason my memory has dressed Christine in a ridiculous lime-green fleece. She asked impatiently, Where's Joy? And in response I offered to go and chase her up.

When Joy opened the door to her room I saw she was still wearing the pearly bikini she'd lounged in by the pool.

What do you think? she said.

It took me a second to realise she was gesturing at the outfits laid out on the bed.

Difficult to say, I replied. Give the locals a treat and go out as you are?

They stare enough as it is.

They're probably in love.

They think I'm a white whore, Joy said, and I mumbled some word like Gorgeous, and we got into this flirty battle about whether whores are ever gorgeous. Accused me of being drunk, I think, and I told her Chance would be a fine fucking thing, and she, what was it . . . ?

You're a lecherous drunk, Peter. That's what she said, and I moved a little closer, seeing her adjust one of the see-through straps on her bikini top.

Stop it, she said.

You're gorgeous, I said.

I'm not.

You are.

This is silly.

And then I kissed her, I kissed her with a sincerity I'd never felt in myself before, moving my hand down her back very slowly, nibbling her neck, glimpsing the shaped skin underneath her briefs, so white it almost glowed. A silly, highly charged sort of kiss.

But Dennis, he won't know about Morocco, and the point is . . . What's that alarm beep? Is that yours?

Ah, Doctor Odd, time flies in your company like a hijacked plane! Too fast, too easily. I'm starting to feel a cold kind of thrill in these sessions of ours. Fun, aren't they? Fun fun fun.

11 a.m.

'DOES OLD Dennis still sniff things? Before he puts them in the trolley?'

When Joy gives no response Peter grins, a hard shine to his teeth like the building itself. 'It was the sniffing of non-perishable items I could never understand.'

'I'm sure you weren't this much of a cretin, back then.'

'When I first fucked you, you mean? In that skimpy bikini of yours?'

'I'm surprised you can remember a moment so fleeting, Peter.'

She looks at him across the circular table in her office, then goes back to focusing on the Handicom Full Duplex Conference Table Starfish Speakerphone (metallic grey) which lies splattered at its centre. She is so lost in the perforations she misses the next thing he says.

'You heard me. Is this one of your little games?'

'It's a handover meeting,' Joy explains, twirling a pen to keep calm. 'If I went on holiday without handing things over to someone the whole case would collapse. I didn't know Brian was going to pick you.'

'What was yesterday afternoon about?' he says. 'All that

stuff about how it's time to be honest with yourself. Your crazy response when I mentioned the promotion announcement. Never seen you so agitated during office hours. I was just trying to talk to you.'

'Best not.'

'What?'

'Best not talk to me.'

'What are you up to?' he says.

'How's your new trainee?' she says.

'Whatever you're planning, scrap it. Think of the pain you'd cause . . . others.'

She half turns in her chair, takes a breath, counts to five, surveys her yucca's more spirited leaves, her desk, her shelves of velo-bound documents, hoping to lull her heart's skittish beat. But when she turns back he is staring at his own outstretched palm with the same expression he wore yesterday by the Coke machine, a look of such pitiful studied sorrow that she can't resist breaking his spell.

'Don't talk to me about hurting others,' she says.

'And why shouldn't I?'

'Because you've always been a selfish, uncivilised little sex pest, that's why.'

His hand slaps wood with surprising violence. The table shakes. The Starfish shudders.

Some things you can't take back, there's no returns policy for them, but all the same she's been jolted into thinking of retracting 'uncivilised' when a shadow floods her thoughts and her red-soled high heels. It is Mental Brian, their walrus-cheeked Head of Work Allocation.

'Campers,' he says.

'Brian,' they say.

'Sorry to keep you. Trying to plan a skiing holiday. This Make Law Fun Day is no fun at all, gets one hungry for a break.'

'Good cause though,' Joy says. 'Getting kids into . . . legal stuff.'

'Precisely,' Mental Brian says, pulling up a chair.

Precisely? It wasn't even precisely to her, and she's the one who said it. She looks at the oily skin of his forehead, creeping crownwards like rising damp. There are more wrinkles than hairs, at least one rivet for each ski season in his life, unevenly spread, full of bloated blackheads. Hard to resist leaning over to give that big one above his eyebrow a squeeze, but feeling the strain of restraint in her neck Joy sinks her gaze down to some bullet points she's prepared. As she does this Peter and Brian exchange a few further words about the Make Law Fun Day, a misleadingly named afternoon of City-related lectures presented to state-school students, and their discussion seems to conclude with Brian saying, 'Terrific you purchased the lizard.'

Joy says, 'Purchased the what?' but the two men ignore her. However high you climb as a female lawyer in a City firm, there's still this residual sense you're on work experience, precluded from appreciating the full picture. This feeling is particularly prevalent when Brian is in the room; his brain seems to run on its own exotic logic, and conversations with him tend to snag in one place rather than evolve. Irritating though this is, part of her enjoys exercising the inventive vigilance required to unstick a subject, or to head it off several sentences in advance.

'Your articled clerk,' Brian tells Peter as an apparent

afterthought. 'Jessica, is it? Rather charming I must say. *Must* say.'

'Anyway, Brian, Peter, very kind of you both to spare ten minutes of your time, and I just wanted to fill you in on Project Poultry really.'

'Project Poultry,' says Brian, somehow confused.

'In advance of my holiday. I understand you've lined up Peter to help.'

'Help.'

'To cover me. That's why we're here, after all.'

'Here. After all. Yes! Poultry. Thinking about the slopes. Peter here has kindly offered to keep things ticking while you're away.'

'That's what I thought,' Joy says. 'Thank you, Peter.'

'Over. Ticking over.'

'Yes. That's great.'

'Tickity-tickety-boo.'

'Lovely. Thanks, Brian. Thanks, Peter.'

'Tick-tock. Tick-tock. Tick-tock.'

Peter and Joy exchange the sort of look that used to be frequent between them, a flickering sense of being appalled and amused by others, greedy to be alone, but, scared of dwelling too long on their shared past, on the refuge she once had from her unhappiness, Joy cuts the glance short and redirects her attention to the detail of the case. She alone speaks, keeps speaking as Mental Brian, distracted perhaps by some black run in his brain, retains the glazed look of a shop-window dummy, keeps speaking even when she loses Peter to his own reflection, talks and talks and bores herself, searches out her former lover's eyes in the only window her office possesses, sealed shut to stop jumpers, chemically treated to dim the daylight. Layered behind his reflected features are squat chimneys, antennae skeletons, crystal towers, metal entrails, the whole robotic Square Mile shivering under a January sun. She wonders whether Peter sees these things too, whether he sees anything other than himself.

'Anyway,' Joy concludes, 'one thing to look out for in terms of managing the client is that they really hate any suggestion that their factory farming and nugget-making practices are cruel. Hate it. As far as they're concerned, they are putting food on people's plates. They are giving them fuel. That's the thing the CEO keeps saying: There's not enough fuel around, we're mid-recession, no one can afford to worry about these birds. The publicity hurts though. Disclosure is six months away and we'll have to see what our doc review turns up, build a settlement strategy that will keep the campaigners quiet.'

'Been meaning to ask you,' Brian says, producing an unrelated sheet of paper from his jacket pocket, 'if you wouldn't mind looking at this. It's a one-para pitch to you-know-who for any CDO-type work they might have. Kind of area that's in your, dum de dah, partnership plan.'

Joy picks up her pen and scans the twelve lines of text. '*Extensive amount of experience* sounds arrogant,' she says quickly, 'and it's not – don't laugh – that kind of bank. Better to say *fair*. By contrast, *reviewing papers for* sounds understated to the point of weak. How about *managing multi-jurisdictional disclosure exercises for*. Now, let's see, *several key clients*' – she guillotines all three words with a single streak of ink – 'is perhaps a touch non-specific. Try *leading financial institutions*, then add something about our corporate governance experience, so they know we're on message about the need for greater transparency in the City. And rather than *took the lead on your biggest piece of banking litigation* put *assisted your in-house specialists with*. It'll make Chloe and Co look good, and they're the ones who dispense mandates. Finally you might consider a fourteen-point font. The Head of Legal is half blind but in denial.'

She pushes the marked-up paper back to Brian. He is slow to take it.

'Just suggestions, of course, Brian. I could have Barbara email them to you in track changes?'

'I think you'll make an effortless partner,' Brian says. '*Effortless*.' Turning to Peter he adds, in a deeper voice, 'I have no doubt you'll find Project Poultry in excellent order.'

'Marvellous,' says Peter. 'Happy to help. Not my specialism, not remotely, but a fascinating case. Always harboured a soft spot for chicken libel. Remind me where you're off to, Joy?'

'Pardon?'

'Holiday. Remind us where you're tottering off to?'

Tottering off. The phrase takes her back to Wimbledon, she doesn't quite know why, someone must have said it, kids totter around, little tyke can't have tottered off far, and though in this office on this Friday her tongue is shaping some easy lie about getting sun and feeling sand between her toes her mind has rewound five and a half years of footage and she is there again, joining the search, trying to explain to the police which shades of blue her nephew wore, getting the gates shut down. After the tears a sudden calmness came. People needed her to be calm. They spoke in a series of nervy surges – tell us where exactly; who and when; think, think – and it was as if the panic leaching out of her had found a home in these obscure bystanders, their determined faces. There was an unspeakable collective excitement in the air. Child, missing, we must find the child. People wait their whole lives for such a sense of direction.

There might have been a man wearing army boots that afternoon, wandering between the quieter courts; there might have been a woman with a lost look in her eye, pushing an empty pram; on the CCTV two teenagers make small measured movements around something on the ground, a strawberry or a toy or some innocuous trick of the light.

'My office,' Brian says, 'to chat through that lizard presentation,' and he and Peter disappear through the door.

When a child goes missing there are daisy chains of images and lies and half-remembered things, all loosely linked. Your brain is a room full of theories, flimsy as the paper pinned to walls: ticket stubs, staff lists, security logs. Pictures too, from cameras in streets, hospitality rooms, waiting rooms. She heard a line once – 'Every room is a waiting room' – but until Wimbledon the full force of its meaning eluded her. The hours in which her nephew went missing became bloated by the business of waiting, were made slow and fat with the experiences of others, their hearsay and think-I-saws and hopes. The accounts of each given minute vary in every conceivable way – *I saw a man with him; I saw three kids with him; He was alone wandering out through the turnstiles* – and it makes you wonder, when someone disappears, whether they were ever really there. Posters in bus stations, shop windows, local papers, his features going soft in the sun. So much paper! Hundreds of pages of testimony, an inhuman haul of tip-offs and mental debris. Anonymous reports and images that expand to fill the space his disappearance has left. No wage slips, tax returns, appraisal forms – none of the documents that make up an ongoing life – just fragments from the past, mind-scatter lying around the event.

Sometimes Joy looks up at the big flat screens that hang in braces outside each Hanger, Slyde & Stein employee coffee pod, installed during the credit crunch to better monitor the markets, and thinks that the twenty-first century is no more than a vast structureless datastream. Oil up. Copper down. Gold holding. Somehow the white spaces on the graphs, cracked by ragged red lines, seem to breathe a kind of sadness. And what would it mean, exactly, to be one of the people both in and out of this datastream, everywhere and nowhere, waiting to be identified or found?

There is no need to invent some convoluted plot or clever conspiracy. There is enough mystery in the facts themselves, their loose ends, dead ends, spaces where the known world fades. Joy knows this now, has known this ever since that tennis match in 2005. She knows that England's capital, more than any place on earth, exists on film; that in the City of London alone there are around seventy CCTV cameras for every thousand people. She lives in the most watched city in the world (she saw a documentary that said this was so) and yet more than ever she feels there are parts of society which cannot be recorded, which lie outside the frame, lost from view. Cameras caught twenty-seven images of her nephew that day, starting from the moment Joy took him from her Hampstead home, boarded the Tube and then the train at Waterloo, met Christine, silly-hatted, leaning into the ticket machine. But there is no confirmed footage of him after 14.57.

Missing posters; ground searches; tracker dogs; street work; the images of Joy's sister, fierce with grief, giving the public appeal. Utilities up a touch; telecomms down a tad; consumer goods unchanged. The ordinary recorded written-down world.

14.57, reported lost.

15.24, gates closed.

Mass search throughout the night.

Only five years old.

They often are five years old, she's learnt, trawling public records of vanished children, searching for some strange comfort or clue. It was said, in one trial transcript she had a paralegal find, that two boys, themselves only children, tried to insert batteries into their victim. This detail, like so many details, she cannot forget.

Dennis

I'M NOT sure, Counsellor – tell me if I'm wrong, of course – but I'm not sure (are you?) whether I ever finished that anecdote I was telling you about the encounter I had in the first-class carriage, you know the one, the day before my wife's accident, not the William Hague experience (ha ha, sounds like a gruesome fairground ride, does it not, the William Hague Experience), but no, rather I'm talking about, yes, quite, the Beverley Badger encounter.

As I suspected. I was thinking that just as I was working my way through the foreword to a classic yesterday (which was actually a way of putting off rereading the classic itself, in the same way that the idea of rereading the classic itself had sprung up as a means of avoiding rereading the draft text of chapter seven of my highly commercial but hopefully nonetheless insightful study of Shakespeare's language), I was thinking that even as I hear myself reciting one of my own anecdotes, even as I enjoy hearing myself recite it, I find myself hoping for its (the anecdote's) end, for it is the same highly modulated but oddly empty experience you have when reading a book, Counsellor, the way however much you are loving the book, loving to linger in its pages, you are also hurrying through it, flicking occasionally to the end, comparing your page number with the final page number, flicking fairly frequently between your page and the end page, flicking pretty much constantly, never wanting it to end but desperately wanting it to end, hoping unreservedly that you never have to put it down but at the same time without contradiction thinking Oh My Merciful Lord I Can't Wait To See This Story Sewn Up.

Now, come, let me be brief. Half an hour outside London, a mere twenty-four hours before my wife's accident, I told Beverley I too was an author of sorts.

Oh terrific, she said. Who's your agent?

No agent yet, I explained. I haven't managed to find an agent yet, unfortunately, although I've barely started sending out material, there are still some agents I haven't tried.

Did you send it to mine? she asked, meaning her agent, Abby Aardvark (you'll appreciate I've changed the agent's name, Counsellor, though I hope without cheapening the surrounding facts) of Aardvark Alexander.

I sent an outline and sample chapters to someone there, I said – it was true, I had – but I received nothing back from them.

Looking at the streaks of silver in my hair, she asked me if I had published books before.

Purely academic ones, I explained. My last was *Shakespeare and Sir Gawain: Ships Passing in the Knight*.[6] The current project is aimed, I told her, more at the general reading

[6] Sadly now out of print, Counsellor, but nonetheless available from one persistent seller on Amazon's esteemed second-hand marketplace.

public. My goal is to make Shakespeare's language exciting to a new generation, to frame my textual analysis with commentary on developments in the English language since his plays were first performed, developments which latterly would include, of course, email abbreviations, textspeak, status updates, Tweetings, et cetera.

Interesting, she said, tracing a finger idly down the spine of her book. At the other end of the carriage was a pinstriped, painstakingly tanned man who managed to squeeze the word *dickwad* into almost every sentence he spoke. His coarseness reminded me of my wife's colleague Peter.

Now, to get to the crux of the conversation, I explained to Ms Badger over the rat-a-tat-tat of the carriage and the incessant dickwads that I was deeply interested in the means by which inarticulacy in Shakespeare's tragedies can be linked to the inarticulacies in our daily lives. I had been to Bristol, that morning, to listen to a lecture which skirted around the edges of that very theme. You see, Counsellor, I find that Shakespeare himself, as the examples of *Hamlet* and *King Lear* illustrate, does not seem to associate inarticulacy with the failure of reason, with individual madness, but instead identifies it as a symptom of a *world* in a state of chaos, which is what the modern world is in, yes, no? In chaos, words splintering and spiralling, the physical struggle to *heave the name of father pantingly forth*, hmm?

Thank you, Counsellor. Too kind. Ms Badger said something similar.

Your book sounds very interesting, she said, polite and considerate and musical of voice, eyes asquint against the gust-rush of a handbag brushing past her button nose, the train pulling into Paddington.

You haven't even heard the twist, I said. Have a guess. What's the twist?

No, no, not you, Counsellor – though you are welcome to join in if you wish – but I mean to say I directed the question to Beverley.

She was stumped, no idea, so I told her.

Iambic pentameter, I said. The whole book. I'm writing it in iambic pentameter.

Needless to say she (Ms Badger) was suitably gobsmacked.

You really like the idea? I asked. My wife – top City lawyer – says it's silly.

Oh don't listen to a City liar! Beverley said, chuckling.

To this I responded, a little annoyed, just a little, by reminding her that we are lucky, she and I, that we know we want to spend our lives wrighting words.[7] I explained to Beverley, Counsellor, that my wife is highly intelligent, and imaginative, but she has never really found the thing she would love to do, and has gone the way of many of her

[7] *Wrighting* being used by me in the sense of the word *playwright,* Counsellor, and I'm sure I don't need to tell you that if we dissect that word, the word *playwright*, we find that the noun on which the verb *play* leans refers to a person who makes, constructs, or repairs, e.g. a wheelwright, or a shipwright (or, presumably, Frank Lloyd Wright, Orville Wright, Wilbur Wright), and thus the prefix and suffix mingle to describe a person who has wrought language, ideas and character into a dramatic form. The homophone with *write* is in this case no more than an interesting coincidence, an example of the way that language itself is preternaturally wrought in all kinds of interesting ways.

generation, becoming trapped by the dark treasure that is her own talent, and the more her employers recognise that talent through pay and praise, making her feel it is lived up to not lost, the more fenced off she feels from that feral beast Failure, and the harder it is for her to find a way out.

Beverley was silent awhile, but when she saw me gather up my coat she said, Let me scribble my agent's email address on this.

She handed me a tattered receipt for two magazines and a Curly Wurly.[8] Email my agent, she said, and mention me. She'll think it's a bit highbrow, but if you're keen to break away from the university presses she might suggest some suitable publishers.

And that, pretty much, was the last thing Beverley Badger said to me.[9] I ended the journey feeling rather sad to see her go, but also a little uplifted, changed in some small way.

I stood waiting for the 205 hoping, hoping against hope,

[8] Making a comeback, I'm pleased to note.

[9] Yes, let me think, *pretty much*. Her actual last words, uttered on Platform 14, following the gift of the tattered receipt, were probably – and of course recollection is more imprecise art than solid science, the human brain tending to *reweave* as much as *retrieve* experiences – Well, nice to meet you, to which I replied (I think), And lovely to meet you, following which she said, See you then, to which I said, Yes, thanks, see you, following which she said Bye, and I said Bye, and she gave me a half-wave with her body rotated at one hundred and eighty degrees, and I stood waving too, and pretending to need to phone my wife urgently, just to let the awkwardness of our passing pass, when in fact I knew that my wife would be working for a good few hours still, even though Thursday nights are – were – are – *our* nights, and there was no real rush at all.

that Ms Badger's literary agent would like my manuscript, and would help me sell it for a fair sum of money, at which point I could look back on the last few months and say to myself, Dennis, Dennis old boy, something good has come out of your suspension.

Pardon?

Ah.

I meant *sabbatical*, of course. This is the true condition of Western civilisation in 2011, is it not, everyone caught between two or more inadequate words for the experience itself, nobody quite sure if they are on sabbatical or suspension, torn between free will and circumstance, ending up using different words with different people ha ha ha?

Well, it's more that the Dean tends to use the word suspension. Him and, well, yes, everyone else at the university.

I see.

Granted.

Yes.

Now technically, Counsellor, it *is* a suspension, but only in the sense that a Jaffa Cake (which is good for you, I've read) is technically a cake when, in fact, most self-respecting tea-drinking snack-dunkers know it is in essence a biscuit, for they are not satiated by just one Jaffa in the way they would almost always be content with one slice of cake, yes, you see my point, yes?

You really think so? I mean really? I've heard that one before, Counsellor, and on this subject, with no disrespect to you or to the VAT Tribunal, I do not find it persuasive simply to restate the old entrenched argument that over time biscuits go soft and cakes go hard, but to answer your initial question in the most succinct way possible, without further delay or diversion – it was like this when Joy-Joy's nephew went missing, every straight route to the facts obscured, eyewitnesses saying this man looked like a paedophile and the next person saying he looked like a kind-hearted chap and the third person saying his eyes were blue and the fourth person swearing blind they were brown, all concision and precision obscured by images from all angles and split perceptions and the force field of inconsistent asides in which every powerful happening is enclosed – it is all down to a mix-up with a female undergraduate. I say mix-up, but in actual fact she (the female undergraduate) has a vendetta against me, is telling all sorts of lies – that I felt her up, yes, that I said lewd things, yes – as a way of punishing me for not giving her the grades which she in her pretty prim misguided mind thought she deserved, and although there is not a jot, certainly not a lot, of objective evidence against me it is my misfortune, my great bad bloody luck, that her father is some bigwig fat cat on the London restaurant scene who has a whole wing of the new Arts and Social Sciences Library named after him and also happens to sit on the university's Board of Governors. The Dean is on my side, I'm pretty sure he's on my side, he seemed at first to be on my side, less so now, but he is hamstrung, he says – hamstrung – because it is her (the misguided undergraduate's) word against mine, and they (the university) are forced to investigate it, and it (the alleged groping) must of course be investigated fully but with this restaurant magnate kicking up an almighty fuss and getting seven of the twelve independent board members and five of the eight co-opted members, one of the two academic nominees, the student nominee and the Vice Chancellor on side, notwithstanding the Board's alleged commitment to the seven principles of public life as set out in the Nolan Report, Gerald says that at the moment he can't see me getting through the disciplinary process with my career intact.

Sadly, Counsellor, your sympathy is not what I need. Not unless it is backed up by a fat cheque and a refund on my self-respect.

Joy-Joy? No no, I couldn't possibly have told her. If she thought I was skulking around the house eating Jaffas in the glow of the television on an indefinite basis she would be unduly concerned for me. Because she has done it herself, you see, the moping and TV watching, and knows how it can gnaw at your self-esteem, just like ailments gnaw at the hirsute, humped, hunched and halitotic people you meet in the street; just like the hands of hospital clocks nibble away at the day.

Beg your pardon?

In 2005, in the wake of Wimbledon, when she needed time off work, Joy-Joy watched a lot of television. All the hot bustle of the prior period, searching for her nephew, all that thinned down and cooled and she barely left her Hampstead home, did not leave her home at all for many many weeks, and I would go over there straight from the university and sit slumped next to her and worry, for we had been seeing each other for several months, long enough for me to worry very deeply, and almost everyone was worried, including her sister, who seemed at that moment ready to forgive her, worried that Joy-Joy might never come out.

She was at her weakest, her most see-through, that autumn. Grief can do that to a person, I think. Drain all colour away. Leave them so thin that light shines through their skin and out the other side, the way the sun shimmies in and out of a jellyfish. Through madness or miscalculation her hair was shorn unflatteringly short, and the only things she seemed to take pleasure in were cream crackers. I sandwiched them around lemon curd, a snack my mother used to make me when I got one of my killer colds, and Joy ate them staring at the news or a wildlife documentary, hungry for facts not fantasy. Eventually she progressed from cream crackers to soup and mentioned going back to work, and we made love one lunchtime on the sofa, the first time in months, and that very afternoon I went to touch her chin and look meaningfully into her eyes and she swatted my hand away and said, Why has everyone picked up this habit of touching my chin all of a sudden? And in that moment I knew she was segueing back into her old self.

To me it seemed apposite that, soon after her return to the office, we discovered Joy-Joy was pregnant. She greeted the development with a sense of shock and guilt, but to me it felt fitting, redemptive, exhilarating. And it felt similarly fitting that on the weekend after the pregnancy test proved positive, when we went for a walk along Regent's Canal, all the way from Victoria Park to Angel, I should point to a For Sale sign outside a surprisingly spacious, split-level property and ask her to be my wife.

People questioned our motives, of course. Some went so far as to imply I'd deliberately asked her to marry me when she was still too weak to say no, phrased it (the big question) in a faintly manipulative way, snuck a promise of security into her mind before that mind regained something like its full protective strength, and light no longer went right through her, and she seemed less like a memory of herself . . . and the lemon curd got struck off our shopping list . . . and her hair regrew, shiny and thick . . . and marmalade became our household's conserve – preserve? – of choice . . .

Anyway, that's the story of my meeting with a famous author, and my trouble at the university, and how my marriage began.

11.45 a.m.

Running out of fuel, Joy thinks, tugging a sports bra over her breasts. Humanity itself is running out of fuel. The half-dressed girl on the next bench is taking gleeful greedy swigs from a bottled mixture called Rocket, the downward slope of the 'R' accented with a bright lightning bolt, but this fragile-looking brunette isn't heading to Mars or even Marylebone, is simply looking for a kick to get her through half an hour of exercise and then back to her desk, to her computer, to the two dozen emails she'll have been sent since leaving her seat. Hardly that different from the cycle of Joy's own daily life, and yet the scale of Rocket Girl's assumed ambitions strikes her, in this moment, as heart-breakingly small. An almost-pretty young thing; trainee, probably. Elegant shoulders. Hard to keep those through your thirties. It's clear as Joy turns to the mirror, clear what a decade huddled over QUERTY has done, the knottedness that comes from typing out late-night notes with titles like 'Frozen Meats: The Regulatory Landscape'. The poultry industry is under pressure to investigate new ways of improving sanitation and minimising feather pecking. It hopes to avoid recourse to beak trimming. It is best practice for broiler companies to consider the relationship between (a) strain of bird, (b) housing environment, (c) stocking density and (d) feeding regimen. I mean, really, *who fucking cares?*

She cares and she doesn't care. Increasingly she agrees with those intense walking-boot wearers who campaign for standards and transparency about standards. Sometimes even agrees with the ones who use that grandest of words, Ethics. There's a product liability lawyer in her team called Tiny Tony – taller and better-looking than Peter's nickname gives him credit for, actually – and he has a new office-mate, a guy who really is one of God's cruder pet projects, a guy who on his first day at the firm tacked to his pinboard a motto which reads 'Consumers are Fools; Client is King'. And while Joy realises that life is too messy for anyone to be perfectly *good*, it's apparent, taking this new recruit as a case in point, that some people are making more effort than others. She is not aiming to deceive the public in the way he may be, but her job nonetheless involves sneaking around the boundaries of what's true. There's no expectation to lie, exactly, just to find ingenious means of disguising reality, remodelling unhelpful facts by dressing them in helpful facts and half-truths and the odd nicely caveated view. Unlike the painful paperwork, internal politics and antisocial hours, this part of the job – the exercise in reality management, the ritual of transforming one thing into another – used to make her happy, and for years she really did believe all the John Locke, Thomas Jefferson stuff about life being the pursuit of happiness. Only now, too late, does she feel that chasing this most conformist of ethical aims, of societal demands – *Be happy! You deserve it! You can do it!* – has taken her on a savage, obscurely sadistic path. Through her twenties she approached every dark desire and unhappy thought with the self-help-book belief that she could will it away; could, through a series of further choices, win herself the contentment she deserved. But every time she's gone full-tilt in pursuit of bliss, believed those fundamentalists who rule luck out of life, everyone has ended up getting hurt. *Side effects may include disappointment*: this is the health warning our search for happiness should wear. *Disappointment and selfishness*.

Is she still selfish? Maybe. But she is convinced, almost convinced, that her present pursuit, the hunt for something beyond happiness, incorporates an altruistic desire to leave things in good order, to make life easier for others. It irritates her that by mislaying her tennis racket she has let her lunchtime tennis buddy down and created a glitch in the structure of the day, this day that's supposed to be about her rediscovering some kind of goal and control. The error niggles like unironed linen on a Sunday night.

Before summoning the special effort required to leave her BlackBerry behind in the changing rooms, Joy tries to phone Christine. This time there is no instant voicemail greeting; two rings and the line connects. It's a line saturated by static, though, her friend's words periodically obscured.

'Joyous? Sorry, darling, I . . . Joyous? . . . I'm in . . . still there?'

Mimicking these pauses and resumptions Joy begins to explain that they'll have to cancel their match, but it isn't clear how much Christine hears; her reply, when it comes, seems to spring from an entirely different subject: 'Honestly, husbands. Peter's such a clever . . . *cunt*, sometimes. I'm sorry if that shocks you.'

'No, no,' Joy says, though people's choice of language constantly shocks her. Her nephew would sometimes come out with peculiarly adult words: *drainpipe; muesli*. They had always arrived in her ears as lessons: he would grow up, change, hold conversations with plumbers and . . . muesli sellers. 'Cunt' has given her a little glimpse of another Christine: older, angrier, less willing to submit.

Beginning again she says, 'Christine, I . . .' but the crackles kick in and before the double beep of the phone call dying she only has time to add, awkwardly, 'You're lovely, you know.' She blows her nose and ties her laces.

Samir is sitting behind the fitness centre's only computer. He is doing some kind of neck-stretching routine. The visible sliver of PC screen shows an image of his Antipodean manager – Jock, *Jack*? – smiling.

'Hi, Sam,' she says. 'Just you in charge today?'

'Oh hi Miss Stephens! Jack is not back until later.'

A shame not to have one last look at Jack, at those cheek-bones that remind her of a cunnilingus-loving IT genius she made love to one summer. He was a Systems Interrogator, but the joke wore thin.

Samir closes the world wide window and says, 'Very very big day today Miss Stephens!'

'Sorry?'

'Your brilliant promotion! I got the email.'

'That went to everybody?'

'Champagne at five it said.'

'Prosecco, probably. It's not 2007.'

'No it is not,' he says, an earnest blink revising his eyes. 'Would you like to start with a run?'

She nearly says something about it being her last session with him, but instead merely offers a nod. Is this why she's bothered coming into work today, to try and say goodbye? Do normal people exercise before taking their lives? Is there a set of agreed rules for the process she's in? A partner in Structured Finance is doing sit-ups, holding a medicine ball to his heart. Sweat has made his T-shirt a hundred shades of grey. In this mirrored room five or six others are running into their reflections, lifting weights, loading bars with Olympic plates. Strange places, gyms: hideaways where people look to develop aggression, or disperse it. Hard to say which category she fits.

Stretching, she listens to Samir talk about his dad. His mother comes up often, but this is the first time she's heard about the father, and she always likes to hear about people's fathers. Sometimes, noting her rapt attentiveness to such stories, she wonders if she's hoping to apprehend noble paternal attributes she can transfer to her own dad, embellishing an evasive image of him with borrowed details. Talking to Dennis about her childhood, hearing her voice falter into the confidential fizz of a confession, she has on occasion found imaginary anecdotes creeping into her speech and taking on – through the effort of invention and the feat of repeating them – the authenticity of actual memories.

'You think he'd like to go back to what he was doing in Bangladesh?' she says. 'To teaching?'

'Perhaps it is too late now Miss Stephens. Father still likes to teach people things though. Even if it is only teaching junior waiters how to carry three plates.'

'And what does he like to teach you?'

'Me? For a while in Sylhet it was algebra. And then English. Now mainly it is marriage and things of that nature. He is keen to introduce me to a nice teenage girl.'

'As in, arranged?'

'That is the idea. I suppose it has its advantages. I would like to share everything with somebody one day.'

'And what's in it for this girl, exactly, to get hitched to a stranger, married off with no part in the process?'

Oh, God, listen: every time she aims for Virtue she misses the junction, ends up in Selfish Bitch.

'Um,' Samir says, disinfecting the machine and programming her run, choosing inclines and distances, setting the calorie count. 'In terms of what she would get I suppose there is perhaps protecting her chastity. Family honour. And the matter of lower household expenses. Not that I am financially that brilliant yet but . . .'

The temperamental treadmill starts with a jolt. She jogs. She will go at her own pace. It won't matter what Samir says, it will only matter that he is saying something, because as her laces start to wave and her heart grows hard this is precisely what she needs, a noise beyond her own body, a thought beyond her own head. His voice always carries a sweet, stirring note of enthusiasm, speech somehow animating not just his face but the room around it, and only in silence does the positivity of his presence seem to wane; peering in at him as the gym door swings open she has before now noticed how gaunt and scared he looks, half drowned in a tracksuit, eager for his next client to come. Communication gives him courage, it appears, and some of it he feeds into her.

Joy runs. At first she feels her muscles as burdens on her lungs and bones, but slowly, slowly, the legs begin to lengthen, buttocks begin to tighten, breasts buoy and lighten the load on her chest and strictly held by nothing at all she feels loosely bound to the room around her, suspended between the basement gym of Hanger, Slyde & Stein and somewhere more like life. A series of beeps mark her progress towards top speed. Her own motion becomes a kind of inward fluttering, the dissolution of all physical resistance, the wall of mirror making light caress her clavicle as clogged thoughts rearrange themselves, the surf-like sound of the conveyor belt creating space for her to breathe and think. I mean it is not that I agree with arranged marriage. I mean I am not certain it is a brilliant idea. Some fertile presence within Joy is kicking back at Samir's speech, finding friction in memories of Hampstead Heath. When her mind is searching out happy times it always seems to find its way here, to the Heath, thoughts spinning, wheeling, the air streaming with the smell of cold glades, woodland, heathland, meadow, as if she's running fast through its landscape, all this air submitting to her body's own eloquence, and it *is* a landscape, it is a landscape containing dreamy trees and formless clouds and a picnic blanket loaded with cheese and ham and olives in brine and one or more cheap boxes of wine, it *is* a landscape containing her sister and her nephew, the three of them in their favourite quiet clearing eating and talking, islanded in newspapers and games, the soft swelter of summer in the air, flocks of birds mixing with other flocks, and amid the dozen-birded blur you are almost feverish, ill, deliciously ill like the times you were a child in your parents' bed, alone but not lonely, everything hyperreal, moments folding in on themselves, minutes like paper or Morse code or music, and it is a landscape, close up it is definitely that, but from far away the Heath itself looks like a face, your sister's face, full of puffy eyes and swollen cheeks and twisted smiles, and from where you are – not close, not far – running, running, you can see the landscape and the face, both at once, one and then the other, and it makes you so tired you have to close your eyes and dip your head and imagine you're a poplar leaning in the wind. Eyes closed, your limbs are the things that are moving but the movement can feel more near and slight than that, the way different stories move through your thoughts on the nights you can't sleep, when you're lying there or sitting pillow-propped and thinking of people the police should be speaking to, gestures you could have made towards your sister to make it all OK, thinking about how the vanishing of people, their death or disappearance or dwindling, makes you aware of your being here, making stupid circles round the stray grey cells of your mind, running through scenarios, listening to the faint thunderstorm of your husband's small-hours snores – Do you perhaps plan to run any marathons? – I am running the marathon for a charity – spaces – perhaps they still have spaces – fancy dress – the brilliant things people wear – are you OK? – are you OK? – are you OK? – Joy looks up into the mirror and runs into its deep light space, into her own self, a floating effortless athlete, and like one of those bulldog recruiters who constantly calls your direct dial, takes a hint you give and turns it into an emblem of some bigger thing, keeps you talking, tries to lead you into the murky outer circles of friendship by talking talking talking, she is unstoppable, breathless, so persistent that in the end everyone either hangs up hard or cries or kills themselves or says, Fair enough, why not, I'll send you my CV.

'Are you OK? Are you all right? Miss Stephens? You are very focused today.'

Focus. That's it. Not desperation and despair. Clarity, focus, expedience. That's why she's picked today, an anniversary of sorts. Anniversaries are nice neat shadows of prior days – flat, exact, with the muted truth that distance gives.

'Miss Stephens allow me to get you a towel and then perhaps it would be a good time to –'

'Rowing,' she says, slowing the treadmill. 'Next, let's do, rowing machine. Shoulders. I'm keen to work on my shoulders.'

Samir

Allow me to wipe that. It has dripped a little coffee. No wait it will not take a second I have a napkin here. *Wait!*

Sorry. I . . .

No your suggestion was . . . Why not just leave it. Forgive me.

Yes.

Yes I suppose. Even at school. My teacher in Sylhet. Not my father they would not let him teach me but a friend and colleague of his. He used to say An orderly pencil case Samir! Very good to have an orderly pencil case! But in England this seemed less popular. It was better to have a disorderly pencil case and to embellish it with Tipp-Ex pictures. Skulls. Body parts. Diagrams of that nature.

When I left school I did not have brilliant exam grades and I had missed getting waiter experience. I was behind some of the other boys from Sylhet in this respect. So when I began to work with Father at the Raj while I did my fitness diploma Father's manager decided I should not do front of house. Not until I had gained experience. Instead I cleaned. Kitchen and toilets. This is why I am grateful for the very clean toilets at Hanger, Slyde & Stein. I see the Brazilian lady come in every two hours. We smile at each other. Once you have cleaned a toilet professionally you know what it involves and you make sure to smile. If she enters the lavatory while I am in the cubicle I do a quick Astaire so that she knows to wait. Then I smile on my way out.

Well some aspects were brilliant. The free food was very good. I was close to my father. But there were the smells. Those could be very bad. Meaty smells and trails of paper that got dragged across the floor. Like . . . bolts? Bolts of paper lightning. And people blowing their nose into the sink. Bits in the sink that remain after rinsing. Bits in the bowl that cling through the flush. The freshener that makes the smells worse by making them a little sharp. It is trying to improve the air but it makes it much worse. Sickly. Sweet. Whoever invented the toilet air-freshener made a mistake. Not a mistake as bad as some of mine but a mistake nonetheless.

Examples? There are so many! Only last Friday I . . .

I have been trying to tell Jack about a problem that occurred on Friday. But then I thought. I thought what if this on top of all the other little things makes him ask me to leave. To leave my job. I love my job. Drawing up the schedules for my clients. The seaside sound of the ergos at top speed. The click of the coffee machine behind the fire door. If they knew what I had done that might all disappear.

And then there are only moments! We have only moments to talk together. Jack has to conduct his boxercise class. Or I see the water cooler needs attention. Every now and then I have asked Jack if he would like to come to my home sometime. To talk about important issues or perhaps nothing at all. I have checked with Father and he does not seem to mind if Jack comes round sometime to watch a DVD and drink something cold. But Jack is a busy man. He plays a lot of sport. One time the other week he said he would visit but he got held up. He said Sorry mate you know how it is. I know how it is. It was no problem. I had set aside a pile of DVDs we might watch but it does not take long to make or unmake a pile. It takes no time at all.

One of my mistakes is I probably ask things in the wrong way. When I see people like Miss Stephens asking things they have a way. A way with large dark eyes and a decisive neck of getting people to listen. I always look at her on the treadmill her cheeks blushing just the right amount and think how unaffected she is by her brilliant looks. They seem to have a very small effect on her if that makes sense. By which what I mean is it is in others you can see the big effect. The way Jack smiles at her complete in his attention saying yes to everything. The way he disappears into a sort of tunnel of her making.

If you are thirsty I could go and get more water? It really is key to stay adequately hydrated. I was reading an article about hydration in *Testomuscles Monthly*. The marathon special issue. It had advice for treadmill training too. Pulse pace calories incline distance speed time. It is important to monitor these things. Like the final run Miss Stephens did for me. I monitored her heart-rate and it went very high. I was worried for a moment.

Yes. That was the day that Miss Stephens went into the coma. When I saw her around midday for a last-minute PT session. But my mistake had nothing to do with letting her heart-rate get high. My mistake came later. It came when

I saw her for the second time that day. Not the third occasion which is when she went over the railing. No. It was the second time. Number two of three.

It was 3.35 p.m. I think when the trouble began. It must have been 3.35 p.m. because I had just completed my biweekly review of the lost-property cage. The review can be brilliant sometimes. In past years we have found among the T-shirts and socks a prosthetic foot a stuffed fox and a mains rechargeable scrotum-hair trimmer. But that day there were only half a dozen T-shirts and socks to add to my inventory so within a few minutes it was complete and I was heading to the towel room. The towel room is where I go after the lost-property cage before then circling back to the gym to give the equipment the end-of-week wipe-down with the blue spray. But as I was walking along the corridor I saw Miss Stephens. She was just inside the goods entrance. And Barbara her PA was there too. Jack calls her Battleaxe Barbara but her weapon is in fact a stick.

I do not think Barbara or Miss Stephens saw me. Miss Stephens was crouched over. She had her head in her hands and Barbara was standing over her holding some clothes on a hanger. I think Barbara was trying to stop Miss Stephens crying. I do not like it when people cry. The way it melts their face. Crying is not how people are supposed to look. And when Miss Stephens finally stood up I saw she was muddy. Normally she looks brilliantly clean but her clothes were very very dirty. I decided to stop monitoring her. I went to the towel room as planned.

I unlocked the towel room. Have you been? It is a warm safe place. All the nice clean towels are always hanging and drying completely white. It is lemon-fresh in there. And I went to the nook in the far corner as I always do and settled down. There is a kind of lemon-fresh lack of mess about the place. A simplicity. The kind you could get for a small while in the Raj bathroom if you really really scrubbed. I took out the little zip bag. I keep a small zip bag lodged by the boiler. I took out my antibacterial gel. And the antiviral gel. I . . .

OK.

It is not that it is just I do not want you to think . . .

I sometimes do this. Go in and unzip the gels so as to then cover my hands and lower arms. Purely as a precaution. To ensure cleanliness following the lost-property review. In case I have handled unpleasant socks or touched a hair trimmer in non-refundable condition. But while I was applying the gels I could not get Miss Stephens out of my head. Muddy. Crouching down. Crying. All that usual power she has that I wish I had even a shadow of. All of that gone. Later that Friday doing her speech she looked clean and pretty again drawing people into her eyes with that way she has but at this stage of the day when I committed my latest mistake she was out there looking muddy and sad and I could not shake the memory of her. So to try and shake the memory I did some counting. Just a little quirk I have. Nothing important but sometimes it is very nice to sit somewhere quiet and dark and count to seven. Perhaps try it. One two three four five six seven. You may think it is strange but it is just a little thing I do in the towel room sometimes after applying the gels. One two three four five six seven. A very small thing to relax. Some people smoke a cigarette but I like to count.

Rules?

Oh no rules. Except. Well. The only definite thing about the counting is that I have to do seven rounds of seven. That is very important. And sometimes as in the case of that Friday I have a propelling pencil in my hand. To tap out the seven on my knuckles. It would be a mistake however to think the pencil is always present. The important bit is to do the gels and the counting. I mean none of it is important it is just a little habit after all but after the gels and counting I can go back to the gym and spray down the equipment with the blue spray and everything will be brilliant again. Does that make sense? Do I sound very insane?

Thank you! OK. That Friday afternoon I am in my hiding place and I only achieve three rounds of seven with the pencil when the door creaks. The door creaks and a shard of light comes in. The light is beautiful in a way but it shows up a lot of dust which I did not know was hanging in the air. This is less than brilliant. I am not a supporter of dust. And also less than brilliant is the fact that I must have left the door unlocked. This fact justifies the thousand previous times I double-checked thinking I had forgotten to lock but actually I had. It gives sense to all those times I checked and checked so I know going forward I am going to have to build extra lock-checking time into the schedule. I am not complaining. I love my job. But the schedule is already very terribly tight you see? And anyway the door creaks. And the light comes sharding in. I see shadows. I hear two people giggling. One high giggle. One low. The low giggle is similar to the unusual noise Father makes if Mrs Hasan from Flat 15 says something amusing on our way to mosque. And then the light sort of shrinks but is still there a little.

And the lock locks from inside and the one with the low voice says something very strange.

I think he says.

He says. Says something like I fancy.

Yes. I fancy Peter the Great is going to enjoy it here. He says that which is perhaps a Russian reference or something of that nature? And then between two hanging towels I . . . well . . . I glimpse the lady kneeling down.

Act Two

COLOUR HER HAPPY

. . .'twas all one; – in whatever form or colour it presented itself to the imagination . . .

Laurence Sterne,
The Life and Opinions of Tristram Shandy, Gentleman

2.05 p.m.

WITH JANUARY clouds closing in low on the road it doesn't feel like 2 p.m., more like 2 a.m., the narrow slice of night in which everything has a smudged, unreal feel. This is it, the long-planned trip that will clarify all her confusions, and yet it feels so insignificant and vague – a small-hours stagger for a sleepy wee.

'Wherebouts on de Heath you lookin on?' her dread-locked cabbie says.

'Near South Hill Park,' Joy replies, horrified to perceive a hint of imitation in her accent. There is a song on the radio about New York – Tribeca, Harlem, Knicks and Nets – and the waves of pure, colourful sound wash up piecemeal memories of her seven childhood years there: taxis that are yellow not black; her dad's unabated insistence on his girls saying 'cars' not 'automobiles', 'petrol' not 'gas'; birds perched in the wires of Brooklyn Bridge like notes on a musical stave. One of the last times she was over there the news reported an al-Qaeda operative's plot to bring the bridge down by blowtorching through each supporting cable. You hear a lot about these highly sophisticated terrorist networks, but Joy struggles sometimes to shake that image – a scrawny guy on a hopelessly big bridge, his weapon of choice more useful for a crème brûlée than a terror attack. The rap music continues, wordplay linking and flowing with rests and gear changes that generate an oddly smooth structure.

In the back of the cab she clutches her Marc Jacobs bag. Through the window she sees other designer bags glide by. Make-up, BlackBerry, cigarettes, chewing gum, keys, iPod, tissues. She once asked Christine and some other girls from work if they found it funny, the way all of them bought the same bags from the same shops and filled them with the same stuff, but they just did the 'she's mental' eyebrow raise and changed the subject. People are so unknowingly identical in what they sling around their necks it makes Joy feels queasy sometimes, as if she alone is in possession of certain intense secrets about the way the world is arranged. She wonders if any of the other intermittently visible Marc Jacobs bags contain, in addition to the usual, sedatives and a suicide note. Maybe even these contents are not unique. The taxi turns and climbs a road lined with expensive Hampstead houses in pastel shades, a stucco staircase leading up to the sky.

As she falls asleep in the woods today her few true friends will fall, oblivious, into different things: married men's beds, sunloungers in the South of France, those little tubs of organic falafel. She has no doubt they will be better off without her. You can hear it in their long silences and sighs, their repetition of comforting clichés, the requisite reminder that Things Could Be Worse: you have become a burden.

She checks her pills, hoping they are strong. She refolds her note, hoping it is kind. She zips her bag, closes her eyes, swallows down a stubborn knot of sadness.

Lump in your throat. Joy never used to understand the phrase. But then when she was twenty-three her father, having his weekly shave, found a lump below his Adam's apple. He had become wealthy by investing in pubs and clubs, Brooklyn's only traditional English boozer to start with and then, in the nineties, the sorts of Soho nightspots frequented by It girls with mono-nostrils. Before all this he'd pulled pints and saved pennies, and if someone on the darts team he joined when Joy's mother finally agreed to move to England said his story was one of rags to riches he'd always, always say it was more like lads to bitches. He was famously thick-toned from years of raising his voice above the clatter of glasses and chatter of crowds, so his GP found nothing unusual in his patient's hoarse hello. And he felt no lump in his throat. 'Nothing,' the GP said, 'nothing at all.' A touch of hypochondria at worst. So, proud and private and not one to seek help twice, Tony Stephens (Anthony if you wanted to talk business) took himself home. He phoned Joy and said all was OK and asked what the best thing was about her new job, and only half joking she said, 'Nothing, nothing at all.' The following June he put a pistol in his mouth and blew a hole in his head. The autopsy showed advanced thyroid cancer. They said it must have been a struggle to swallow or sleep. And Joy, hearing this news, already spending each night wandering through the rooms of her own mind looking for a place to rest, worrying about her career choice and lack of boyfriend and the two pounds she'd put on since spring, felt nothing ahead of her, a doctor's mocking nothing, the nothing she did, the nothing she could do. You spend your life distrusting clichés and then they come true. Lump in your throat. Sick to death. So close you can taste it.

Death by misadventure. Coroner's sensitive verdict. Thought it possible the trigger went off accidentally, while he was cleaning his gun. Joy's sister, whose soaring career in PR had already left her depressed by second-rate spin-doctoring, responded most succinctly: 'Interesting choice by Daddy: to clean a gun with his *tongue*.'

From the moment she started planning this day she knew she didn't want to go by gun. Nothing noisy, nothing messy. She didn't want to jump in front of a Tube train either. You were screwing with people's schedules, not to mention the driver's mind. And it seemed a bit mean to rent a car just so she could fill it with fumes (plus it raised all sorts of new questions: how expensive do you go? hatchback or saloon?). No, what she needed was somewhere quiet, intimate, but at a distance – not her home, not her office. And then it clicked: the Heath.

It really is a nice handbag and maybe she should have left it for Christine to say sorry for the cancelled tennis and all the other unspoken stuff. No one will want the bag that accompanied the corpse. She should perhaps have brought her fake Fendi instead, a souvenir from a distant trip to Morocco where, amid the cries and shouts of market life, the barking of unchained dogs, the bird squawks, the voices of men calling out 'Asda prices' in cultivated cockney accents, she got ripped off but still felt good. Started to feel good for the first time since her dad's suicide. Except when she looked at Christine. On that holiday she did not feel good when she looked at Christine.

'You sure bout dis?'

She has given the driver a tip that's bigger than the fare.

'I'm sure,' she says, stepping onto the pavement. 'It's yours. Have a good day.'

As she slips into flats he winds the window down.

'Hey,' he says. 'Everybody have problem.'

'I'm sorry?'

'What I say, girl. Everybody have problem.'

He leaves this message hanging in the exhaust fumes and eventually she walks away, wondering.

By the time she reaches the gate, her fingers are swollen with cold. They ache when she presses them against the rough wood. The gate swings back with a groan and she steps forward, passing from the Heath into a private back garden shared by three homes. A few metres in front of her are some low hedges, then the curve of a familiar stream, and beyond that, over to the right, where grass stops and patio begins, the house she lived in between her seventh and eighteenth birthdays, now occupied by her sister. The walls and windows, aged five years since Joy last saw them, still look in fair repair. Before marrying Dennis Joy rented the top floor of a period conversion one cul-de-sac further back from the Heath than this one, and if you stood on tiptoes in the study, where the wall became the window, you had a weak sightline across the road and into the loft conversion her father finally got sorted the year before his death. It has since been reverse-converted back into a loft. To Joy this seems, like almost everything, to be a metaphor for modern life. After decades of wanting to turn storage spaces into living places we're going the other way again, realising the value of hideaways for all the odd lonely debris from our lives: notes from estranged friends, impulse purchases, deferred DIY.

Her sister's husband – a fat, forgetful man who is nonetheless an expert joke-teller – likes to tinker with motorbikes in a shed which stands on his side of the garden (too close, the council once claimed, to the property's perimeter). One such machine leans out of the shed door now, shiny black plastic caping it from the cold. She lurks behind one of the low hedges and a smell of petrol – or is it diesel? – reaches her through the intricate circuitry of twigs and brambles. As she crouches here, breathing hard, the coastal sound of traffic drifting in over rooftops, over satellite dishes cupping clouds and aerials raking sky, this scent from Jamie's bike shed begins to mingle with something deceitfully sweet, almost like fresh-cut grass, a suggestion that spring is much nearer than it is.

Joy means only to survey the scene from a distance and then get on with the day's business, but hearing laughter and a dog's barking she becomes intrigued – she didn't know they had a dog – and while lining up little things she'll say if caught she passes through a gap in the hedges and steps over the stream, watching out for frogs. There are no frogs, of course, just water which trickles so slowly over rocks it seems afraid of getting hurt. Excited by her own prying she moves past the children's swing and a smaller-than-remembered pond and lingers behind a tree. Dad, a fair-weather believer just like his daughters, used to say God was a great follower of fashion and that the lowest branch of this tree, dipping dramatically over the roof, was His moustache: in June the Almighty liked it Burt Reynolds bushy; in January, smart Clark Gable was the thing. The seat of the swing wears an inch of dirt. It shares with the leafless branches all around a lonely look inherited from winter. False expectation – maybe her sister will see her, run out, say Thank God you're here, I've wanted to get in touch – makes her heart beat childishly fast.

Then she sees her. The living-room window is a box of light in which she plays. Not her sister – a little girl, playing the piano. She heard they had a little girl. It was some small measure of comfort to hear that, fresh dressing on a wound. The child is not really playing the piano, admittedly; it's more a case of pressing one key repeatedly. Joy takes another step forward. She is pleased she has had the chance to see her niece. It doesn't matter that it is from a distance. The distance is a safe distance and even a step or two more would probably be OK. The tinkling noise the piano key makes acquires bass from the barking of the unseen dog and, desperate to see more, Joy takes three further steps, almost out in the open now, risking being seen. The little girl looks – can it be true? – a little sad around the eyes, like she's inherited some of her mother's mournfulness, but Joy's mind must be trying to find signs of misfortune in the face, mustn't it, for you can't inherit a trait borne from events.

The back door opens and a brutal-looking dog totters out: black, heavyset, carrying too much skin. A hairy arm puts food on the patio. Were Jamie's arms ever that hairy? The door snaps shut and with its balls swinging magnificently the dog bends into the bowl.

Joy takes a step back, twigs crackling underfoot. The dog turns, looks – yes – straight at her. There is a moment of total silence. The beast does not blink. And then it growls, and the fact that it growls after this thoughtful pause makes Joy feel that everything which is about to follow – the dog twisting towards her, tensing its muscles, starting to run – is part of some deliberate design. The animal has a plan.

It takes her no time at all to feel afraid, the mouth of the dog stretching back over ominous intimate teeth as it bounds at her, takes her no time to decide she needs to turn and run – human nature to run rather than hold your ground – and as her skirt rides up her thighs, legs lifting high, she trains her gaze on the hedges, she'll be all right if she can get to the hedges, and she just hopes she gets to the hedges as in one prolonged and airy and discontinuous instant she leaps over the stream and feels the hard soil shock her shoe-soles and turn her calves tense. Running, this whole day of planned composure turning into a run, skirt hitched and lungs burning as the hedges get closer and a second arrives in which she sees herself as the black dog must see her: a mass of moving monochrome, spooky-soft, another animal to bite and rip. How could they let this thing near their daughter? Her muscles go hard at the thought of their own ripping, her brain fear-charged, everything tight and trembly, and it feels like the dog is ten yards behind still running but maybe less. She is panting and navigating the unruly sprawl of roots underfoot and in a split second she'll have to decide what to do about the ragged wall of hedge – where's the gap in the hedge gone? – she half jumps half skips with her shoulder leading the way and comes out the other side with a slapstick bit of bush around one leg and knuckles lashed and grazed. Blundering through the back gate she risks a glance behind her and sees to her horror that the dog, closer and closer still, its muscles quivering, is bursting straight through the hedge mess she's thinned – straight through it and through the gate too – closing ground. She thinks she hears a growl but it might be the sound of the air in her ears as she sprints across shadows on half-frozen soil, handbag banging her thighs, fully into the Heath now and the fucking thing still chasing and this is when, pulse racing, unable to stop herself turning back for another look, she trips over her own feet and comes down hard.

Let it happen, is her thought. Let it happen. And as the dog leaps on her and thrusts its face down into her neck she has only that thought again: Let it happen.

But it does not happen. No teeth meet her throat. She is not being mauled.

Lying here with the dog on her chest, three facts reveal themselves: one, this dog is grey not black; two, this dog is smaller than I thought; three, this dog is licking my face.

When her breath has come back she lights a cigarette and pets its head. It looks pleased to have company. So much sagging skin it's like a taxidermist got bored mid-project. The long cone of ash leans close to its paw. The dog's eyes – sensitive to smoke? – go nervy and bright. She listens to the hum of its lolling tongue. Thought only cats could purr. She massages its back with long slow strokes.

Her grazed hand lifts the lit stub, hovers it above the paw, the ash about to drop. She has an urge to press the stub deep into the fur. She has an urge to hear the dog let out a small yelp, to see it run back to the house looking hurt.

She fears she will do this to the dog.

What if she did this to the dog?

She stretches her fingers out on the soil next to its paw. She looks at the back of her hand. She presses the stub into a vein.

Barbara

HALF THE staff are liars. Liars or – worse – fools. I know you're seeing some of them so I thought you'd like to know.

A fall and a jump are as different as a stapler and a hole punch. If you confuse the two you're either an Italian with mozzarella for brains or someone looking to mislead. She never did that to herself. Never did any of it. If there's foul play it was probably that Samir. When he held her feet during sit-ups he wore – he really did – gloves. Gloves! Wouldn't be surprised if he had something to do with her looking all beaten up in the basement that Friday afternoon. Only killers and lepers wear gloves. Him or Peter, both dark horses, both obsessed with her in their own way. Peter was down near the gym that afternoon. I know for a fact he was. Saw him going down there with his trainee, her wearing a dress that made no compromise with the weather, him carrying a bag with some bulky green thing poking out of it. Going fast with his head down, pretending he doesn't hear me calling him. Couldn't get hold of anyone to deal with the issue on Project Poultry. Had this key document and no one – never is! – to give it to.

I'm implying nothing. Implication is not a pastime I

partake in. We all have enough to worry about without getting into implication.

Me?

Since Friday?

Well the whole thing's been on my mind, hasn't it? At my age I've seen it all. You get older and men don't give you the glances any more, it's like you've become invisible, but the lack of incoming attention frees you up to be alert to what's around. To watch a pretty young woman falling from such a height, though. The impact was . . . the noise was so . . . real. Whole room seemed to vibrate. People went slack, dropped their champagne. Lawyers round here, corporate types with interchangeable heads, they stand so rigid most of the time. But seeing that happen they went all loose and childlike. There's no easy way to shrug that memory off. It's half the reason I need a break from this place. Do you think when I was a girl I imagined I'd still be stapling documents at seventy-three? That I'd have to practically beg these people to let me carry on for a few more years? That I wouldn't even be able to afford to go and visit Jackie, would instead be stuck working with fools with no regard for English? Yesterday I saw Alfredo looking at something on the Internet Explorer and I say, Hey, Alfredo, how about some work once in a while? And when I get close it turns out he's looking at flights. *He*'s looking at flights! And he says, I've got all these-ah air miles to use from my-ah trip to Australia last-ah year. Australia! I wish he'd go down under and never come up.

What? What do you mean?

You don't listen, do you? It's like a rule of the twenty-first century: don't listen. You're just like Alfredo. He doesn't listen.

You remind me of him, actually. The way you sneeze, it's like you've both been to the same Sneeze School. Perhaps on account of his similar nose you think you have something in common with him, do you? He's one of the group rushing to therapy, is he? I'm genuinely traumatised and he's coming here just to sit and chat and drink espresso? Well, lemme show you something that's going to change your mind, make you realise what a joker this Italian is. I told you I'd bring evidence and I have. This is what he's been doing when he's on the Visualise software. Debs, our Team Supervisor, she makes allowances – he's been selected for the Visualise software training – too busy for this – too busy for that – Joy Stephens wanted him on the Visualise Support Staff Trial. Well, fine, but is he actually using the Visualise software for proper business purposes? I had an obligation to go into his workspace. It was my duty to find out. And I present to you – yes, take it, have a look, you can keep this copy – Exhibit A.

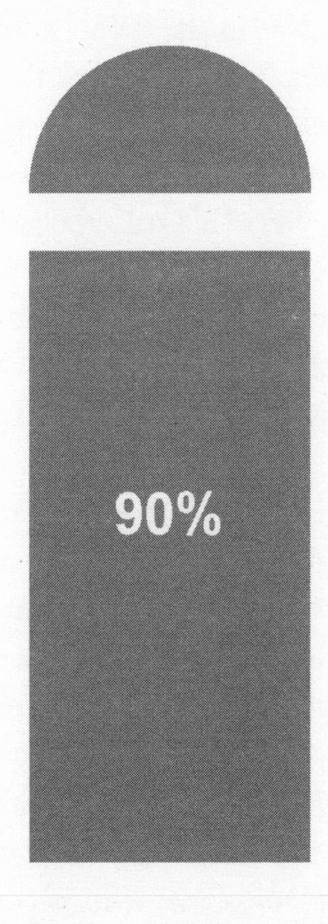

Percentage secretary* who think
Italian = better lover

*** Barbara abstain**

Exactly! As the fee-earners would say, smoothing out their costly hair, I rest my case. And there's more where that came from. You want to see?

Makes no difference to me. Why should I care?

Maybe, maybe not. Have a cup of this and tell me what you think of the exhibit. You want a cup?

Well, that's possible. Finally you speak some sense. We all need an outlet. We're all still children deep down. But either way – you doing one of those no-caffeine things? – either way there are days when my new hip causes me no trouble at all. There are worse things than a new hip. I'd take a new face if they'd give me one. If our National Health Service is so great where's my platinum cream! There were weeks when she'd come in, tell me she'd given up caffeine, meat, water. I'd just nod. She'd have me running around at lunchtime on a new hip to find her some bread-free, meat-free chicken sandwich, or sushi with no cardboard footprint. Would give me maybe ten pounds and with the juice it would come to maybe seven and she'd say, Barbara, you're a star, and Barbara, keep the change, which quite frankly is somewhat patronising, don't you think? I wanted to say to her: Joy, do I look like someone who accepts tips? The only tipping I'm worried about is the toe-stubbing type that sends me flying down the stairwell. And if it wasn't for the fact I needed it, the money, I would have refused point-blank to take it. Plain as day I would. It's a strange universe they live in, don't you think, where their own pride is so big they can't see anyone else's?

I think there might be an issue with the heating. If you're OK – natural insulation and so on – don't worry, I don't fuss over weather. Alfredo is Italian and I have nothing against

Italians but, like Joy, he thinks he's the heart of the world. Always laughing that our English weather doesn't suit him, fussing with our section's thermostat like he's the Lord God Almighty. Well, I'm sorry to disappoint, but next Monday, when I have enough evidence, I'm going to put a stop to his grinning. Nothing brings me down like that man's grin. All that flirty nonsense with the younger girls in my section, who does he think he is? He creeps up on them like global warming. Invades their environment. Though in truth when people talk about global warming I think about how much further my winter-fuel allowance might go. I mean generally on the question of global warming I take the standard English perspective – I'm in favour – but when it comes to visiting Jackie and the little ones on her side of the family? If a special summer offer from a travel company was advertised in the *Mail*? Well I wouldn't want to go in summer. A New York summer? I'd boil! Now if I was a fee-earner – ha! – if I was one of them I'd charge flights to business development and go whenever I wanted. Don't even get me started on business development and the things they can claim. I've got four fee-earners I look after plus the Halfwit Peter Carlisle on temporary cover while Lauren's off with irritable bum syndrome and one of them – remains unnamed – he gets Booking Desk taxis with his hedge-fund friends to – to? – yes – Private Liaisons – buys them all sorts – they leave voicemails the next day – say, oh – oh, Peter – that girl – that girl was *hot*. He thinks I don't know what Private Liaisons is but I do. I've seen the fake money on his desk, with the G-string where our Gracious Queen should be. You want to dish out some therapy, you should dish it out to him. All these lawyers. They're not people. They're professionals! They're the opposite of people! Is it fair that he gets ferried back and forth, charging champagne and nipples and who knows what, and I can't get to New York to see Jackie? I wouldn't fly in winter. Too cold. Was saying that to Dennis this morning at the hospital. Leave winter to the Eskimos. One of Alfredo's favourite pastimes, analysing the Eskimos. He should try some work once in a while – stop drawing stupid pictures with his Visualise – stop talking about people of no consequence like the Eskimos. Never trust a people with sixty thousand words for snow.

What was that? Speak up. You're too nasal for this world.

Yes, yes, at the hospital this morning.

Well, if you'll permit me to speak once in a while, that was the unusual thing. It wasn't actually in that bit of the hospital. I'd been to see Joy at the whatschacall, *ICU*. She was much as she'd always looked, despite the coma. Her skin was still smooth and girlish, and the chin was raised a bit. Gave her a look of anticipation. Only the tubes and beepers made her strange. And those plastered legs, all raised. So I sat with her a while and told her various things, including the Alfredo business, the fact someone's got to put a stop to it, and then on the way out I manage to get lost in the corridors. I don't know why the NHS doesn't invest in some *signs*. Hospitals are full of people who'd be happier if they knew where they were going. So I'm wondering where to go and I get approached by some boy-nurse and he says all kindly, Have you forgotten which room's yours, dear? And I chuckle, and he chuckles, and then I thwack him with my stick and keep walking. Then finally I get to a reception desk with someone in uniform behind it who's thankfully older than twelve – black as the ace of spades, poor girl, but with a friendly face – and I go up to ask her where I am. But just before I speak I see that in this little waiting area to the side of the desk there's Dennis. And I think about just ignoring him. Lemme tell you, to give that man a minute is to give him your best years. But anyway I decide I should say hello. Maybe make him feel valued by asking his views on the best airlines going to New York these days and what have you. All a theoretical, of course, for when my fair share of overtime comes back. And you should see the surprise on his face when he sees me. His eyebrows and his ears – almost as big as your ears, to give some context – they float up.

Barbara, he says.

Dennis, I say.

You're here, he says.

And I tell him let's not get into philosophising, it's too early in the day.

So we talk for a bit but – *but* – it's not the usual wading through mud. He keeps his sentences all short. Mainly little asides the mind forgets. The only thing I truly remember him saying is that when Joy slept next to him she'd often jerk awake. You know, sudden movement, two or three times a night. He said in her dreams she was falling all the time. Those were his words. Falling all the time. Probably fancies himself as a poet. And he looked off into the distance like he really was some kind of poet, rummaged in his pocket all suspicious, got out his phone, and tapped something into it.

I've always been conscious of avoiding tactlessness, so I

didn't ask him what he was tapping into his phone. Me and the girls keep a spreadsheet to avoid tactlessness, a list of fee-earners who are going through difficult times, to remind ourselves that if we're surly to them we could get sacked like what happened to Teri. At the moment there's three lawyers with cancer, two on nervous breakdowns, one who's recovered from self-harm but isn't allowed scissors or staple removers, four with a recently deceased parent and twelve with chronic fatigue syndrome. So with my heightened awareness of impoliteness I don't ask Dennis what he's tapping, I ask instead why he's sitting in a different wing of the hospital to the one his wife's in. And do you know what he says?

He says – wait for it – Peter normally visits around this time. That was it. No further explanation. Peter normally visits around this time, he said. As if that explained him sitting in a completely different wing of the hospital.

Isn't that one of the strangest things you've ever heard?

Well, it got me thinking. The Halfwit Peter Carlisle must have had something to do with Joy's accident. Must have done, mustn't he, or else Dennis wouldn't have said that.

Don't you think?

Who knows.

Your guess – if you believe the phrase – is as good as mine.

2.25 p.m.

SHE FINDS the area easily, making only one further stop on the way, a quick look at a tree-tacked poster for a missing cat. Already wasted enough time today on people's pets but she's a sucker for these posters; more than tsunamis or earthquakes they make her maudlin. Something deep and dreamy about this realm of woodland. Trees bunched like troubles. They crowd around unexplained clearings in which only earth seems to grow – within itself, swelling against its own skin.

This is the clearing she wants to view. She will get this right. It will be her focus however tired she gets. Licks the cigarette wound on her hand. Wedges herself between two tree stumps to face the right place. In a final shuffle to remove a twig from under her bum she grazes her jacket sleeve. Everything grazed – clothes, skin, Marc Jacobs. Chips of bark lie about wearing downy flakes of frost. She imagines how in a few hours her nylon tights will shimmer like stalactites. Tights; stalactites. The pun gives her a weak little stab of satisfaction.

She has trapped herself well. It hurts to flex her right arm but she can manoeuvre her wrist just enough to access the bag. She has a hundred-strong tub of sleeping pills inside. Enough to kill a whale. Enough to send the whole of Dispute Resolution sailing down the stream. Her left hand has to balance the BlackBerry on her legs so that it can join the right and open the tub. Press. Twist. The motion and the click make her think of the time she found her mother's tablets, played with them a while as the adults argued downstairs. Bitter and bulky. Not like her yogurt raisins at all. At Lenox Hill Hospital on East 77th Street, as Joy slowly woke, stomach pumped, feeling her throat had been torn open by the tube, her mother said the same line to any medic who'd listen. 'The thing about child-proof tops is that they only work on retarded children.' Cold is settling into her fingers and toes. 'Does my child look retarded to you, Doctor?'

She will get this right. Nothing will distract her. Except perhaps if she sees Brambles the Cat, in which case she may take time out to return him.

Wriggling her skirt upward she pinches the tub of pills between her knees. She settles on a method whereby the tip of her index finger rubs each drug up the inner plastic wall and through the container's neck, at which point the thumb has room to assist. Each pill torpedo-shaped. White. The cigarette burn, a little pink crater of collapsed flesh, has a twinkle in it. She must remember to tug the skirt back down when she's done. No appearance of sexual interference.

Pill number one. Chalky-bitter in her mouth. Gets a blood rush from its foul foam, pauses to let air allay her nausea. Should have brought water. Expert dry-swallower but not with these. The website said Easy Swallow, Easy

Sleep. Internet: just a sticky web of half-truths and hard-ons. Should have lined her stomach too. Couldn't eat that chicken sandwich. Felt she could taste the bird's terror in the mayo. Two: *disgusting*. Three: less bad. The fourth and fifth pills add padding to her own closed world. Six catches in throat, comes back up on a cough. Stay positive. Bilesurf on the tongue will help seven and eight slip down. Amid the dark raftered trees her heart beats quickly. The sweet-scented silence is endless. The light moves. A squirrel pads its harmless face. A leggy crow steps over twigs. A single drop of thawed water shuffles down a branch. But none of this peculiar beauty is enough, not today, not for Joy, and she will make sure she gets this right.

Perhaps this is why she's picked a place she was once happy: in order to challenge herself, to be certain she is not blind to the consequences.

The shuffling drop of water is a rehearsal for some greater gesture. Damp wind catches her collar and the air it brings is new, full of turning earth and wet wood, the very same scent that wafted around Centre Court that day. Odd thoughts of crows wearing acrobats' tights are washed away by a pronounced rush of rain tapping on leaves, slipping through sleeves, running the rivulets of trees. Ever since her teens she's made these wanton rhymes in her head, a weakness for learning lyrics to Pearl Jam or Nirvana, little poems where the sounds mattered more than the meanings. You supplied the meanings yourself, so they fitted the exact love-struck predicament you were in, and there was something consoling about wearing headphones, lying in the dark of your den, your field of vision reduced to the size of a fist, rain touching the window as it touches her skin now, more insistent every second. The sky cries like a sulky child and she feels a sluggish frustration in her veins, clotting into anger.

Anger. Good. Anger will keep you focused, a pinball in your system. Show the Heath who's boss. Show the sky you're serious.

She will get this right.

She will make the call. Planned to take more pills first but worried now the rain will get the BlackBerry wet. Dropped it in a glass of wine once – sex with Dennis or was it Peter? – SIM card didn't fare well. After the gym she put her desk phone on voicemail and shut her office door. The plan is to call that phone, leave a message saying here I am. When it gets past five and they realise she's not going to be there to make the speech Barbara will check Joy's office and see the red light on the phone and listen and tell the police and it could, should, *will* avoid some poor unsuspecting woman, looking for her cat on a crisp sunny Saturday, finding Joy here all soaked and blue. Later, in her desk drawer, the police will discover a second identical tub of pills, together with a printed Internet receipt, and with the suicide note these pieces of the evidential puzzle will help them rule out foul play straight away. Couldn't stand the thought of some tawdry investigation dragging on, facts unravelling in her absence.

Joy makes the call. It rings once. She prepares to hear her own voice. To hear your own voice on a machine: one of life's many small tortures. It rings twice. It shouldn't ring twice. It should go to voicemail. It rings three times. It really shouldn't –

'Joy?'

What the fuck?

'Hello? Joy? Is that you? It's your number, but I can't hear so well.'

'Barbara?'

'Joy, I don't know what you're doing there, it sounds like you're in a hot tub or something, but wow am I glad to have you on the phone.'

'Barbara, I . . . I'm in the middle of something.'

'Well I've got to tell you that sits kind of strange when it's you that called me.'

'I didn't call you! I called me!'

'Well it seems double strange to interrupt yourself but there you go. I didn't go to law school or get fancy grades. So this chicken man's been phoning *me*. Everything urgent and so on and complaining your phone goes straight to voicemail. So I check and he's right so I call-forward it straight to mine while you're in your hot tub or whatever and then he calls you and it comes through to me and still I've got nothing to say except I'm not sure where you are.'

A fearless squirrel with perfectly alive eyes seems to have taken an interest in her tub of pills, advancing across the picnic spot she and her sister used to love. Bad squirrel! She shoos it away, tries to reimagine her nephew there crouching in a square of sun, digging with a twig, same long lashes as his mum, weird how traits like that pass on, a kind of budget immortality, saying 'Auntie, is there colouring books for my birthday?' Wants to remember but doesn't want to remember. Hurts her to think about it – his fifth birthday, colouring books unwrapped – physically hurts her like the memory is a living thing clawing at her head. Leaning over him to see the picture of the tree.

Reading him the instruction Colour It Green. The outline of the smiling woman. Text underneath saying Colour Her Happy. Handing him the green crayon, handing him the pink; checking he knew leaves were green, checking he knew lips were pink.

She unsticks a wet curl of fringe from her forehead and says, 'Tell him to email me or I'll call him later.'

'He said it's urgent, Joy. Those protesters keep leafleting about his company. The whatschacall.'

'Meat Musketeers.'

'The Meat Musketeers keep leafleting the street. He said there's this new leaflet out and he wants to injunct or something. He emailed me the leaflet. It says they genetically alter the birds for bigger thighs and breasts. Sounds good to me, it means more meat, none of my concern, but it says they mess up the birds so the bones can't support the weight so they're all mangled all the time until they die. It says chickens are put in cages the size of this leaflet. It's an A4 leaflet. What kind of name is Meat Musketeers? Then it talks about the slaughterhouse and the way fully conscious birds are hung upside down on an assembly line, it says assembly line, and that the millions of birds that don't get killed by the hit-and-miss mechanical blade die in boiling hot water and are called redskins.'

'OK.'

'He wants to know whether that's defamation slander or a libellous what-have-you. I don't know if it's relevant but there's lots of fonts and colours on the leaflet and miniature designs bordering the page. There are cracked shells with words like immoral, addictive and poisonous on them and little chickens emerging. There is a pair of hands cupping stuff about Third World starvation. Also I've picked up your dry-cleaning and put it in your office.'

'Christ.' She has been through this. It is raining. To be defamatory it needs to be false. It needs to be untrue. The client knows this. Rainwater is streaming down her fingers and face and the squirrel has taken shelter somewhere behind her. 'Tell him it's possible we could get them on the mention of it being "poisonous". They may have gone too far on that. And ask him about whether it's really "millions" that aren't killed by the blade. That sounds high. Tell him to check up some statistics with his farm managers. And ask Peter to get a trainee to look up the legal definition of "poison". In fact get Peter to call the client. Make sure Peter's up to speed, tell him I'm relying on him.'

Relying on Peter! What a joke!

'Joy, this client's excitable. My hip hurts. Also the trainee's gone to the doctor's and left me with this document from the document review he said you should see. Are you sure you don't want to come back to the office for a minute and –'

'No. I can't. I simply can't. And, Barbara?'

'Joy?'

'I'm sorry. Really I am. There's money in my desk drawer for the dry-cleaning.'

Fuck the woman looking for Brambles. She doesn't care who finds her. Doesn't even care if her sister finds her. Teach the vindictive bitch a lesson. Forgiveness. Where was the forgiveness? How can one mistake in a life cock up the whole canvas? She takes another pill. Some rain has got in the tub. The ground is getting muddy and a puddle – no, a swamp – has formed by her left knee. She shivers. She wants to stop thinking about chickens. This is not the life that is supposed to flash before her eyes. *Redskins*. She takes one more pill but it's soggy and bitter and she retches and retches until the last three pills maybe four come burning up her throat and make a broken yellow yolk in the rainwater.

She is trying so hard to get it right but tears are stirring deep in her ducts and she feels herself failing even at this. She tries to think happy thoughts. She remembers Dennis asking her to marry him along Regent's Canal, his knee unwittingly picking a puddle. She was accidentally pregnant, desperate to make a change, and genuinely relieved and touched that someone who knew how careless she could be wanted to spend their adult life with her. She might not have loved him before, but in that moment, when she said 'Yes, I love you', she meant every word. Some feelings are like this – they become true when you say them. She wanted to be his wife, take his name, wipe her identity, start again.

Cages the size of this leaflet. Bones can't support the weight. Birds all mangled all the time.

She sent people an email saying she was engaged. Her university friends wrote *Joy, congratulations!!!* Her school friends wrote *Joy, where has this come from?* One of her friends wrote *Joy, you sneaky sausage*, and attached a picture of two chipolatas on a plate.

The chipolata friend had introduced her to Dennis. They went on a few dates, and then there was the tennis match and everything after. She tried to stop him visiting, but he kept visiting. He chased a journalist down the street. He went with her to see scientists and psychics. She was in love with her best friend's husband, but where was he now, why wasn't *he* making tea in her kitchen and leaving plates of stew steaming under sixty-watt bulbs? Dennis did stews; Christine did cakes; Peter stayed away. He stayed away for the first couple of months after her nephew went missing and for this brief period she could not imagine ever speaking to him again, let alone sleeping with him, but she had a religious attachment to self-destruction, it seemed, to the risky moments you had to fight for, the seconds so sneakily stolen they became precious. She read somewhere that approaching orgasm most of a woman's brain shuts down – the emotional parts, the fear centres, they go blank on the scan – and if she was ever taken to trial she'd cite this in her defence.

Her attraction to Peter pre-dated Hanger's and Dennis and her friendship with Christine. She recognised him immediately on the first day of their induction at the firm, knew he was the boy she'd kissed at a drunken law-school party the previous summer – tall, offhand, tanned – the one she'd hoped would call but didn't. She spotted him despite the all-transforming suit, felt her heart trip a little, and within a minute he'd slipped through a clump of tastefully dressed trainees and was standing before her, the only one who'd chosen beer over wine, strangely nervous in this setting, tilting forward on his toes.

'Hi Peter,' she said. 'How's things?'

He looked thrilled that she'd remembered his name.

'All the better for seeing you,' he said.

'You look the same.'

'Do I?'

'You look exactly the same.'

No one knew they'd kissed before and that secret was

the seed from which, over the years, so many bigger lies branched.

In the middle of all these lies Dennis remained dependable. She loved thoughtful docile Dennis. The appetite for risk was within her, but so too was the need for someone safe and kind. He brought her things when she got depressed: flowers, crackers, perspective. His sentences were full of the outside world. He had secretless eyes and an upright nose. He was conceited but not really. He was serious but not really. There was a quiet compassion in the way he moved. There was warmth and hesitancy in his voice. He carried no storage space for past pains. He wore corduroy with tennis shoes like her father used to do. He liked the Eagles, he really did. He wasn't interested in stock-market trends or the biscuits they give you at Goldman Sachs. He wanted her deep in his big dusky bones. He knew things about books she'd forgotten she loved. He felt like someone she'd known since school. Her school friends said *Joy, where has this come from?* – but he was honourable and alive, a mystical jumble of quirks and qualities that appeared in her life at just the right time, and from where else, exactly, can a relationship come?

Has it stopped raining?

It has stopped raining.

Reaching out once more for the pill tub she remembers the last few years as a ten-second segment of time: marriage, pregnancy, infidelity. The long cold slide into loneliness.

She listens to the leftover drip of leaves. She looks at the goosebumps on her hands. Cold has blanched the cigarette burn, made it bland as the paling sky. She thinks of her nephew and stares into the clearing and – God! Go away! – the squirrel is sniffing around the yolk of sick and as her body contorts the tub between her legs topples and pills spill into the mud. She thrusts a hand forward. The fabric of her jacket rips. The rodent darts ninety degrees up a tree. Pain spins through her nerves. Tablets sullied, sinking, cased in dirt and only one or two still clean and whole and in the confusion her phone starts ringing and trying to stab it dead she hits speakerphone and into the dark damp wood Barbara's voice stutters obscurely into life:

'JOY WILL YOUR HOT TUB BE FINISHED BY FIVE BECAUSE IF NOT I REALLY NEED TO KNOW.'

Peter

So I've remembered a weird thing about that Friday: some kleptomaniac stole the firm's brand-new pet reptile.

The day of Joy's suicide attempt was, with a touch of gruesome irony, the firm's Make Law Fun Day. Once a year, to coincide nicely in the PR calendar with its partnership promotion announcements, Hanger's buses in a load of underprivileged kids from all over the country and makes them sit through aspiration-raising talks about life in the Square Mile. Journalists come and take snaps and it tends to bury a few of the usual stories re 80 per cent of new partners being public schoolboys. The 'Life in Law' session I was due to put on for these rat-tailed little snotbags that Friday afternoon tenuously pertained to tropical wildlife; I was to entertain them with anecdotes about a recent Madagascan case and its associated environmental issues. Thus Mental Brian decided that what the session needed was, you guessed it Doctor Odd, some tropical wildlife. A visual aid, as he kept saying.

After giving up hope of purchasing our first choice of beast – a genuine Madagascan chameleon – I had Jessica source a small lizard. She installed it in the towel room by the gym. Hot, dry, perfect. But when we went down there to pick it up in good time for our talk, and also so that we could photograph it sitting on Barry 'No Relation' White's forearm, which bears an incredibly intricate tattoo of a snarled tree branch he attributes to a night spent in Utah, we found someone had stolen the thing. Well, that's what we discovered the second time we went to get it. The first time, Jess and I got a bit distracted talking about some billable issue and forgot about the lizard entirely. When we came back a few minutes later the cage was still there, locked, but with not so much as a kiwi fruit inside. Photographing it on Barry's arm now seemed like a distant dream.

Point is, there are clandestine lizard thieves among us. And from that simple observation you can, I suggest, extrapolate a wider truth. The truth is that every single person in our office has something – however plain, however puzzling – to hide. In any office, secrets are like electricity, the strange currencies that keep the lights bright, but it's especially true in the City.

Let me take you back to my induction day at Hanger's. The famous eye-lock moment in the movies. I think I knew, secretly, instantly, that I had to have her. I was chatting to one of the other new trainees, exchanging perfunctory politenesses while keeping a finger or two on my down-tilted chin, a way of embedding sincerity in the choreography of our exchange, when I saw these fatally pretty legs and rushed – mid-sentence – to be with them.

Hi Peter, Joy said. How are things?

And of course I knew instantly that she must be attracted to me. She'd clearly studied the little photo bios that HR had handed out. How else would she know my name? She even made a comment about how I looked *the same*. Interesting tactic, I thought to myself. Not even trying to disguise that she'd been pawing at my picture, comparing it to the real-life me. Later on it turned out we'd met before, in hazy circumstances, but the point is the attraction was intense and we both felt it instantly. Too intense, too concentrated, to squander in the diluting context of an actual relationship. No, what we felt wouldn't have fitted in a homely old boyfriend–girlfriend scenario, not at all. Secrets: they're the thing we live for. Two people are in a perfectly happy marriage, supporting each other, making each other Lemsip when winter kicks in. What more could they want, I hear you cry. The answer? Something else. Secrets. Lies. Risks. Small breaks from the known. They have to be small, mind you. On special occasions I love to have a bath – nothing better than sinking into the heat, letting the water swallow me up. But if I had one every day? Baths would become routine, like showers.

Christine was always my Lemsip provider, my daily shower. Which isn't to say that I don't love her. I love her very much. When she gets back from this silly space-to-think sojourn at her parents' place, or answers one of my bloody phone calls, I'll tell her that and I'll mean it. But even in the love-filled moments in your life, the ecstatic headline moments, there lurk secret desires for something different. In fact, especially in those moments.

I'll give you an example: my wedding.

The big day. Christine was desperate to have a big day and I gave it to her. Big days don't come cheap. I spent a fucking fortune. You plan a wedding and you find that even the flowers come in two-grand increments: a couple of thousand for the cheapest, four thousand for the middling ones, six thousand for the wall-to-wall full-colour floral floor and table displays with reinforced stems that wouldn't even wilt if Alan Allan (aka 'Alan Squared') caught them with his Human Fire Hose party piece. Some prissy-mouthed harlot takes you on a tour of the venue and says in her Surrey sing-song voice that it's really just a question of what you can afford for your special day. I went for the six thou option. Of course I did. I wanted her to be happy. I wanted to celebrate our elevation into the bouquet-buying classes. And she *was* happy, walking up the aisle. I could see it: her happiness was undisguised. Which made me happy, because I loved her. But part of my happiness – a quarter, say, or a fifth – was derived from somewhere other than her, from glimpsing the gorgeous Joy off to the side, nervously twirling her order of service in the second row. Part of my joy was Joy. She was not marriage material – no, Joy Stephens was too impulsive and unpredictable for that, liable to crack a plate over my head at a moment's notice, the skittering defiance that women from well-to-do backgrounds have, daring to be damned – but I still felt . . . privileged, if that's the word, to have a secret connection with her. It was my wedding day. One hundred people staring as I said my vows. A grin on my face, happy as could be. And no one else there, not even Joy, knew that part of my happiness was down to the affair. I was secretly suffused with her, my lover, the way something gets suffused by colour, or water, or light. Joy Stephens's presence at my wedding amplified my happiness. Strange? Perhaps. But true. She was part of me, forbidden and true. This is not heartlessness. This is a statement of the way people, moments, can become a hidden part of who you are.

Not convinced?

Let me give you another example. Wimbledon. Summer 2005. There is an official version of events, and then there is the reality. The official version is that Joy was queuing for the toilets with her nephew, just the two of them and a bunch of strangers. She took her BlackBerry out of her bag. She looked at it. She felt something at her feet. She thought it was the boy, tugging to get her attention. She looked down. It was just chocolate wrappers. He was gone. There was a huge police search. Public outcry. Some public outcry, anyway. A girl in the Home Counties had gone missing the same week. The papers prefer girls, apparently. But even with this other disappearance splitting the journalists' resources, there were already photographers outside Joy's sister's home when she got back from France. One of the neighbours, a public-spirited little Hampstead busybody with a view into their lounge, rented out her spare room to a few of the more persistent paparazzi. Ten pounds an hour. Long lenses leaning out of windows, trained on a crack in the curtains, checking that the grief was real. These days you always suspect the family, don't you? And then of course all the freaks came out to play. The constant caller who pretends to be their son, wailing for help. The faith healer who says the body's buried under the Houses of Parliament. The Egyptian pimp who sold him to a king.

All these pieces of the story – police search, paparazzi, crank calls – are known to those close to Joy. This is the official version of events. But the whole narrative is built on that initial image, isn't it? Of it being just Joy and the boy, standing in the queue, her checking an email on her BlackBerry, feeling something at her feet, seeing her nephew was gone. But that initial image is false.

Doctor Odd! Come on! You heard me the first time. It isn't true. It's been – for want of a better word – doctored.

Do me a favour and put your pen down, will you? We both know this has nothing to do with my so-called trauma. I'm merely telling you how the world works.

I know because I was there. I was taking clients to the tennis. Joy and Christine were having a day of annual leave but I was in the hospitality suite, actually working. And I happened to . . . well, there Joy was, running up and down the queue, in a complete state, saying she'd lost the boy. But she'd been chatting to someone moments before, when it happened. It wasn't just her and the kid. There was a third person, a source of distraction. But, as I told her at the time, she would have been mad to say that to the police. Sorry, officer, I left the five-year-old to play with a bit of litter over there while I was having a nice chinwag. Come on. They'd massacre her. Criminal negligence, it could be argued. Her sister, as it turned out, massacred her anyway, but that's beside the point. The point is I had the presence of mind to look around for a camera and, when I saw there wasn't one trained on the queue outside the loos, advised her accordingly: Listen, Joy, you were in the queue, just you and the kid, and you may have briefly checked your BlackBerry but otherwise you were focused.

Not one of the witnesses contradicted her. Proof, if you ever needed it, that some people on this earth are revoltingly wrapped up in themselves.

Simple as that. The truth becomes a secret. A lie becomes

the truth. And the official version is built up from those shaky foundations.

I predict the same with Cuthbert the Lizard. An official explanation for his disappearance will emerge, and then several counter-explanations will be floored, and soon everyone in the office will be giving their version of the circumstances in which he slithered away. It'll be fun for a while, everyone trying to be entertaining in the telling, adding their own splash of colour to the few known facts. Like a tireless TV show – crocodile tears, canned laughter, pretend happiness – there'll be a certain fake energy carrying us along. And then we'll all get bored and switch off. Even Mother, who with Dad taking to his bed has found herself wedded, instead, to the television, will switch off when the soap writers have recycled the storyline one too many times.

Have I heard from who? Mother?

No. You raise a good point. I need that phone number from her. For Christine's parents. I must admit, I'm beginning to get the feeling I am at the sore end of some kind of conspiracy. Christine's hiding out at her parents' house, refusing to return my calls. My own mother won't call me back. Emails disappear into cyberspace to no noticeable effect. What's everyone hiding from me? How am I supposed to get my marriage back on track?

There's something wrong, something missing. I'm just too busy on Project Poultry to work out what. And . . . Hang on, I'd better read this.

Oh for fuck's sake.

Shit fuck bollocks cock.

An email from Charles Jestingford! Saying we should grab a coffee!

Because Jestingford is one of the most feared and revered partners in the firm. If he wants to buy me a coffee, it means he's got a new case for me, and if he's got a new case for me, it means I'm not going to see a weekend until spring.

Tiny Tony and I peered into Jestingford's office this morning. He's just had it fitted out with all this new stuff. Tony kept going on about the antique mahogany desk and how he'd like something similar for his attic conversion – a domesticated beast at heart, old Tone, an asexual romantic with a fondness for furnishings – but the thing that really bothered me was that glinting whiteboard hanging above it, complete with marker pens and foam eraser, seeming to suggest that the old-fashioned pinboard in my own office was now a reckless relic of less enlightened times. I am going to ask my PA to procure one. Bill it to Office Optional Furnishings. Before this coffee meeting, if I can.

3.05 p.m.

'I MEAN,' says her second driver of the day, 'people will assume a certain ignorance of your basic cabbie. No, no, hear me out. Not everyone. But some. Many. The snobbish or selfish. Whereas in fact I know drivers – we're not talking the minicab boys, of course – with degrees from Oxford and Cambridge. I myself have qualifications in ancient writings. I did a course on the Romans and I still find – we'll do a left here, it's chocker to Cheapside – that Seneca's writings are a whopping great reserve of strength.'

'Seneca's bollocks,' Joy mutters.

'He's the bollocks all right, couldn't agree more.'

His face hangs big and rosy in the rear-view mirror, a pink planet of people seen and people judged. With a twitch of its twenty-five-foot turning circle, an engineering feat he's already explained in lavish detail, the black cab banks into a thin dark street. Death-shaped cameras are poised on posts. Her heart beats distastefully in its chest. How has she failed at this, the easiest of pursuits, the long falling into nothing? She'll go to the office, pick up the second tub of pills from her desk drawer, head back to the Heath and see the job through. Maybe buy a knife too, in case she needs it as a fallback, or for killing troublesome squirrels.

'Of course,' he continues, 'Seneca remains one of the few popular philosophers of the period. There are many works since in which he's referenced. Many works.'

'Appears in Dante,' she says, feeling the need to show a little knowledge.

'He's in Chaucer, he's in Dante. Very quotable, like Virginil.'

'Virgil.'

'My set reading included the old Erasmus edition. Yeah. Found it bloody fascinating.'

Joy has unclipped her seat belt. She is trying to use a wet wipe on her shoe. The portion of properly swallowed sedative is making this tricky. She has begun to see double of everything: twenty polished pink toenails, four ankles, and two signs about the fouling charge. She may well have to pay if they continue through dizzying backstreets, tyres hiccuping over welts in the road, the whole vehicle inviting her to vomit.

'Don't take this the wrong way,' he says, 'but you seem messed up. Is that blood on your shirt?'

'Mud.'

'And in your hair?'

'Moss.'

'Moss?'

'Moss.'

'I see . . .'

Why isn't everyone blowing their brains out? Why don't they make bigger wet wipes? With the driver forced to pause at traffic lights she asks him for another one from the glove compartment, and with his face bathed in a red glow which with dreamlike speed becomes amber, then green, he passes it through the perspex window like that Chinese client of hers always gives his card: two-handed. A small fly, one of those that's little more than a speck of dust, hitches a ride in the wet wipe's airspace. She claps it dead mid-flight. You kill the things that bug you. The taxi driver is beginning to bug her. She wishes she could get her old driver back, the mysterious taciturn dreadlocked guy who condensed the entire history of human thought into three smiling, unsettling words: 'everybody have problem'. She decides her best tactic with the current chatty cabbie is to tee up a soliloquy, turn their patchy interaction into an ignorable white noise.

'Tell me about Seneca,' she says, and hears, as she sometimes does, her sister's tone of tart disinterest. It is how her family approaches conversations with strangers – from a distance, scared of suffocation.

With an edge of scepticism he says, 'Yeah?'

'Go ahead. Please. I have unexpected time on my hands.'

'OK. Seneca. Right. Well, in lesson one of these classes of mine . . .'

Dennis made reference to Seneca one night. They were – that's it – sitting fireside on the rug, with Riesling and carrot cake, one creepy jazz track shy of a romcom cliché. She'd recently had an abortion, and as they sat there talking she felt surprisingly untroubled, grateful to have her body back. The conversation began with *Othello*; they'd been to a matinee earlier that day. Her own recreational instincts tended towards *Heat* magazine and Häagen-Dazs, or at most a subtitled film and reduced-fat hummus, but under Dennis's influence she was starting to take pleasure in becoming (in his phrase) a Proper Culture Vulture.

'You know,' he said, 'one thing about Shakespeare: he was rather keen on suicide. Like Seneca, he saw exit routes everywhere.'

This interested her. Dennis had things to say and, back then, he took less time to say them. 'Othello kills himself, but who else?'

He listed some: Cleopatra, with the venom of the asp; Juliet, with Romeo's dagger; Mark Antony, with his sword; Romeo himself, with poison. 'It's like Elizabethan self-murder Cluedo,' he said. 'Ophelia with the willow branch in the brook.'

'Ophelia fell! It was an accident.'

'She made no attempt to swim.'

'Lessons were scarce, Dennis.'

He looked at her expectantly – a hint of the rapt, nervy child she'd later come to see him as – and, at that moment, the subtext sank in. She took his cue, talked to him about her father's death those years ago, and he listened, nodded, fetched more of Christine's cake, and they were fine for a while, more than fine at times, on that rug in their Islington home, newly married, living within civilised walls. The house was large and simply furnished. They liked to keep space for their own pretensions.

'We need more Riesling.'

'It really is a fine Riesling.'

For a while they spoke like this. But then work got busy. She decided she would love it. She would do well. They'd been good to her after Wimbledon, when she needed compassionate leave, and finally she could stop worrying about raising the prospect of maternity cover, could focus on showing how good *she* was. She swapped cake on the carpet for desk-bound dumplings. The noodle place at the Icarus delivered to reception. They started giving her free spring rolls with every order. She had money and no time to spend it. *So*, she thought, *let's invest in refurbishing the house*. It made sense to have more comfort in her few hours at home. It made sense to have more colour.

'. . . Raining again. Even Seneca couldn't explain the rain, the way it can get you down. Same everybloody-where I drive today. Woking. Wimbledon. Wandsworth. All rain . . .'

She got up early to buy paint online. They tried it on a wall. It wasn't quite right. She bought more. It didn't quite work. She reassessed the palette. With their home in a state of stalled redecoration Dennis spoke of best-sellers with brains and having kids when the time was right, but his presence had become an abstract thing all around her, like mood-lighting, or the sky. And in truth she didn't appreciate the sky any more, only noted its colours. Teal Tension, First Frost, Mint Whisper, Sugared Lilac. The names themselves were colourful. Who needed sky when you had paint like this? He spoke only of Shakespeare, and children, and impressing the Dean.

'. . . I wish I could say this job doesn't get to you some-times. My cab's my life. People shit in my cab, or puke in it, or wank in it, or throw their kebab over the floor, that's my life they're soiling, littering . . .'

She had Barbara block out her lunchtimes: one colourful hour in each thin grey day. She went from hardware shop to hardware shop, showroom to showroom, buying pinks and reds and violets, blues and greens, oranges. There was always another colour, a shade with more depth and personality, stylish yet comfortable, vintage but modern. She purchased paint with reckless abandon, causing Dennis to fear for his retirement fund. She reminded him how much she earned. He looked depressed and pleased, mentioned only once the six thousand she'd paid to a con man promising to rescue her nephew. She admired Dennis the way you might admire a well-made French film, one where everything's shot from odd angles. He was unashamedly intellectual; he believed the mere act of thinking could redeem things. At the start a mutual possession had given their marriage momentum, but now it was this quality – detached admiration – that kept the relationship chugging along.

'. . . Sleep in this cab half the week, trying to make enough. When people foul up the back seats it's fouling up my bed, like a drunk student pissing on a tramp, laughing and pissing on his sleeping bag on Lavender Hill, mates with camera phones, laughing . . .'

She purchased for urgent fantasies and remote contingencies. He said she was becoming self-absorbed. Self-absorbed! Her! After the walls were just right, she'd get sleek new furniture and a washing machine that didn't make a noise. These were the things that would make her feel at home. And, for a while, curtain fabric and doorknobs and phone calls from needy clients lit up her eyes and flushed her face. She wanted so badly to feel at home. She found reserves of determination and ambition that her few remaining friends, making quick visits, mistook for happiness. She was sick of her friends, wanted to see Peter again, so she did, another drunken night ruining her resolve, his heedless teasing making her feel edgy once more, his stare emitting an unpredictable flicker as they sipped champagne, as she let it wash and warm and flatten on her tongue, her throat alive with its hot sweet bite. He never seemed to doubt his right to live.

The driver's single supine eyebrow floats up and he says, 'Sweet fucking Seneca, I've had enough of this arse in front,' and – for a moment, a long casual moment, lying in wait for the whole journey, casting a shadow over the whole cab – she sees what will happen. Blinking to blot out the doubling effect of the pills she sees that, having weaved a route in and out, having swerved here, having swung there, her philosophising cabbie will veer back in, into the bus lane, hand on the wheel, hand on his shoulder, scratching an itch, fingering fabric, and, picking up speed, the number 100 to Elephant & Castle will stay dead straight, will put its big red nose right in their path, will –

Impact. Joy somersaults over all four feet. Dirty heads over dirty heels. The screeching birdsong of brakes and tyres; streets tangled; the dirty double world all upside down. Horns. Headlights. Wheeling shapes where she had sat. The City all shuddering colour: wine, carrots, rusty blood.

Another long moment. Tennis ball at the top of its arc. Energy waiting, withheld.

Big big car comes into view, spinning spinning on its side, a giant coin shedding light. This second car has, must have, clipped the bus, and it comes wildly towards them, looking strangely wavy as it spills, heads and tails. Waits, it waits, expanding one corner of her vision with its glow, and then, here it comes, holding her own body in a knot she sees it, sees it will crush her and her driver, that they both will die, that she'll go to hell with this driver, that he'll talk all the way through the afterlife, that he'll talk talk talk through nine turning circles of suffering until they go skinny-dipping in the lake of fire. Redskins redskins redskins – *Smash*. Sort of sound that's always an impersonation – button on a radio deck – *Smash*. Side caves in. Lack of space all around. Melted-looking metal. Tinfoil trap. No room to breathe or swallow. Joy's tongue like a rug rolled back, back into the dark space where her dad's gun tickled, back, back to the black waters where lost syllables bubble, back, back to all the silly deep-pitched shit you'll maybe never say. *I'm sorry, it's my fault, keep going with your book.*

Dennis

PROBLEM WAS, Counsellor, I'd decided not to think about things. I'd come to the conclusion, after meeting Beverley Badger on the train, that I'd spent too much of my life thinking, had in fact during the last year or so become a procrastinating Nabokovian caricature of myself, over-thinking my cover letters, my sample chapters, my sales pitch, my blurb, my career, my marriage. In short, I'd overcomplicated the whole tawdry business of living. The proverbial proof was in the proverbial pudding. In the process of trying to distract Joy from past traumas – by not mentioning the traumas, by mentioning everything else but the traumas, probing at issues only obliquely, via obscure philosophers and Shakespearean characters – I had allowed my marriage to acquire the distracted character of the distractions I'd engendered to distract her.[10] On the job

[10] I'd been caught out by all these things happening at once, Counsellor, that was the thing. In the space of a few months there was Wimbledon and our marriage and the nephew news and the abortion (she decided after the wedding to have an abortion, and I protested but relented, always do relent, just like when she decided to stick with her maiden

front, I had analysed the situation with the student I now refer to as the CAUB[11] for many weeks, deciding what I should do about her veiled threats to make me sorry if I didn't up her grades, hesitating as to whether to speak with the Dean given her father (the CAUB's father) was such a powerful figure on the board, and amid this perfect storm of variables she (the CAUB) got in first, citing leg-stroking and attempted nether-region-groping, and suddenly I was in this massive professional elephant trap. And the book? Months had passed in which I'd revised and re-sent and waited and revised and re-sent and waited and had received not a word of encouragement from anyone and then – then! – on the one occasion when I'd decided *not* to think something through, to just come right out and without hesitation or pre-planning or delay say hello to Opportunity (in the elegant guise of Beverley), I had walked away with the email address of a top London literary agent, and the memory of a quite lovely train journey to wind through my mind forever. It was, yes, a sign.[12]

---

name, to tie herself to Stephens, to pass up the chance to change). All this in a few months, the implausible way significant events have of clustering, like ailments, like mosquito bites, around each other, and then there was my job, yes, the distractions on the job front . . .

[11] Complete And Utter Bitch.

[12] And I began (though I digress) to look for other signs, signs deep in my past, began to wonder whether my own tendency towards overthinking hadn't been the metaphorical fox in my tuck box ever since boarding-school days. I began to think about the summer of my twelfth year, when my friend Charlie was having a birthday party, one component of which was an afternoon spent at the public swimming baths. I had a crush on one attendee, a girl called Angela Rogers. We

So, Counsellor, with Impulse as my new God, on that Thursday afternoon before Joy-Joy's fall, I typed a quick three-line email to Abby Aardvark. I read it back to myself only once, and felt sure that it would end the run of

---

all had a good time splashing around, Angela included, and then some gung-ho friend of Charlie's suggested we boys take turns jumping off the top diving board. I should emphasise that no one was talking about *diving* off the board, just jumping; bombing as we called it. Gung-Ho was the first to go, teetering on the edge of the board's mottled white tongue, the thing sending him into the air with such a sharp upward flick that I remember thinking it (the tongue) was revolted by his courage, just as I was, and he came crashing down into the silky green skin of the pool hugging his knees, causing that skin to bust and foam. And, one by one, the other eleven boys went up to the diving board, and did the same, squealing with delight, one even having the nerve to dive, Counsellor – dive! – until it was my turn. And I made it up the steps. And I made it onto the trafficked board. And I made it to the edge, smooth from all the feet that had paused there before. But then it happened. I made the mistake of pausing to think. I thought about the violence of the impact, the possibility the water would flood up into my nose, sweep through my brain. What if I somehow did it (the jumping) wrong, differently somehow to the other boys, so that I went straight to the bottom, broke my legs, and the water with that way it has of repairing its own surface took me in and never gave me back, and as I stood thinking about this, the other boys jeering below, the tiny Angela Rogers sidling up beside the sinewy stick-man that was Gung-Ho, I found I could not do it, could not do it all, was frozen, could not move, shame burning my brain, ruining this playful day I had so looked forward to for weeks, and I'll tell you, shall I, the strangest thing: when I bumped into Gung-Ho a decade later, at a fund-raiser in a barn that smelt of soap, still sinewy but with more fear in his face, he did not remember that day at all. He did not remember it at all.

twenty-seven straight rejections from literary agents. I thought about waiting to press send, but then the more I thought about it, about whether five-ish on a Thursday was a good time to catch a successful agent (what if she was heading off for a long weekend in her Courchevel chalet?), the more I also thought (in parallel with the thought about whether to wait to send the email) about my resolution not to think. Ergo, after thinking things through but also *not* thinking things through, I just sent it.

Now, pleased with my new personality, I took myself downstairs, passing the paint pots that always hug the walls and nestle in the corner places, and got myself a glass of really rather good deep ruby red. It was not yet past my own self-imposed watershed for snifters and chasers (6 p.m. weekdays; 11.30 a.m. weekends) but I felt I deserved a drink. I'd spent too much time of late worrying about the generalities of grammar, and about even bigger things too, like Death. The chrome-framed photographs, the symmetrical lamps with their porcelain curves, the precious glass figurines with their special see-through grace, they had all acquired the sorrowful sparkle of some big ominous thing beyond my control, and it is hard to explain how the glint of this mystical thing (this thing which I will call Death) had become such a distraction in my field of vision of late, but it had. And here I was, the night before my wife's own encounter with Death, feeling powerful and focused and suddenly free of it, free of mortal fears, ably assisted by the second, third and fourth glasses of wine swilling through my system and my soul. I did some drunken bicep curls, keeping my back straight and my elbows tucked, and hoped this would add a year or two to my life.

So far so good, yes, Counsellor? But around twenty minutes into my exercise routine I received a terrible shock that punctured my bubble of new-found fearlessness.

Jesus Christ, I said.

Evening, Peter said.

I was, yes, hanging upside down, shirtless, for I have this contraption I can set up in the living room, you see, that allows one to work on the abdominal muscles from a tilted position.

How did you get into my home? I asked.

You *are* funny Dennis! he said. The killer question is why you left the front door open.

Oh, I said, remembering that, given the heating was on the blink, I'd opted to let some of the hot air out.

That'll be why you're sweating so much, he said.

What? I said.

Is it always this silent in here? he said.

We were going at cross purposes like that, him leaning forward on the Jacobsen as if he owned it, me by now sitting on the carpet beside my contraption, wiping my chest with an exercise towel, feeling that the continuing need to hold my head at such an upward angle was putting me at a disadvantage.

I think it shows real guts, he continued, for the two of you to live in such silence.

It's only silent during the day, I said. When it's just me here.

The famous sabbatical, he said. Yet more courage. You're my hero, Dennis. If I too had some sort of creative gift to exercise, I would surrender the professional respect and enormous base salary plus bonus and just, you know, *do* it.

It was unclear, Counsellor, if he was being sarcastic.

Peter smiled and said, Your lovely wife said to me once you were a tortured genius.

Ah, I said, that's very –

Without the genius bit. She has such spot-on timing, your wife! Makes her a thrilling litigator. Knows when to attack, when to hold back.

I said nothing, nothing at all, for really, truly, what could I say to this, this, this repugnant yuppie?

Joy's not here? he asked. I was hoping to catch her. I'm awfully sorry if I disturbed you. You seem a little on edge. Are you expecting a guest, or something?

Absolutely not, I said.

He explained (which I found deadly strange) that he wanted to borrow Joy's tennis racket, that he had been passing by on his way home and Christine had said, if you pass near Joy and Dennis's place, be sure to take out Joy's tennis racket on loan, because I've got a game tomorrow – this is what he said Christine said – and Joy won't mind. He gave me this explanation, which even I would argue was long-winded (the explanation), and then said, with a smile, Christine's is getting restrung, you see. Not as highly strung as your wife's, probably, but it needs more tension. I'd loan her mine, but it's far too big.

He said something along those lines, an imprecise lewdness lurking in the words, and I replied by saying Joy normally plays tennis herself on Fridays, with Christine, but he interrupted yet again and leant over and slapped me on the back, said the loan of the racket was appreciated, and he slapped me really quite hard because the sting crept round to my chest, and he said, My, my, you are sweaty, aren't you?, something like that with a certain snarkiness in his voice, but then a second later he was making some general statement, about how he found it fascinating the places moisture collects on a woman's body, and then again just like that he was back to the specific. General, specific, general, specific. That was his modus operandi.

No doubt she'll be sweating tomorrow, Peter said. You should come see her speech. Or will you be busy packing for your holiday?

I explained, Counsellor, that we had no fixed plans to holiday this winter.

Surprising, he said. Do you like surprises, Dennis? Personally I *love* them.

I'll get the tennis racket, I replied, but stayed sitting on my hands for a moment, just a moment, to stop the fingers (my fingers) shaking.

I had been humiliated. Humiliated by a yuppie asking for a tennis racket. Pathetic, isn't it? You have to laugh, do you not, at this comico-sentimental life of mine, full of tiny daily battles, things which don't matter at all in the grand scheme, silly local issues?

Yes, I'm inclined to agree with you on that, although as Miss Badger said to me on our train journey most of our fears *are* local these days, don't you think? Despite the bombs on buses, the ash clouds over Europe, our gradually warming globe, they are local, are they not, among the vast anonymous bustle of mouse-clicks and updates and downloads they are local: will this man attack me, will this person steal my child, will this food make me ill. These are the local fears, the primal terrors revived, are they not, Counsellor?[13]

What I haven't mentioned so far is that on that Thursday night I *was* – despite what I said to Peter – expecting a visitor. I had a message from Joy-Joy saying that she'd be home late, and in light of that I, yes, really should have cancelled said visitor, a visitor who was in the . . . services industry, shall we say? But determined to rediscover that all-powerful state I'd experienced prior to Peter's arrival, still tipsy on wine, recommencing my shirtless sit-ups, I became increasingly reluctant to do so.

[13] And in fact Beverley also said – and you might be interested in this, Counsellor – that she wished more fiction addressed these local concerns. She has a bit much of a pet hatred – a touch unfair, I think, though as you know I'm not much of a fiction man – of the same literary tropes being recycled by writers over and over. Tropes such as, let me think, she listed seven, yes, seven . . . Number one was little-known wars in distant lands. That's right. Opening: period detail and hints of a cross-cultural inter-generational love affair that transcends the contingent concerns of race and religion, time and space. Middle bit: guns and memories. End: stunning revelation that, ultimately, all war is unpleasant. Trope two was Man's epic gap-year-esque journey to find himself, and lose himself, preferably at the same time, in a much-ignored corner of the Commonwealth. Beverley explained that, in the eyes of prize committees, this type of fiction is much enhanced by colourful references to jams, chutneys and pickles, as well as the use of foreign words of great texture and rhythm, at all times without recourse to explanatory notes. Three was . . . no, no, four was . . . something to do with artistic types reconnecting with the world? Gone, sorry, the rest of them are gone. And. Where was I? Thursday. Thursday . . .

3.32 p.m.

SHE KNOWS how it began: the front of the bus colliding with the cab. And she recalls how it ended: climbing through glass, realising with indifference that the driver was dead. But running shoeless and shaky through New Change and Cheapside the experience is already unfastening itself from who she is, becoming part of the air passing through her hair. The crash might come back to her at some point, of course – she has learnt to anticipate the moment when past events return as strange, rousing gusts of memory, engulfing her sense of self, dragging small parts of her personality away – but for now the few images that glimmer in her mind have the feel of something indulgently decorative, irritatingly extraneous to the substance of her situation. Collapsed bodywork, reflections snagging in the metal's depressions. Wheels spinning, light unscrolling around them. It is hard to focus on these details. She is alive. This is the key thing. Maybe she blacked out for a while. Maybe she didn't. Difficult to remember with this curious gaseous pain in her head, a new unsteadying heaviness.

Must get clean. No Dennis. No police. Need a Plan B.

Trouble is, the Heath *was* her Plan B. Suicide was never

the Plan A. It's the thing she kept for the rainiest day; the comforting shadow, always trailing behind, forever there to fall back on. You've been told by a grief counsellor that you need to give traumas five years to heal, so you wait five years, still seeing the counsellor now and then, less and less, demeaned by your need to buy empathy, and when half a decade has gone and your pain gnaws even deeper than before that shadow is still there, dark and simple, more appealing than ever. She needs a Plan C, and who in their right mind has one of those?

She stops outside a dry-cleaner's to catch her breath, that shadow of hers settling against a Credit-Crunch Special poster. In the cut-glass British bank opposite a lift falls softly from floor to floor. She sees a tramp approaching her on the zebra crossing which rolls out, like a tasteless eighties carpet, from the bank's electric doors. He is huge-haired and filthy, powdery bruises lurking where stubble meets cheeks, neck and forehead wearing that sailor's tan you get from living beyond borders. There is a way of walking through this part of London he has not learnt: purposeful, harassed. He is stagger-swaying in his own unprepared way, looking for someone to address, and he chooses her.

Losing saliva between words he says, 'This is my spot lady,' and after waiting a beat starts laughing hard, his breath full of excrement. When the laughter stops as abruptly as it began he gives her a clean bare stare, a look that's uncluttered by background facts. Here she is, a woman in expensive ruined clothes, he does not care how or why.

She runs. A scene swims up from a puddle she passes: driver in seat, sagged, rag-dolled, eyes blank, single eyebrow a dead beast above. Under the rear-view mirror, a cardboard air-freshener in the shape of a Christmas tree. Everything glass-sharded, glittering away, his blood adding colour, the whole mangled vehicle looking faintly festive. God has an eye for the absurd.

For a moment, as she backed away from him, as she began running from the pristinely twisted metal, a savage structure full of gaps and bends and breaks, leaving the second car upturned, wheels still spinning, head hurting but body working (working!), she felt an unfamiliar sensation: gratitude.

The security guard at the Service & Deliveries Entrance sees her coming. He starts with her muddied tights and scans upward, eyeing every stain and missing button. In her more serious smoking days she used to stand and examine *him*, and he in turn would be examining newly arrived packages. She has noticed that he likes to find the imperfections in a thing, the nick on a corner or suspicious extra weight.

'Miss Stephens,' he says.

'Hi,' she says, smiling.

'You look . . .' he begins.

'Yes?'

'Different. Is everything OK?'

His walkie-talkie sputters to life: *Police have cordoned off New Change; your three thirty's running late.*

She decides to respond with a lie: 'Afraid I've left my security pass in the gym.'

'In the gym?'

'Gym changing rooms, yes. Whole handbag there, in fact. So if you could wave me through I'll wander down, into the goods bay bit, get to the gym through there.'

'Everything's OK, then. You just need your handbag.'

He is patient and measured. Some of the neat weightiness of boxed stock has pressed its way into his being.

'Everything's fine, I promise. And if you let me in I'd avoid walking through reception with this drowned slut look I've got going.'

When he smiles his features lose shape, melt into the excitable boy she feels he used to be. He rummages in his pocket. She half expects him to pull out a conker.

'You'll need this temporary pass,' he says. 'Maybe I can pick it up from you Monday. I mean, it's nuts how many we lose.'

Even now, panicked heart pumping, she has that way of getting what she wants. In a slightly flirty show of gratitude she squeezes his forearm, then walks through the entrance and down the ramp towards the gym. Call Barbara, that's what she'll do. Her head should not hurt this much, the airy ache becoming a sharper sort of pain. The mud on her tights, on her thighs, looks like dried blood.

Blood on her thighs, blood on her thighs, blood on her thighs. Reminds her of lying on plasticky sheets in the treatment centre, seven weeks pregnant, legs spread, hearing that awful sucking sound. She didn't look at the bedpan then, couldn't believe they'd use a bedpan and didn't dare look, but the following week she had to return, transpired they hadn't properly emptied the womb, had to lie there and pass what they called 'the retained products of conception' (all this talk of eggs and products and waste, like the whole place was a sick supermarket), and on that occasion she made the error of glancing down at it, the him or the her, the sinewy red unforgettable mess. Unmentionable, that mess. The words describing it existed only in her own head. And, months after the abortion was complete, her relationship with Peter – if you could call it a relationship, those years of secret meetings, prudent break-ups, aborted confessions and heady pitiful collapses back into adultery – that ended with blood too, didn't it? She'd practised a unique, sensitive speech so many times but at the key moment her rehearsed words fled and she used the same television-drama dialogue as everyone else: 'I'm sorry', 'I can't do this any more', 'It's over'. She said these things to Peter. He was silent. She said them to him again.

He wanted one last go. That's what he said, one last go, and at first she thought he meant the relationship generally, that after all this time spent clinging and hating herself for clinging the roles had been reversed. She sat on his sofa, on Christine's sofa, and thought about saying yes. There was a twitch in his smile that could have been pain. A boyishness to his words.

She thought about saying yes, but she said no. And he said Come on. And she said No.

'Wrong time of the month,' she explained, remembering it was true, wanting to reinforce her refusal with a physical detail, beginning to feel afraid of his level expression.

As he leant over her and unzipped himself there was this great stray voltage in his eyes. Whisky-glazed. Risky.

He tickled the nape of her neck and pulled her head – too hard – into his waist. His other hand found a space between the buttons of her shirt. Fingers cold. Prick warm.

'Fuck off, Peter, I said no.'

His thumb and forefinger pinched her cheek with a pressure poised between affection and aggression, and the imposition of this gesture, weirdly familial and old-fashioned, startled her so much that she wasn't aware of being pushed backwards, missed this moment entirely and realised she was lying flat, wriggling under his weight. He did not show her his eyes. His eyes were buried in cushions and his shoulder was in her mouth and she was biting hard but the pain seemed to reach him as pleasure. He gave her no moment of anticipation or connection. No attempt to get her wet the way he had the first time, kissing her nipples in Essaouira, everyone waiting outside. Peter gave her no secret moment like this, just pulled the tampon out and as she delivered the muffled words 'Peter listen' his thrust caused a dull blunt pain that surged from her pelvis to her jaw. That's the moment she stopped biting him, became silent and submissive, his moans merging with the gassy groan of buses stopping on the Holloway Road. Then or shortly after.

And pulling his jeans back on, throwing her a tea towel for the blood, he said, 'Will you stay for another drink?'

There's a phone at the bottom of the goods-bay ramp. It is tricky to remember Barbara's extension so she dials reception, gets put through that way, listens to a speech about how Alfredo needs to go, and explains exactly what it is she wants from this vigilant senior citizen of whom she's oddly fond. Only then, after that, does she cry, dabbing the sides of her eyes with the burnt back of her hand, cigarette wound stinging from the salt.

Barbara

I've already heard what I'm getting. My gift presentation – that fruit is going to waste – isn't until Monday. But Liz was tasked with buying it, the gift, so I already know what it is. Do you want to know? Wait for it. Wait till you hear this. Just wait.

Bath oils!

Did you not hear me? I said bath oils! Forty years. Forty years at the firm. And they give me bath oils. Is it bad? Is it bad? Of course it's bad! It's about as bad as that shirt you're wearing. Worse, even, if you take an objective whatschacall, *perspective*.

Hmm?

Well, that might be true. But do we mean hate, when we say hate?

I've always loathed this place. Four decades of tedium and paper cuts. Meeting requests. Lever-arch files. Spines. Labels. Sandwich-fetching. Mistake-covering. Fee-earners and their mistakes! Lemme tell you, mistakes are their vocation. You cover for them, they're all grateful, and the next day they've forgotten. They don't know the meaning of thank you. Like Mr Ignorant. He never knew the meaning of thank you. A musician, my husband, when he wasn't in uniform. Did I tell you that? A musician of sorts, anyway. Did the rounds for a while. Banjo. Loved it. Five string. Like the minstrels had, Joe Sweeney and the like. His whole life was a tune played on those five strings. Over-twangy. Improvised. I'll tell you this, if you're thinking of getting involved with a creative type let me tell you this, you can have this for free, it's the best advice I never had, it's been a rule of my adult life ever since he died, men throw themselves at me but I follow this rule: if you're thinking of marrying a person who's into the arts – poems, trampoline, banjo, whatever – you *must* – believe me – I know what I'm talking about – you must not do it.

Well then. Good for you.

A question? Of course. Ask away. Ask anything.

Now all credit to you for asking, but there's that word again. *Feelings*. I'm going to be clear. I'm up here with you because it beats being down there working for James O'Brien, photocopying invites to his son's birthday party. I was told as Joy's PA I'm entitled to come and speak with you. But I am not comfortable exposing my feelings to a man I barely know, and I'm tired of you focusing on Friday. Joy Stephens is a minor character in my life. You might think everything I tell you can, through some clever note-editing or flick of perspective, be connected to what happened last Friday, but it can't. There have been plenty of interesting unrelated developments before and since then. And I don't just mean on the Alfredo front – though I'm going to make him sorry he ever came to this office, that much is definite – but all sorts of areas.

Well hold on. One thing at a time. Let's deal with Friday

first. There are still plenty of questions about that day. Questions like this: why did she look all beaten up that afternoon when – as you point out – she hadn't even had her fall yet, when it was a good couple of hours before her fall? I could barely believe it, when I got down to the basement and saw the state her clothes were in –

There he goes again! The human alarm clock! Studied it at your fancy university, did you, the art of interruption?

Good. About time.

Friday. I was thinking maybe I'd phone Joy. This Project Poultry thing was getting tricky and nobody was around. The client was calling and the trainee had left me some document he said was crucial. I'm forever left holding the fort. I'm a modern-day Penelope. And then, as if I've got psychic powers – which by the way Jackie's always said I have, partly on account of me predicting the bullet that hit Mr Ignorant's brain, no easy target – *she* phones *me*. And it sounds like she's in a car wash somewhere. This is around lunchtime, and technically I'm on my break. I never have a break, which is why I want to see New York so badly. Reliving the old times there, seeing lost family, it would restore me, see me through another few years. So Joy's speaking to me from this hot tub with all this splashing and trickling all around and, if I'm honest, the things she says, they're unhelpful. Tells me to speak to the Halfwit Peter Carlisle, that he can sort out my poultry issue. But I know Peter Carlisle's off somewhere with his trainee. And, furthermore, I know that Peter Carlisle's a halfwit. So, once she's put the phone down – is that the way to treat your PA of eight years? – I have a think and end up phoning her back. She puts me on speakerphone, so I can hear every soap sud on the bonnet, and then brushes me off all unhelpful again. Almost – if I'm honest – rude. She was, at times, a very rude person. And then an hour or two passed and I was thinking about phoning her again and – yes – what happened next? – guess what happened next.

Exactly. Those ears aren't just ornamental, eh?

The phone in my cubicle goes and it comes up as Basement-ex-two-six-six-something and I pick it up. Joy. It's Joy. She can barely keep her voice smooth. Her words are obscure and full of gaps – more than words generally are, I mean – and she begs, *begs* me, to grab the dry-cleaning from her office, plus one of her pairs of fancy heels, and come downstairs to meet her. She even gets the dry-cleaner to do her shirts. People are so wasteful. It's like when the young girls in my section are doing the tea run and use a separate bag for every mug. Eight separate tea bags! You could keep Africa awake with that!

So I do as she asks, obviously. Lemme tell you, I'm a good PA. If one of my fee-earners needs help, I help. And when I finally get down to the basement on my stick and my hip, her appearance gives me a real shock. Her shirt's dirty and wet. It's see-through to an indecent degree. The flesh beneath looks grazed. But it's not the physical side that tells me something really serious has happened. No. It's the breathing. I'm a great believer in breathing as a way to get by. If you want to relax you've got to breathe properly. In through the nose – sinuses permitting – and out through the mouth. Oxygen calms you. I tell her this. Breathe, Joy. Breathe. Calm down. Some old man from the canteen walks by and tries to help us. Men are the worst at crises, aren't they? I haven't known many intimately, but I've heard bad things. Especially old men. I'm not a fan of old people. Problem with the old is this: they have every door open to them, yet all they feel is the draught. So Joy's breathing is gradually calming down and I'm holding the dry-cleaned suit, shirt and shoes. And then I see that behind one of her ears there's this ugly cut. Small but deep, a purply bruise around it.

Obviously I tell her she should see a doctor. It seems like she's knocked her head. She's all dazed. Her speech is a bit . . . watery. But she won't let me call a doctor. The most I can do is get her to the women's changing rooms.

I get her to the women's changing rooms. Luckily there's nobody there. I tell her, Give me your clothes. And just like a little girl she obeys. She takes her clothes off. And them, I say. And she slips her knickers off too. Women these days with their fancy nether hair. It's none of my concern. And for some reason she says, Don't look at my shoulders. Completely naked and she's thinking of the shoulders. And she's shivering like it's cold, and I take one of the spare towels on the side, all warm from being in the towel room, and I wrap her in it, surprised how small she is. I walk her over to the showers and get the temperature right, then rest for a few minutes on the bench, waiting for her wash to finish. The whole thing reminds me of when my daughter was little. She travels a lot but she phones sometimes. And while I'm getting her dressed and putting some of my own make-up on her – my best stuff – to cover up her bruise and so on, she says something, and I have to ask her to say it again. And she says, voice a bit better now, looking clean and almost composed, she says, Barbara, I think I killed someone. And I say, Joy, lemme get this straight, what are you saying here? And she says, He wouldn't stop talking, and my BlackBerry flashing, always flashing, so I threw it at the perspex screen, I think, to make him stop.

Joy, I say, come on, what are you saying?

And she says, He turned and swerved and hit the bus.

She couldn't explain any more than that. Couldn't explain, for example, about the burn on her hand. Now I'm no expert but that looked like a cigarette burn. It had the shape of a burn Mr Ignorant left on the sofa after a Mets game, back when me and him lived two blocks down from my cousin Jackie in New York, cousin Jackie who I'd give anything to visit but can't. And how are you going to get one of those in a car accident?

Anyway, she was dressed. We had hair and make-up covering the cut behind the ear and she was seeming more calm. So I leant in close. I said to her, very quietly, I said, Joy, listen, you need to speak to the police. One thing you've got to really do is speak to the police. And before you do that I think it would be an idea, don't you, if we went to your office quickly, you owe me this, to resolve what we do on Project Poultry.

Hmm?

Well, don't misunderstand me, she took some persuading. Sensitivity's the key. I tell her, I'm not getting left with this dodgy document while you're serving time. And although she agreed to come back upstairs with me, I'm sad to say that when we got in the lift, she switched. She became old cold corporate Joy again. Laughing and joking all insincere with one of the lechy partners. Ignoring me completely. I've just washed and dressed her like my own child and she ignores me.

Did it hurt, her coldness? Of course it hurt. I would be justified, would I not, in hating her. Sometimes I hated her more than anyone in the world. Not that I don't appreciate she's been through things.

No, I don't mean the nephew! Who told you about the nephew? That's none of your concern. You have no business delving into people's private pains.

We go upstairs, she presumably deals with the document direct, I leave her to it, it's no longer my concern, and the next time I see her she's up on that viewing platform thing starting to speak. I'm not really listening. I'm nudging Debs and saying, See those police over there, I know what that's about, it's all going to get messy after this. Because there were two police officers in the crowd at her speech, did you know that? And then I add – casual – that we need to talk about Alfredo too, that I've got some information she'll want to see. Joy's up there speaking and I'm thinking to myself, Do I need more evidence before I dish the dirt on Alfredo? Is it too risky to do it now? And then, well, we see this thing happen, this thing with Joy, to remind me, to remind us all, that life is one big gamble, and the odds – the odds! – they're pretty awful at the end of the day.

First to move, we were. It felt that way, anyhow, that the four of us were the first to move towards her when she hit the ground. Me, the Asian, Dennis, the Halfwit. Which is maybe why we tend to visit her more regularly than the others.

I decided to take less risks with the Alfredo thing. I started to compile my whatschacall, *dossier*, so I couldn't be accused of prejudice, or having improper motives. And now I've got all I need. I present to you Exhibits B and C.

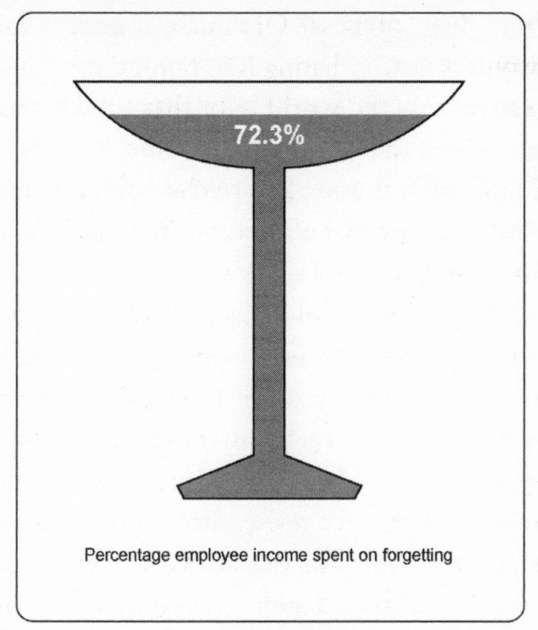

Percentage employee income spent on forgetting

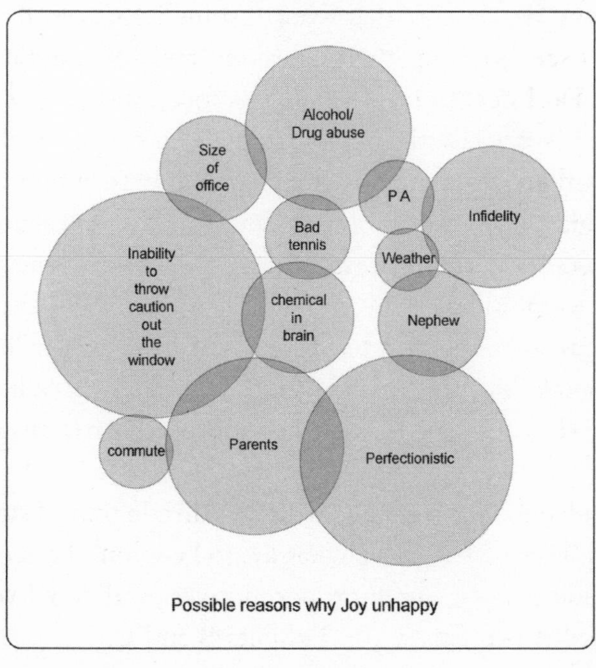

Possible reasons why Joy unhappy

Have you ever seen such an improper use of firm whatschacall, *resources*?

There's more where those came from, much more. And on Monday, right after they give me the insulting box of bath oils, right after I make my rehearsed quip about how a bath is just what I need after forty years at this place, a long bath with a brick and no snorkel, right after that I'm taking Debs to one side, and I'm showing her the evidence. I'll give it a week, maybe less, before Alfredo's sent packing.

We are all born idle. Some remain so. That's the point.

4.02 p.m.

She loves the affection Barbara gives her, is desperate and grateful for it. The old woman waits with a towel as Joy showers, the crashing of the water half disguising her remaining sobs and sniffs. She despises the sound of her own grief. Reminds her too much of the noises accompanying her mother's frequently contorted face, its athletic upset. Lydia Stephens cried so much during Joy's early teens that Dad expressed concern she'd bleed out, go crusty like an old sponge wrung free of all moisture. To emphasise his point he would, during his wife's more dramatic fits of self-pity, bring glasses of water to her bedside, a tactic that was deemed sarcastic and thus made the wailing worse. Joy's mum wanted to be an actress, but even family contacts on Broadway told her she was ill-suited to the profession. Surprising, really, because she seemed to have all the requisite mood swings and insecurities. Broadway remained her dream and she'd often say, as Barbara sometimes does, that leaving America was a mistake, would say it so often and with such ugly grief-soaked snot in her voice that when she did finally abandon the Hampstead-based family, in the middle of Joy's GCSEs, the thing that shocked most was not the loss but the pleasant aftermath of silence that came with it. The kind of quiet calm that hangs in the steam now, after the squeak of the shower tap turning. Joy would cook nutritious food, her father would read the paper, Annie would flick through university photos – all in serene silence. Joy got eleven A grades. A*s were introduced a couple of years later. Irritating, really, the flightiness of Perfection; makes you feel like the dinner guest, corner-seated, who must forever lean to hear the out-of-earshot jokes. Mostly they're not even funny.

Would moving to New York be the answer, leaving Dennis and her job? On some nights, trying to find a way into sleep, nostalgia stirred by darkness, she thinks it could be, even wonders about it now as Barbara cloaks her in the beautifully warm towel. She has a yearning to return to something, some prior swaddled state. Her life began there, maybe it could begin there again. Lying beside Dennis she has weighed up so many possibilities – new careers, new lovers, new continents – so many ways of hurling herself into the unknown and proving she exists, and New York, the prospect of tracking her mother down, asking her questions, giving her a hug or a punch in the face, rediscovering an unexhausted part of herself, used to loom large in these imagined escapes. But visiting friends of Dennis in Brooklyn Heights a few years ago, all four of them drinking chilled Coors and studying lower Manhattan from the terrace, the city seemed changed, suddenly too fragile to house her rehabilitation. Back in 2001 Bennie and Jen had emailed Dennis footage from this vantage point of theirs, a mid-September morning through which oily smoke rolled south from the collapsed towers, obscuring Liberty Island. Now the air was clean once more and the skyline had shaken itself out, settled into its new spaces; yet with this revision came a vulnerability that was somehow sadder than the raging mess it replaced. The emptiness was stifling. Surrounding skyscrapers stood unmoved – stony, glassy, mute.

'Weird,' she told Peter back in London, 'to think how quickly those towers vanished.'

'My uncle died on September eleventh,' he said solemnly.

'He did? You never mentioned.'

'Nineteen ninety-one. Gallstones.'

Another cloud-like patch of memory gathers mass, obscuring her sense of getting dried and dressed and entering the lift, until eventually a man's voice, addressing her with excessive energy, pulls her back into the present.

'I mean, Swindon's another planet, another universe. It has roundabouts and supermarkets, but no irony or proper coffee. People are loud and animalistic without recourse to cocaine. Everybody has a cold. They get their hair cut by people whose own pelts and manes are harrowingly ill-advised. My dear Joy – are you feeling OK? – it's like stumbling onto the set of a horror film, a British one, after the funding has gone. And, as is the way with horror films, the more you see the more grisly it gets.'

It is Charles, a senior partner in her team. The chicken-pale flesh of his throat is taut at the Adam's apple, making every swallow look contrived. He stares forlornly through the lift's glass doors, bits of the office sinking from view.

'This young Swindon client,' he continues. 'He does all this pensive chin-stroking. Whatever the context, he's always quietly stroking his chin, with that sort of bland philosophical puzzlement that doctors have when you're telling them about kidney pains or stool trouble. It's this little gesture he's picked up from some adult or other. I mean, there is no beard, there never will be a beard, it's impossible!'

Charles's great accidental strength is his oversized outrage; he has the comedian's gift of making little things matter and big things disappear. A combination of his colourful performance and her recent shower has left Joy close to relaxed. Barbara, the only other person in the lift, is the one who looks tense, refusing to meet her eye and share a smile – embarrassed, probably, about her boss's meltdown.

'Peter grew up in Swindon,' Joy says, focusing on Charles again. 'His first contact with Hanger's was through the inaugural Make Law Fun Day. You know, as a schoolboy.'

'*Really?* How did he survive to tell the tale? Luckily for me Project Rioja is coming to a close, so I can shortly abandon the West Country Hellhole and return full-time to Planet Earth. You may recall Projects Claret, Merlot and Malbec? Same client. Of course, I've got a Junior Partner and a Senior Associate working with me. I'm there to provide a bit of grey hair, really, and it's just unfortunate that the grotesque finger of fate has, this time round, pointed me sixty miles up the M4 to Poundland Central, rather than in the direction of Mayfair, say, or Hong Kong. Of course, my main Hong Kong contact, Steve Lurie, popped his clogs last week.'

The lift stops to pick up a canteen girl holding a tray of pastries. Lost for a moment in the half-moons of croissants, Joy thinks about the cabbie, Charles's mention of death casting a shadow on her improving mood.

'Although,' says Charles, the floor beneath them moving

once more, 'the one plus in working for this client is that when you finish a bit of litigation with them they give you this deal toy trophy thing which is actually a bottle of extremely good grape suspended horizontal by this, this' – he makes a hammock with his hands – 'clever curve of plastic. Last time I got back from Swindon I downed the Claret and Merlot right there in my office, I was that depressed. Alas, I ended up a little worse for wear . . .'

'Julie had to clear that up,' mutters Barbara.

'Belinda! What a pleasure! Didn't see you down there.'

'Did nothing for her whatschacall, *knee joints*, scrubbing that carpet.'

'I'm dreadfully embarrassed. A sixty-three-year-old man acting sixteen! But Julie is so very big of heart. Big of everything, in fact. Fourth floor, here we are.'

The offices and meeting rooms are arranged around a bright atrial space. Builders have almost finished installing a viewing platform on each floor. The idea is that employees at all levels will be able to look down into reception and the ground-floor function space: an opportunity to see if your client has arrived, or to deliver a speech to the assembled crowd below. The pastry girl goes left. Joy and Charles, followed by Barbara, head right. They pass a serenely smiling Julie, red-lobed as if to prove a person's overhearing ears really do burn. She's big of heart, it's true. Joy remembers receiving a letter from her after Wimbledon. A surprising number of people, including some supposedly close friends, decided with humorous awkwardness it was best to say nothing at all. Julie's letter, like many others, conferred a bleak but special benefit on Joy, the unique indulgence owed to the bereaved. The attention came perilously close to pleasure, at times. For a while, a short while.

'Now we're having a sort of Friday partners' meeting at half past. Just a fifteen-minute job before your ceremony. Small on content, big on pain au chocolat. Has anyone mentioned it?'

'No.'

'Well, you're one of us now – will be shortly, anyway – so you should join. We're due to resurrect the old redundancy debate. Room 4.57.'

'Thanks, Charles. I have to finish something for a client, but I'll try my best.'

'Finish something,' Charles repeats, drifting away. 'Good for you.' He isn't a fan of work, but doesn't mind it in other people.

She likes Charles. He was the one who first put her forward for promotion. It seemed to Joy then that joining the partnership might give her a sense of belonging. There were no real female role models, but there were partners like Charles who were, at least, at home in their own skin. Then it dawned on her: his career arc, which reached its zenith at a time when fax machines seemed sci-fi, was not comparable to hers. During the partnership interview process she got to know a sample of lawyers the firm had made up in the last ten years: Arianne, who cries in the ladies' loos each morning; Eddie, who is on his fourth wife and second ulcer; James, who reads stories to his kids via speakerphone. She realised what she always, in the depths of her bones, suspected: that the younger partners, raised in the age of email, were having as terrible a time as the associates below them, and that partnership at Hanger, Slyde

& Stein would provide her with none of the tools she needed to make a happy life, none at all, it would be like receiving a gift box from God containing a squashed kumquat and a novelty ultra-heat-resistant hand-puppet oven glove and being told 'Best of luck'. She wanted to complete the partnership process, prove to herself she could do it, but she did not want to spend the next decade eating kumquat off an oven glove or using the oven glove as an impromptu kumquat-storage device or whatever other scenarios would emerge as she muddled into old age with whatever was to hand. She became envious of Dennis, whose job at the university seemed to come from an urge in his heart rather than an idea in his head. She'd always wanted to do something special with her life, she never quite knew what, baulked even at stating this vague plan out loud, but she certainly did not intend to end up doing this, a career which divorced her, daily, from her own temperament, the way a puppet is divorced from the true self pulling strings up above. Someone like Dennis, or Samir. They have less inner clutter, she thinks. Less mess. And as she walks into her office and switches on the lights, sending yellow splashing across piles of paper, this is what Joy wants: less. Happiness, that thing she's always associated with outward acquisition, is maybe just a shrinking deep inside.

'Yours I believe,' says Barbara, dangling the plastic bag with Joy's muddied clothes inside. The folds of skin under her chin, they dangle too. With age our layers get looser.

Joy takes the bag. Barbara turns to exit. And it is only then that both women see a third figure – hardly human – lurking in the corner of the room.

Samir

YOU MUST promise not to think I am insane. I feel with the discussion of the bowel difficulties and the counting to seven I have conveyed a very bad impression. The tracksuit also perhaps does not help my case. In a shirt and tie I could seem merely eccentric. Father says elasticated trousers do not do a man any favours. But this is my uniform. This is my skin.

That is kind.

You are a brilliantly kind man.

Well I was . . .

Before your timer did those three neat beeps I was telling you how it felt to be behind the hanging lemony towels. In the towel room by the gym. I had just seen Miss Stephens outside crying with Barbara. And I was counting to seven with my pencil. Two people had stumbled in so I was . . . yes I would say I was hiding. From my mother I have learnt truthfulness. From my father how to disappear. And I was beginning to realise that Peter Carlisle would engage in activities with the young lady with nice hair.

Then I see something else. Crouching as I am I notice under one of the benches to my right a cage. Not a lost-property type of cage. No. Something much smaller. The kind of plastic cage Mrs Hasan uses to take her cat to the vet. Mrs Hasan's cat is named David Cameron. She says this is on account of him only licking his own bottom and the bottoms of other cats of a similar breed. And I cannot quite stretch to see inside the cage which has a blue plastic top. Not without being seen by the two visitors. At one stage it might have been good if they saw me or I made a noise to alert them to my presence but now it is too late for that. It is too late for the Astaire. It is too late to perform the Full Bollywood and in their moment of surprise and wonder shoulder my way out of the room. And it is also too late to zip up my cleansing gels and hide them again.

Oh yes very. I hate to hide things but I have already lost the Fitness First job with this kind of thing. So I try to sit and wait while they whisper things such as I knew you would be a talented trainee and Well the Make Law Fun Day really is fun. Things of that nature. And then Peter begins to make very very small humming noises and the lady on her knees goes quiet. I take a quick glimpse between towels. It is bizarre. He is wearing what appears to be an all-in-one green Lycra outfit. Something suited to the Tour de France. Something not out of place on a marathon runner attempting to be a muscular space alien. It is peeled down to his waist. His waist is where the lady's hair begins. And being present for this performance I begin to feel quite tense and upset. Not very bad but on my way to feeling very bad you see?

My cycle of sevens has been broken. I am trying to say them under my breath but that is not the thing. The thing is to say them out loud and the towel room is the place to say them out loud and if I do not do my counting I occasionally get this looming. I do not wish to make it seem like a big problem but I have been known to get this looming feeling that something bad will happen to someone I care about. A sense perhaps that the Raj restaurant will catch fire with Father inside. He is old now and cannot get in and out of places as quickly as before. And just as soon as I have convinced myself that will not happen that the Raj has a number of modern smoke detectors I get another looming. A sense that Jack will leave the office on Wednesday to go to his five-a-side football and he will be thinking about Miss Stephens's smile all distracted and will be hit by the number 100 bus. Just because I did not complete the cycle of counting to seven seven times. I fear you will think me very very strange but these are my feelings and like most feelings they are not accompanied by a full set of reasons. So I am hiding and getting very tense hoping for a brilliant thing to happen that will make them both go away and all the time there is slurping and grunting grunting and slurping. And I end up spreading out a towel on the floor and lying on my stomach with my fingers in my ears. And I can feel my legs shake. I am there for a while. Shaking.

When I open my eyes I see two things. One thing I see is the shadow of a ponytail wagging here and there on the wall. She has obviously tied her hair back which I suppose is a sensible precaution for the manner of activity she is engaged in. And the other thing I see from this position is what is inside the cage.

Please guess.

No.

Please try again.

No.

Lizard!

There is a small lizard inside the cage and it is looking directly at me with its brilliant little bubble eyes. I have no idea why a lizard would be here. I am very confused. And there is no movement from the lizard at all. It occurs to me it is dead. Then *whoosh*! In one of the little squares between the criss-cross wire bars his tongue comes. Just a second and then gone. And suddenly I feel the need to do a movement of my own.

You have understood.

So I am dreaming of a nice clean bathroom but instead I am lying here on my stomach and unfortunately the towel keeping me from the carpet is picking up fluff. And then a further bad development. I feel in my nose the itch of a sneeze coming. Very very bad. I pinch my nose with finger and thumb. I hate to block the airways it is a far from brilliant strategy but there is no choice. And I am very tense because I am recalling once reading in the TestoTrivia section of *Testomuscles Monthly* that by holding your nose during a sneeze your eyes could pop out.

I keep on pinching my nostrils. Then it happens. One two three four five six seven *boom*! The sneeze finds a way through. The noise is muffled but loud enough that the lizard disappears to the dark back of his cage. The shadow ponytail stops wagging. So I am thinking this is it. This is not at all brilliant. I am going to get sacked it is going to happen again what will Jack say. All these worries whirring in my head. One second. Two seconds . . .

Then I hear the voice.

Peter's voice. After perhaps two seconds Peter's voice says Well come on do not stop. And I think he is telling me Do not stop watching us you pervert. Something of that nature in the sort of smirky way people at school had that makes everything sound like they are keeping secrets.

But then the wagging and the sucking recommence and I deduce he was talking to her.

Can I please take a tissue?

Thank you. Thank you very much.

So following further unbearable noises they laugh in an awkward way and Peter says something strange such as That is not in the pastel care manual and finally they leave me with a neat click of the door. But it is too late you see. It is too late to recommence the counting. The counting is ruined. And not that it is important . . . it is just a few numbers . . . but I have carpet dust on my hands and I am shaky and upset. I pick up the propelling pencil and if it was not metal I might break it into seven pieces right there. That is how upset I have allowed myself to become. And what I wish to convey is every second that passes after you fail to count in accordance with the set schedule is a second where someone may be chosen to be harmed. I know how this must sound to a man of your expertise but I do believe in the possibility. That someone can be harmed by small failures of this nature. I am not very religious but that does not mean I do not see reasons for things. It does not mean I do not see consequences. So what I do next is I lay a further lemony towel a completely fresh one in front of the cage and I kneel on it. I am thinking how the last time I failed to conduct the counting properly Mrs Hasan's grandson got sick almost died and this time someone closer to me is at risk. And there are clips on the blue plastic top of the lizard cage which I click with my thumbs.

With the top open I held the propelling pencil in the manner of a dagger like this. I peered forwards and there he was. Tiny and still. Not even a flick of the tongue. Little eyes like those fish eggs they tried in the canteen only once.

Not roaming. Just still. And I was amazed to find that my hand was not shaking. I could not swallow smoothly and my brain felt swollen but the shaking had stopped and I could see very clearly what I would have to do. I would have to choose the lizard to be harmed. Before Jack or Father was chosen instead. I half closed my eyes. I hovered the propelling pencil with its sharp little metal point above the lizard's speckled head. I lowered it. I lowered the pencil slowly until the tip was perhaps two inches above him. And I waited there. He looked tiny and harmless and somehow lovely but I had no choice but to hurt him. I had to bring the metal pencil tip down. One two three four five six seven and I would thrust it down. I would put the tip of the pencil through his eye. Pop. The fish egg would burst. I would kill him quickly. It would be easy. It would be bad but necessary. It would save people I like from being hurt. I would have to do it.

But I could not. I needed to even wanted to but I could not kill the lizard in that place of invisible dust.

I closed the top of the cage. I zipped and hid my gels. I covered the cage with a brilliant fresh towel and I carried it out of the towel room and up the goods-bay ramp and past Terry from Security scratching his ear. A sort of tic of his. I ran down the street feeling sick. I could guess at the strange looks of people . . . they always look when you do not want them to look and they never look when you do . . . but I did not meet their gaze. They existed only in the corner of my eye. Panting I entered the small walled space of Postman's Park. There is a tiled wall there that I sometimes like to look at. It says it is a monument for ordinary people who saved the lives of others. People who would otherwise be forgotten. I have memorised some of them. Sometimes at night it is nice to say them to myself.

Thomas Griffin. 1899. Labourer. In a boiler explosion fatally scalded searching for his friend.

John Cambridge. 1901. Clerk in the London County Council. Drowned saving a stranger.

John Clinton. 1894. Drowned aged ten trying to save a friend.

There is a pond in the park that makes me think about swimming. Jack is doing a triathlon but I stick to running because although I once tried I cannot swim. And in the shrubbery behind the pond I found a damp place with plenty of leaves. I opened the cage to let the lizard escape. At first he did not move but then he did. He moved so fast I did not see him go.

And that is it you see.

That is what I did.

And do you not see?

Please try and see. Try and see and ask yourself.

Is it because I did not choose the lizard that Miss Stephens was chosen? Is it because I set the lizard free that Miss Stephens had her fall?

Jack says he misses the spacewoman tights . . .

And even if these ideas are from the nonsense parts of my mind I know my job is over I fear it is over after this mistake.

Because someone important bought a lizard for some reason. Because I took it from them. Because in a law firm crimes have what is the word? Repercussions.

4.15 p.m.

It is an unusual problem, unique in her years at Hanger, Slyde & Stein (though they have had rodent difficulties in the past, and on one occasion an issue with flying ants) to find in the corner of your office, sitting at the round conference table, chewing on a Mars bar, chocolate detritus raining down on the Starfish Speakerphone, a giant lizard.

'Never in all my life,' says Barbara, her walking stick held high in self-defence.

'Calm down,' says Peter, abandoning his chocolate bar to stand. 'I didn't mean to frighten.'

With misdirected adrenalin ringing through Joy's veins she overlooks the obvious costume-related questions and asks instead why he's been sitting in the dark.

'You expect me to sit under a spotlight, Joy? Sell tickets? I'm an eight-year-qualified Senior Associate dressed as a Smith's Dwarf Chameleon.'

'Funny,' Barbara mumbles. 'Always thought of you more as a snake.'

'Barbara,' Joy says, 'you've had a tough day. Why don't you get me that document I need to look at.'

'It's on your desk,' she replies, voice fading as she exits. 'Whole place a whatschacall. Viper pit.'

As the door closes a line of shadow shudders across Joy's practising certificate and a framed print of an Ansel Adams photo: *Ice on Ellery Lake*. She inherited the picture from a friend who left Hanger's to pursue cheese-making in 2004. You hope to keep these people in your life but nearly all of them go missing. To Joy's younger self the glacial landscape seemed evil, some nebulous terror lurking in the black-and-white terrain, but of late it has looked quite different, a thing of bleak beauty, candid and pure.

Peter clears his throat in an exaggerated fashion, as if the room holds a spell of sadness he wants to break. 'Joy, I need to talk to you, it can't wait.'

'Why? Why are you dressed like that?'

He exhales with a great deal of cheerlessness. 'It's for the Make Law Fun Day. You know I worked on that Madagascan mining case with Brian? UK subsid entered a process and we were called in by the administrators.'

'I don't get it.'

'Project Chameleon. Madagascar is home to half the world's chameleons, you see. Used to be, anyway, before the mining company got overexcited. Brian thought it might be a fun case to tell the kids about.'

'Laugh a minute, I'm sure. Must be why you volunteer so much time on this scheme each year – for the sheer unbridled fun of it.'

'He wanted me to crawl around the floor and pretend to eat stuff. I told him straight: no fucking way.'

'What an incredibly tough negotiator you are.'

'Lawyers dressed up as animals, it's obscene.'

'Like that team-building thing,' she says.

'I mean dressed up as animals and crawling round the floor . . . What team-building thing?'

'Team-building exercise.'

'Wasn't there.'

'When we started.'

'Wasn't there.'

'You were,' she says. 'Awful HR woman. Dirty-bathmat skin.'

'Wasn't there.'

'Told us: Pretend to be an animal.'

'Wasn't there.'

'You were Peter the Sloth. King Penguin Christine? Leopards, Lions, Labradors prancing all around. Only me lying still. What animal are you? Awful asked me.'

'Dead one, you said.'

In the silence she becomes aware of time passing: she needs to slip down the fire escape and find a rope, or blade, or precipice. If not today, when will the courage come? She has more pills in her drawer but associates them now with embarrassment, feels she needs to confront a more dramatic death – one with blood, with breakages – to win back some self-respect.

'I think the lizard thing suits you,' she says. 'Makes you seem more human.'

'Where's Miss Perfect's contribution to Fun Day? I don't see *you* dressed as a chameleon.'

'Maybe I'm just good at blending in.'

She's barely seen him smile since 2006, this man she loved, this man who is never more comfortable than in costume. But now, causing his face paint to crack and his lipstick to shine, it comes, cautiously, the mouth making sure there's something to smile at, crimping in one corner and enlivening his eyes, ridding them of the flatlined look all office workers get. He shifts awkwardly in his green body stocking. There's a second pair of eyes above his forehead and he scratches absent-mindedly at one of the sockets. They seem to be made of fruit, glued strategically to –

'Yes, I know what you're thinking. They're pears. Pears stuck to a cycling helmet. The crest at the back is cereal packet. Christine helped me make it. She's very creative.'

'She's one of my best friends. I know she's creative.'

'Yes. Well. One can forget.' There's a cough in his voice and he lets it out. 'At least we're talking again, I suppose, after all this time. I think this counts as talking, don't you? This morning, before Brian bowled up, was more like shouting. With a low word count.'

'Usually you doing the shouting.'

'I tend to project. It's my natural mode.'

He goes to pick up the chocolate bar with one of his specially adjusted gardening gloves, simultaneously batting off the tail that wants to slide around his hip.

'I had to break a tennis date with her today. Misplaced my racket. Tried to call, but dodgy line. Not in her office either.'

'Yes, well. Christine's gone to stay with her parents, so you couldn't have played.'

'Has she?'

'She has. We had a falling-out.'

'And?'

'*And* – do you not talk to your husband? – I took your racket.'

Joy pauses, frowns, tells him to keep talking. In the tilt of his protruding upper lip she reads either shame or disdain.

'I went round to your place, last night. I . . . I don't know.'

'You're serious, aren't you?'

'Always,' Peter says. 'It's the great tragedy of my life, people think I'm joking when I'm not.'

'If you wanted to chat, how about a call, or an email, or walking ten yards to my office?'

'Thought you'd left for the night. I needed to talk face to face. Which is also what I hoped to do this morning. When I saw you yesterday afternoon . . . what was I supposed to think? Was I supposed to leave the conversation like that, to let you charge off like that? Was I meant to not care what you were talking about?'

'You backed me into a corner.'

'I was congratulating you on the promotion announcement.'

'You were being snide.'

'Snide is just the way I sound! I have an adenoidal issue. My second tragic flaw.'

She replays yesterday's conversation by the Coke machine. She is not sure why she said it, the comment about not sticking around for partnership, the stuff about how it was time to be honest with herself and everyone else. Her thoughts fizzed into words and before she knew it they were out there to be heard. She thinks he banged the machine with his hand as she walked away, but maybe it was the sound of a can falling. Angry or thirsty, angry or thirsty: as she moved through the corridor the question circled, stubborn and pointless, through her exhausted thoughts.

Peter licks his lips, a thing he always does under pressure. 'You deliver this speech to me about honesty and goodness. You chat about a mystery holiday your husband seems to know nothing about. I mean, Joy, it's been years. The beauty of what we had was its invisibility. It was perfect because it was secret, because it wasn't altogether real. Which doesn't mean it didn't matter to me. When you ended it you broke my –'

'Did I?'

'Concentration, you broke my concentration for months. Why ruin what it was? I thought we'd reached an understanding.'

'You make it sound like a contract. It's not. It's my life.'

She feels once more that steady hopeless sinking, nausea rising round her throat and up behind the eyes. It's the feeling that comes when she contemplates falling short of perfection, a despair brought on by what is, nonetheless, her most consistently praised quality: a merciless need to adhere to her own high standards.

'Honesty,' he says. 'It isn't always the best policy. There's a Russian saying my man in Moscow taught me: *He lies like an eyewitness*.'

'So?'

'So even if you told Christine about us, you might misrepresent certain key details. It would be irresponsible, and pointless, because I've . . . turned over a new leaf. Not so much a leaf as a tree. I've turned over a whole fucking forest.'

'I see, I see it now, I get it. You take the racket so I can't play tennis with your wife, in case – to put her off her serve? – I mention how her husband is a truly great screw.

Oh, Christine, he fucked me so hard, we fucked all over your flat, he came all over my tits, does he like to do that with you?'

'Christ, Joy, keep your voice down for Christ's sake. You're talking nonsense. I wanted to speak to you and when you weren't there I needed to think up an excuse, the racket thing was the best I could do. You're out of control.'

'No, that's where you're wrong.'

'Who's shouting now?'

'That's where you're wrong because I'm not out of control.'

'Who's shouting now do you see me shouting?'

'I'm very, very *in* control, Peter. I'm not the Oh-I-hate-myself-for-what's-happened type, I'm not Miss Weep Weep The World Is Better Without Me, waiting for Oprah to give me a hug. I'm not making little cuts in myself as a cry for help.'

'What's that mark on your hand?'

'I'm not secretly hoping I'll earn people's pity and love. I don't want to hear solemn unthinking advice like One Day at a Time and One Step at a Time. I own a calendar and I know how to walk. I didn't get dumped by Mr Right or see my cat squashed by a giant tyre. I lost my sister's child . . . I lost a child, and did that to Christine . . . how did I do that? . . . and to Dennis, betrayed him and everyone, there's no precision to betrayal, if you betray one part you betray the whole, and even today I've caused all this pain. I don't recognise myself, or like myself, or want to be me any more. I need to unzip my skin. I need to climb out.'

'You're depressed,' he says. 'We'll get you help. It's depression, that's what this is.'

'Depression's not it. It's not the right word. Depression makes me think of . . . the pressing down of something that wants to get up. I don't want to get up. I'm not all quiet and acted upon, sighing and lying around, all vacant and peaceful and paralysed, waiting for feeling to come back. This *is* a feeling. A dark overlarge feeling that's everywhere at once. It's in my limbs and my throat, like a tumour in my throat so I can't breathe. It goes away awhile and then I feel it come back and I fear the feeling so much. Not sadness, more like terror. Terror at it having happened, at it happening, coming back, until I make it stop, me, and people said give it time and I have and time hasn't worked.'

'So it sounds like maybe some pills are what you need. We'll get you pills and maybe a counsellor. I mean, you have a great career.'

'I want to feel nothing,' she says.

She stretches her fingertips across the piece of paper Barbara has left for her to read, then drags them inward to make a clumsy ball. The veins on her hand look like underwater things, exotic and drowned, and the headache is back, worse than before.

'So on balance you'd probably say, what, that you're not planning on saying anything to Christine or Dennis? About us?'

She realises what she's done to the paper and sits there pressing it flat, reading the wrinkled text for the first time, squinting through the little coloured dots that have been in the margins of her vision ever since the crash. An email from the CEO to the EMEA Head of Manufacturing. It starts normally enough – a comment on the economic necessity of bulking up meat with water and other additives, injecting it with needles, tumbling it in cement mixers to absorb the water, the standard stuff for chicken nuggets. But then, after reminding the EMEA Head that salted meat attracts only a fraction of the EU tariff for fresh meat, the CEO talks about a forthcoming Food Standards Agency sampling process. *The breasts injected with pig and cattle protein, the* – she has to smooth out one of the capillaries in the page to see the next word – *pet-food recycles, the bovine stuff JT uses to make the flesh swell. All that's got to come out for a week or so, or there'll be all kinds of fuss.*

'Joy? Maybe you need to think about a new job. Banking, perhaps? Joy?'

'Tell me,' she says. 'What do you think of the Meat Musketeers?'

'The . . . uh, OK. I guess they have a point. It's not really my . . . Stuff's probably been concealed by the manufacturers? Animal cruelty's become the norm. And there's those pretty distasteful adverts they put out, convincing kids and their parents that Nana's Nuggets will make them happy. But, you know, who cares? Chicken's chicken.'

'Dennis knows.'

'Eh?'

'Dennis knows, about our affair.'

Act Three

MISPERS

But O, how bitter a thing it is to look into happiness through another man's eyes!

William Shakespeare, *As You Like It*

Peter

VARIOUS TEDIOUS developments, Doctor Odd. For a start my PA is having a sick day, as PAs are wont to do, so I've been stuck with Barbara.

Dry-cleaner got back to me, she said this morning.

And? I said.

Unsalvageable.

She pronounced the syllables slowly, each a tiny knowing blow to my testicles and time. The unsalvageable item in question was my suit. It was involved in an accident in the gym around the time I last spoke to Joy, in her office, me wearing a foolish outfit I'd rather not discuss.

His word not mine, she said. Expensive, was it?

Barbara, I said, do I look like a man who wears cheap suits?

Thought maybe you'd spent your budget on the tan and the teeth, she said.

Jessica laughed at a moderate to high volume and, *fun* being infectious, the fire alarm began hooting too. The test runs every Thursday at 11 a.m., for twenty-two seconds. With the noise deafening us all I made eyes at Jess and started silently mouthing random words. Then when the alarm stopped I said: So, slipped my mind, but it's highly urgent. You'll need to draft me a note on the key aspects of a CVL.

As lunchtime approached I decided – feeling a slight sting of remorse about the invented CVL note – that I'd ask Jessica to join me for a bite to eat at the Icarus. I was not in the mood to lunch with my fellow Senior Associates today: Green, Brown, Black. Certainly not Michael Bland, the resident coke dealer. Hanger's has a policy on coke – it's OK – but I leave it to the polo-playing toffs, the Eton-types with more money than septum.

It was a late lunch – we ate only a few hours ago – and the Icarus was half empty. Jess and I were having a fine time at a corner table, eating pan-Asian in privacy, when suddenly – hey fucking presto! – *Dennis* emerged from behind an otherwise pleasing water feature. He sidled up to our table, the posture of a man with no gym membership, and when I offered my hand he gave it his characteristically bone-crushing shake, the only firm thing about him.

Always the gentleman, I told him, my teeth working on tidy glazed cubes of pork.

Gentle most of the time, he said, pulling up a chair and introducing himself to Jess. It's his bubbly manner I can't stand. Voice like a fart in the bath.

I explained it was a working lunch. Most people would take the hint, wouldn't they? Not Dennis. He just said, Yes I thought I'd find you here, and stared at me as I ordered another bottle of Pouilly-Fuissé. Then he asked if fine wines were one of my many fancies.

Grapes are within my scope of expertise, I said. Heard

you like a drink yourself. I like to get into whatever you're into.

There was a long lull. Jessica told an anecdote about her father and an All-You-Can-Eat Buffet. You could tell she capitalised it.

Dennis said, It's a shame, you know, that Christine isn't here.

And Joy, I said. Could have had a double date, plus Jess here to share between us.

You! he shouted, dragging my plate towards him. You really are –

Sir, the waiter said, popping the cork and trickling me a taster.

Dennis sank back into his chair, his chins taking coloured light from my sweet and sour: the peppers, pineapple, rusty red sauce. Advantage Peter.

What a lovely meal, Jessica said, at which point I sent her back to the office.

I drank some wine, looked at him, yawned. I knew I'd win this little mano-a-mano showdown, so it had already stopped being fun. Me and the Big D, we'd had a prior tussle on the Thursday before Joy's fall and I'd emerged with a top-spec tennis racket as my trophy. You know, I try to imagine him and Joy talking, what they ever had to say, and instead my mind always presents me with a picture of her alone, on my sofa, skirt hitched, body delicately twisted, long fingers shielding her breasts. The last time we had sex, years ago now, she writhed under me, aggressive with pleasure. She never failed to surprise . . .

Where was I? Oh yes.

Listen Dennis, I said, barely summoning the energy to

talk, you're the boss here, and in the spirit of evaporating the awkwardness between us, I'm going to tackle the elephant in the room. I *know*, Dennis. I *know you know*.

You're talking about the affair, he said. The one you had with my wife.

I told him, You're a smart man, Dennis, I've always been conscious of that. So tell me. How did you finally get it out of her?

What do you mean, *finally*?

The Thursday before she fell, I said. Or the Friday itself. Whenever it was she told you.

I took a sip of wine – nice aroma of grilled almond – and noticed him smiling.

She didn't tell me about the affair on the Thursday, he said. Or on the Friday.

Tuesday, Wednesday, what's a weekday between friends?

It may well have been a Wednesday, he said.

Well there you go, I said.

But a Wednesday that was, well, yes, over four years ago.

What? I said. My pile of mute rice was going soggy. It had held until now, a perfect white temple, but I could see the foundations succumbing to the sauce.

Yes, he went on, looking bigger in his chair. There's been no need to discuss it of late, because we already discussed it all, exhaustively, in 2006.

I told him, I'm not sure I catch your drift.

Waste not want not, he said, shovelling a forkful of my meal into his face. Is it pork, or chicken?

I asked him whether he was seriously pretending he'd known about the affair for years, and his response was simply to nod and chew.

I swallowed. She told you . . . at what stage?

Oh, he said, almost casual, after we'd been married several months. Yes, we had a good chat, got everything out in the proverbial open. All of it, even the fact you two had been carrying on straight after our honeymoon. But then, it was never going to be a conventional marriage, was it? I married her when she was pregnant and, anyway, I knew she was too young and beautiful for the thing to be conventional.

But, I said, you and I have bumped into each other over the years, many times. We've . . . shaken hands.

Rather firmly, no?

Dennis's fingers were fussing around the stem of his glass, as if shuffling invisible cards. The image stands out randomly in my mind, a small clear detail in a long-buried memory, and yet it was today, this lunchtime, hardly any time ago at all.

He caught my gaze and said, very carefully, I got upset when Joy aborted my unborn child. I thought I'd stay upset forever. But then she told me all about the affair with you, and I realised I shouldn't have been upset about the abortion at all.

I asked him why. He wanted me to ask him and I did.

And he replied, with a half-stifled yawn, Because it transpired it was your dead baby they'd sucked out, not mine.

I felt suddenly gluten-tongued.

Golly-gosh, he said. You did know that it was yours, didn't you?

He said this to me in his teacherly tone, enjoying dispensing a lesson.

She said it was yours, I whispered.

Oh dear, he said, standing up. Sounds like all kinds of things are outside the scope of your expertise, doesn't it?

And with that he walked out. Walked out. Walked . . . he . . . off he went . . .

What?

No. I mean yes. I mean why not.

Expensive, you know.

This water. I'm on the Associate Sundries Committee. It's designer.

Yes.

Yes I feel fine, more or less. More or less totally fine. After Dennis walked out of the restaurant, I continued to drink, alone. I've had a few drinks today. Alone. But I like to drink alone. Don't you? Solitude. It asks no favours. Gives no surprises.

Betrayal. That's the word I'd use. It nags at my teeth, I have to say. I could taste it as I left the Icarus, and I could still taste it downstairs, in our lobby full of glass, shapely ankles, shiny shoes. A fuzzy layer of betrayal. How could she tell him the child was mine, tell him and not tell me?

Leaving the lift, my head began to hurt. The light felt lurid and false, like a film set some technician had made bright. I caught my reflection in two panels of closing chrome. Its shine and precision startled me.

In this dazed state the first person I saw was, alas, Barbara. She told me my eyes looked puffy, like a chameleon's.

And then, as I desperately sought the quiet of my office and the rubber bands that would relax me, Charles Jestingford ushered me into his room.

Take a seat, he instructed. I've got a Project Unoaked

Chardonnay call in ten minutes, but we must touch base. No, please, go all the way. Make yourself comfortable.

The seat was actually a walnut chaise longue of the kind your lot like. He had it installed at the same time as the whiteboard. Such eccentricities are permitted in the truly senior.

Listen, Peter, he said, as I lay on the chaise longue, listening. He was somewhere behind me, and every time I shifted my weight to see him he would move once more out of view. I wanted to do this over coffee but . . . how are you bearing up? You and Joy, I gather you were close?

When I gave no reply, thinking how this was becoming a back-foot sort of day, he asked me about Dennis. Said he'd been phoning a fair bit. Charles was pleased. Thought it was important Dennis should feel able to come in and talk to whoever he wanted. Not just to you, Doctor Odd – though Charles was talking about keeping you on, the obvious addition to our in-house gym and GP and dentist, he said, and a permanent fixture in some stateside multinationals – but Joy's colleagues, friends. He said it wasn't the time to speak of such things as PR angles and reputation management, but that the legal press were asking questions. What were Joy's hours like, and so on. And anything I could do to facilitate a smooth relationship between the firm and Joy's husband would, he said, be looked upon favourably. As would any assistance in keeping up the morale of the team as a whole, letting them know it was personal issues that caused her problems.

Not sure I understand, I said. But I understood perfectly. I am constantly quick to comprehend. It was one of those sentences that fills a gap, nothing more.

I don't quite know what Charles said next, but the memorable bit was this. He said, If I'm completely frank with you, Peter, I think we made something of a mistake. It should have been you that we made up. Joy is very talented. But, man to man, you know what it's like. You were an *exceptional* candidate, but the team could only put forward one new partner this year, and the diversity initiative meant that it needed to be a woman.

I thought you were a big supporter of hers? I said. A mentor.

He remained silent. Of all the dark office arts, silence is the most powerful.

It's funny, he said. Some people are threatened by good-looking, clever, wealthy white males. There are vendettas against us. A woman loses her nephew and becomes a heroine for merely turning up to work afterwards. What can you do? I should like to discuss it with you at some point, the cult of the spirited female, the bland black man, the obligatory Asian.

He came into view, rummaged in his desk drawer for an exercise book, and pushed designer specs up his nose. Then, with a few parting words, he went off for his call.

I lay there a minute or two, then took myself back out into the corridor. A small crowd had formed around Olivia Sullivan, enjoying a glimpse of her snug bloused breasts.

Is it true you were in Charles's office? said Tiny Tony O.

Is it true you were in with Charlie? said Green.

Summoned by Charles? asked Brown.

Made redundant? said Black.

That's what they said, though perhaps not in that order, and I fled down the fire escape, which is generally referred to as the Five O'Clock Chute on account of its clandestine convenience for those rare precious things: early exits. I stood in the cold, with the BlackBerry for company.

I called my mother. This was about fifteen minutes ago, that I called her.

I need that phone number, I announced. Christine's parents' number, I need it now.

She said she'd been meaning to dig it out for me, but had got caught up thinking about the faulty light bulb and my troubles, so I explained again that my life is trouble-free. I earn one hundred and five thousand pounds a year, base. I live in a converted mansion block in an up-and-coming part of Holloway. My cleaner has the necessary work permits.

If you'd really like to speak to Janet and Stephen, she said, they're here now.

They are? I said.

Yes darling, she replied. They say they haven't seen Christine since that business with Joy Stephens happened. I think you'd better come over. If you're not too busy, you know, dealing with your other difficulties.

Beg your pardon, Doctor Odd?

Yes. They say Christine isn't with them.

Well, after Mother relayed that confusing news I went inside, to look in the mirror. Then I picked up my briefcase, told Jessica not to bother with that note. Oh and then, before coming here to see you – I despise people who break appointments – I took a black marker pen from the white-board in Charles Jestingford's office, and carried it into the kitchen, surprisingly heavy in my hand. I counted the number of complimentary bananas remaining on the work surface. Fourteen. And I stood there for a few minutes, workers coming and going around me, to write a word on the skin of each fruit. All this before laying out the bananas in a kind of yellowed smile in front of the coffee machine, putting the words in order.

When they were all arranged the message read something like – this was it – *Charles is a cunt Charles is a cunt Charles is a cunt cunt cunt.*

You've gone awfully quiet, Doctor Odd.

Rash? Really? Well I'm in a rash sort of mood.

Yes. Yes, I'm heading to Mother's now, to work out what all this fuss is about.

No need to say that. It'll all be fine.

No, no, I'm not shaking. If I am it'll be the caffeine. Late nights on Poultry.

If Christine's not staying with them, she'll be with a friend. I am not concerned. It has been a strange day but it's about to get better. I have a good feeling. Time to reconcile things with the wife. Once I've explained my side – about Joy, the mistakes – it'll all be fine.

4.42 p.m.

As Peter struts out of her office cursing, tail swinging, not affording Joy a moment to explain the parameters and depth of Dennis's knowledge about the affair (or the way he has held it over her since, demanding sexual adventures of his own), she starts to feel feverish. The spasms in her legs, tired from the day's exercise, share a rhythm with the swelling pain in her head as she hands Barbara an envelope and tells her to courier it to this address – no, second thoughts, post – not mentioning that the destination is the unofficial HQ for the Meat Musketeers. Being a whistle-blower, a defector, holds a shiver of danger; it's a way, she sees, of being alive. She approaches Alfredo – needs to discuss some bath oils that are being purchased to mark Barbara's fortieth year at Hanger's – and feels her hot pressurised headache as a kind of lightness, a lightening: its intensity blots out huge swathes of the everyday; her usual troubles are newly ignorable. Alfredo keeps beside his mouse and its mat a mirror to facilitate regular hair-combing and she catches herself in the glass, cheeks a clammy pink that could pass for health, her own reflection insincere at the edges, blurry, smudge marks from his hair-gelled hands, perhaps, or is her post-crash eye trouble getting worse? Feels like that time she tried hallucinogens on an island in Thailand and got the sense an aerial in her mind had been re-rigged to tilt and whirr, sending thought signals spinning in all directions, sensory perceptions arriving with random clarity. Hard to hear Alfredo; too many fringe transmissions about flash floods and flu, minor monologues being performed nearby, the aerial with its free-associative motions increasing the sense of fullness in her brain.

The fire escape corkscrews down around its own faint shadow and Joy begins to move with it, blood swaying, temporary pass slung around her neck. She cannot bear another death cab so she'll get back to the Heath via Tube, that's what she'll do, speed-walk although she's feeling pretty queasy to the hardware shop at the intersection of Moorfields and New Something Street, buy a nice sharp knife, get the escalator down into the warm dark Moorgate underworld before the rush of City workers go bar-crawling into places for the happy and sad. Her handbag in the cab. Her purse, Oyster card. Should have scrambled for these things, but instinct made her reach only for the suicide note, took her through the glass and down the street, and now evening is already settling over the City like a mood and there are more headlights making flawed cones of colour on the road than before and ooooh really feeling kind of drugged and dreamy, the headache more like a big numb nothing now, curling round her ears like cheap steel specs. Specs? There's someone else's voice inside her own, a foreign signal, gets her thinking of . . . yes, that half-busted car radio on childhood trips, picking up different voices in different towns, and she's feeling more or less than human now, maybe a chameleon sneaking down a tree trunk somewhere warm, what would that be like, to mess with your colours and be whoever you wanted to be, everyone or no one, falling in love with a fellow lizard, a lizard who blends in with a branch, a branch that could be another chameleon, making you half suspect your best friend is sucking him off but maybe it really is just a branch, or maybe they're innocently drinking from a cool dewy leaf, and you'd never really know who you were and, even if you did, who knows, you could get creative with your scales and reinvent yourself in one cold-blooded beat of a long tensile tail. Paranoid lusty lizard! You'd be in all kinds of thermal worlds at once, a serpent with no certainties peeling off your skin in a cheap slutty striptease, licking out at an amber-green apple that could always be the bulbous nub of something sinister. Pretty dizzy with spots of all colours in her eyes but she'll get herself down this fire escape, back to the trees in the Heath; will get herself back somehow, probably enough loose change in this jacket for something sharp and a travel pass, the Heath is where she'll go, never one to abandon a plan, in her head the cathartic truth's supposed to happen on the Heath – Hollywood revelations, deathbed conversions, the flipbook of key moments in your life played out to Last Judgement jazz or a low-fi lullaby – because you've just got to hope death doesn't let you down, down, down. We all expect something from the Big D – *the big what?* – even if it's hell, we all expect an overwhelming something, something more than a slack whimpering lack of life, a nice Hitchcock-thriller-type moment where in the last reel you get to relive your former trauma and fall into a kind of peace, each crisis unfolded and explained, reasoned and redeemed.

Like a long rambling passage from her husband's published papers the staircase goes on and on, without a clear point or purpose, until she hears familiar diction from below.

'Amazing thing, isn't it?' – a throat full of Friday mischief – 'A little roll of fine-cut tobacco. A twenty-first-century stick to kick-start pleasure.'

She sees Charles on the bottom step, smoking. Mental Brian too, muttering something just the wrong side of sane. They see her and she . . . no, too late to turn away.

'Joy, my dear,' Charles says, 'where do you think you're off to? Only a few minutes till the big speech.'

'Few minutes until the big speech,' Brian adds.

'She's probably having her last cheeky fag as a Senior Associate. Am I right?'

Her dry tongue licks out sticky ums, empty ahhs.

'You missed the partners' mini-meeting,' Charles says. 'The pastryfest. No matter. Not much of interest beyond the baked goods and the fact we're laying off five further paralegals. Though Brian here did give a rather lovely soliloquy on work allocation.'

She thinks she sees Charles wink, though the tremor could be in her own eye.

'Too kind,' Brian says, 'too kind.'

'Now, Joy, with regret I'm not sure you have time for that last salaried cigarette after all. It's full steam ahead to equity and it was decided at our utterly butterly meeting a moment ago that I should be the one to introduce you to the masses. With back-room support from Brian, naturally.'

'Naturally,' says Brian, 'naturally.'

'Old Brian's an expert in back-room support. Loves

nothing more than to bash the back doors in and come up on a problem area hard and fast, isn't that right, Brian? We're expecting a lot of well-wishers from all across the office to be there to welcome you into the partnership – we never used to do any kind of thing to mark the day, can you believe it? – so I've told Julie to forget the idea of holding it in the lecture theatre. I've had her send a chubby-fingered email telling people to crowd into the ground-floor function space. The caterers are redirecting the flow of bubbly as we speak. We're going to have you, and those two double-barrelled Corporate chaps who are being made up, address your fans from the second-floor viewing platform.'

'If the Health and Safety boys cause a fuss,' Brian says, 'I'll dum-de-dah go to war on them. Go to war.'

Joy opens her mouth to try and say she has to go, emergency at home, can't stay, but the powers of expression that have served her here for a decade are vanishing in her mind's lowering light.

'Brian'll be all over the Health and Safety boys,' Charles says, 'whatever warfare's necessary, his weapon in their faces. And quite right too. They want to build a taller railing on those viewing platforms, like we're all a bunch of mal-coordinated clowns. Well, that's all well and good, there are indeed some clowns here and there' – he flicks a quick thumb in Brian's direction – 'but we need the platform today, don't we? And everything's fine, all perfectly safe. There's too much Health and Safety round here. And too many well-adjusted people. Well-adjusted people will ruin professional services in this country. Isn't that right, Brian?'

'Remind me of the agenda,' says Brian.

'Well, Brian, there's no agenda as such, it's not an agenda sort of thing now, is it? But, roughly speaking, I'll say a few words to introduce Joy, then Joy can speak for as long as she likes re how made up she is about being made up, and then old Jonesy from Corporate can introduce his two new monkeys.'

'Corporate might want to go first? Engine of the, ah, firm?'

'Nonsense, Brian. This is the post-downturn world. It's the young contentious and insolvency stars who are the future. Joy here, closely followed by the likes of Perfect-Eyes Peter, then that girl with the mole who always smells of mint, they're the new leaders.'

Perfect-Eyes Peter? She is wondering why until now she's never been privy to that nickname as Charles and Brian, ignoring her inarticulate excuses, sun setting behind and around them like a controlled explosion, lead her down the remaining step, past the Cypriot tailor's and the creepy-kitsch card shop, over a trampled *Evening Standard* predicting the end of the world and a B-list divorce, to within view of the Japanese water garden, its six bamboo fountains and staggered granite stepping stones, and finally the great dust-less revolving door of Hanger, Slyde & Stein.

Dennis

BIRDS IN flight are not in a space between Place A and Place B, but instead carry Place A and Place B and Place C and Place D and all the other places they have flown or will fly *with them*, as part of them, in flight, for they live in the sky, the inbetweenness of travel gives a clue to their being, the flying itself is who they are, at least that is – crudely put – what the architect Vincenzo Volentiri argues, and his point is a rather beautiful one I think, though only tangentially relevant to this thing I'm about to tell you, which pertains to the relationship I have with my wife, and pertains also to what happened on that Thursday night before her accident (the night that started with the wine and the weights and which that racket-pincher Peter interrupted), and it's going to sound strange even to someone who has heard the things you must have heard, but what I would like you to bear in mind, to bear in your open medical mind, is this: a couple, a man and a woman,[14] can get used to slash habituated to slash accustomed to anything. People can become familiar

[14] Or man and man, in these enlightened times. Woman and woman, even.

with torture, for example. People can come to love hot wax and hostage-takers. People can, in really quite surprising numbers, decide that the best way to spend their weekends is in the company of whips and chains, ball gags, muzzle gags, slave hoods, gimp masks, punishment canes, a range of male and female Gorean-style slave restraints, penis restraints, vaginal restraints, punishment implements, whips, floggers, paddles, straps, belts, rattan Koboo public-school disciplinarian cane sets, wases, floggers – did I already say floggers? – Spanker Sausage™, steel fetters, lockable male and female climax-denial devices, penis pinchers, pussy poppers, testicle ticklers, asylum slash military slash religious zealot pattern discipline thongs, straitjackets, medieval massage maimers, futuristic things they've not yet named – can decide they wish to be in the company of such things, on a given weekend, in London's vibrant Vauxhall. All I'm saying is that the human mind, given time, has a great capacity for embracing the strange.

It[15] starts with a tiny nearly normal thing and ripples out from there. Perhaps you haven't made love to your wife for a while. Things have gone off the proverbial boil. Sex, in the language of women's magazines left lying, spine-strained, around your constantly redecorated home,[16] lacks a certain sparkle. Maybe there's an incident in your wife's past that means lovemaking has ceased to bring her much happiness. Some deep evolutionary need to go through the motions of reproduction has crumbled under a weighty sense of despair at what those motions mean in modern life – when

[15] i.e. the pattern of events leading to habitualised strangenesses.
[16] By way of hint?

you may not have time to care for your child; when your child, growing old, may not have time to care for you; when, even if everybody has time, all the time in the world, some cruel external force may interfere. So one night, after a few drinks, maybe seven, certainly more than five, in tacit acknowledgement of your need for intimacy, and the lack of sparkle and boil, you suggest to her that you watch a DVD, and that – consistent with tip number 5 in the 10 Quick Marriage Menders piece you perused – the DVD be of a softly pornographic nature, be in fact a DVD you happen to own, a DVD called *Chalet Girl's Erotic Avalanche*, a DVD which you have hitherto kept covered by sports socks and gleaming white boxers unwittingly arranged into a drawer-sized version of an *actual* avalanche, a DVD showcasing Chalet Girl's ladybits but also (for this is to be a shared experience) some willies. And that (the watching and subsequent intercourse et cetera) goes well, pretty well, and for the next time, in advance, you procure from one of your bearded PhD students a small bag of cocaine, something you and your wife haven't done together for years (snort cocaine, that is, though with sex it's also been a while), and you have some of this cocaine together, in front of the DVD, just enough to put you at a nice elegant remove from reality, and that (the subsequent intercourse) goes well, really pretty well indeed, and so when several weeks later you bring out the remaining cocaine at a small party with close friends, and things have become somewhat jokey and lewd, and there are only four of you left in the room, and the other man's wife – looking not unpleasant in the druggy moonlight – has her hand on your thigh, and you look up to see her husband's lips on your wife's shoulder, one shoulder of the pair of shoulders you've always meant to tell her you love, you don't overly mind, for it is small fry compared to the contact you've seen on screen, and your wife says let's call it a night this is getting weird, and you call it a night but – *but* – feel somewhat disappointed, feel, in addition, surprised by your own disappointment and amazed by your own surprisedness, for this is a time in your life when surprise seemed a thing you could not feel. Months pass. You start to buy a little more cocaine from the PhD student. And long before you tire of the coke, long long before the CAUB moans in one-on-one feedback sessions that you're the only tutor who gives her 2:2s (could you please reconsider; you'd really better reconsider), long long long before the CAUB goes to the Dean of the Arts Faculty to complain of sexually inappropriate comments and gropings (comments you know were not uttered and gropings you know were not . . . groped), long long long long before the CAUB throws in for good measure her suspicions that you have been engaged in on-campus drug deals, long long long long long before you are suspended pending completion of the university's investigations, long long long long long long before your daily life becomes a series of small lies to conceal this professional catastrophe from your young wife – long before all this, you have one night when the four of you[17] go a little further. And when, several mornings hence, you and your young wife sit up in bed, and talk about how this has to stop, not necessarily because it is unpleasant in principle but because it is making everyday contact with Brenda

[17] You, your wife, your wife's friend, and your wife's friend's husband (as hitherto mentioned).

and Anthony rather awkward – at the supermarket, at the Islington Farmers' Market – well, when this happens, you start to consider your options.

What I'm saying is, we had call girls every Thursday. The words Which girl shall we order in for tonight? became as normal as Do you have cash for the cleaner?[18]

Anyway, judge us if you will, Counsellor, but my wife and I are, in my opinion, only slightly left of normal. The little pacts and betrayals one's relationship absorbs are only unthinkable or upsetting when compared to the perfect vision of an uncluttered relationship one has at the very outset (of the relationship). Did I imagine, when a mutual friend first set me up on a dinner date with Joy, explained how successful she was in her legal career, explained how until recently she'd been mixed up in a relationship with all sorts of complications but now wanted to fall in love, clean and pure, did I for one moment imagine that we would one day be reliant on the paid services of a sex

[18] And actually, Counsellor – a side thought of sorts – I wonder whether this phenomena of strange discourse becoming, through usage, akin to everyday discourse hasn't got something to do with the inherent strangeness of *all* language? I am thinking once again of *Othello* and in particular the greatest of Shakespeare's verbal tacticians, Iago, who recognises that if it is natural that one should demonstrate the native act and figure of one's heart in complement extern it is also natural that such a demonstration *distort* what is contained in the heart, that all acts of naming, of assimilating things into a system of language, may involve labelling that thing in terms of something *other* than itself, alienating it from its unspeakable individuality, and that this is one form of the differentiating or stepping aside which all use of language entails, don't you think, Counsellor?

professional to keep our passion for one another alive? No. No, Counsellor, I did not. But then nor did I envisage that she would become pregnant, and that without a second thought I'd offer to do the right thing, and that after seemingly endless thought, as I stared at ducks paddling the canal, she'd say OK, why not, and that as I looked back over my left shoulder shortly thereafter I would see her in white, dappled with light from the high windows, looking barely real, a smile driving her dimples into delicate shadow.

We had a call girl arrive that Thursday night. Joy-Joy wasn't in the mood. We sent the girl home. I don't think that could have overly unsettled my wife, given it was a pretty much weekly occurrence, do you? Certainly after the girl left everything was very ordinary; we had some wine which I feared might be corked but was not, and I nearly mentioned the Peter visit but didn't want to give him the satisfaction of causing us yet another argument, and we went to bed, and woke up on what seemed to be an average Friday, clouds in a knotted posture filling the morning sky, the sun a clementine, no, a tangerine, no, a satsuma hanging low, and I watched her organising some papers at the dresser as I lay half wrapped in my hangover, eyeballs pulsing in time with my heart.

You're asking . . . ?

Yes, I see. Well, Counsellor, I say an average Friday morning, but I would add . . . yes, that she was tearful and affectionate. Careful, I suppose, to leave all our bank statements in five neat piles, organised into current accounts and ISAs. Slow and showy, now I think, in the way she said she loved me, said I love you, often said those three words to me – perhaps you're surprised? – though of course she usually said them (the words I love you) in the quick snatched way hurried couples do, Joy-Joy in particular being a person who employed the same brusque rat-a-tat tone whenever she talked, delivering life-changing eulogies with the speed of takeaway orders. She could dismiss philosophies, order furniture and book a first-class flight in the time it takes me to swallow my own spit, really she could, but that morning, that last morning, she didn't speak so fast, she was different, her *I* and *love* and *you* were more spaced and languid, so perhaps, yes perhaps, I should have known.

I notice I am in the past tense once again. Funny, isn't it, how the literary times are a changing, how it (the past) is no longer the writer's tense of choice – take Beverley Badger's work, *pour example* – and I'd say that despite a few stubborn memories holding her back Joy is by nature a present-tense kind of person, yes, snappy, headlong, with an irresistible forward tilt, hardly touched by time, whereas I'm all about the past these days, the past which never stops happening, treading through its waters with decreasing pace, dragging my legs like lead weights.

I was going to tell you about my impending disciplinary hearing at the university, and the fact that the female student who has been causing me all these issues has been in the press this last week following a somewhat inelegant incident in Peckham, and that particular stopping-off point in the story, that proverbial narrative service station, that definitely has a place along the, er, motorway of who I am, which I suppose is what these sessions are intended to explore (the question of who I am), but the thing I really want to get on and talk about is the police arriving at my door on Friday afternoon. They were waving Joy-Joy's driving licence.

Asking me to confirm my address was her address. Asking me had I heard from her, telling me not to be alarmed, holding her handbag which I noted was newly adorned with complex shards of glass, telling me that she had been in an accident and was missing, *missing*, a strange word that seems to evoke the mystical, which seems to be within yet beyond experience, the way missing people are, a missing person is, the police call them mispers, did you know that, missing persons become mispers in police-speak, on police papers, one word, like childcare, *mispers*. Joy hated it, the fact the world saw fit to abbreviate such a thing, to steal a space and half the letters from a phrase – missing persons – that already felt false.

I will tell you about that, and my journey in the police car to her office, and my phone call to Joy-Joy's sister Annie, if you would like to hear it?

Thank you, Counsellor. You are an open-minded and attentive auditor. As one might expect, I suppose, from one who mingles art and science. You'd be the perfect reader for my new book, I think. If I ever get it published. If Beverley Badger's agent ever gets back to me.

4.48 p.m.

SHE FEELS a curious detachment from the crisp, alert office workers filling out the ground-floor function space – the niceties they exchange reach her only remotely, the vague babble of voices at the edge of a dream – but the cold walk around the building seems to have done her good: that thunderous headache has settled in her ears as a background hum.

'Must freshen up,' she tells them as they pass through the security barriers, grateful her own words sound sensible.

'Have to be quick,' says Charles. There's something tyrannical in his tone that makes Joy want to please him. 'We'll see you up there.'

'See you up there,' confirms Brian.

The grids of champagne glasses look gimmicky but brilliant, sharp and shiny in their lines. There are canapés waiting on the side tables too, appearing fresh and alluring while nonetheless having something about them which suggests fakery: bruschetta should not be that size, and who in the real world would eat hoisin duck from a lettuce cup? But these perishables have all been laid out for her speech, along with branded water and pulpless juice, and as she walks into the ladies' loos she begins to think it's best to deliver the spiel and sign the forms, for is the partnership realistically going to insist on her paying in the capital contribution straight away? Even if they do, which increasingly she thinks they won't, will the firm really make life difficult for Dennis after she dies? There's probably a good spouse-friendly life-assurance policy in place once you make partner – though she'd need to check for carve-outs in relation to suicide – so where's the rush to die today?

She sits on the toilet, wondering if other suicidal people go through these farces of indecision. Adrift in a sea of variables: this must be how Dennis feels every day. She should go to the police. Technically she fled the scene of an accident. As soon as the speech is done, if she does it, she should take herself to the nearest police station. Did she actually throw the BlackBerry at the perspex before they crashed, or did it fly out of her hand during the crash, or did it not leave her hand until much later? She wasn't aware of any drama involving the BlackBerry until she found herself telling Barbara about it in the changing rooms. If you've had a trauma your perceptions get muddled, don't they, so how do you decide what's true and what's not? She feels almost sure now – the post-credit-crunch toilet paper insists on dispensing itself one square at a time, which is irritating – sure that she had nothing to do with the driver's death, has nothing to feel guilty about, it is him who nearly killed her, but all sorts of thoughts are thrashing in her mind, probably must be (scrimping on loo roll!) the shock. The twenty-first of January. It had seemed the right date on which to take her life, and when the partnership promotions were scheduled for today too this struck her not as a coincidence but as a sign of some wider design. Any sense of structure is precious. She would take herself to the Heath, she would get this right. But did she not feel an odd elation, after the collision, at being able to flee that crumpled metal coffin, succeeding where the driver had failed?

She hears someone walk into the lavatories. Flats not heels; you can tell from the lack of clack. A mobile goes, not the standard Hanger ringtone, and the woman says 'Hello?' with that air of faux surprise everyone has in their repertoire.

With shoulders rolled Joy is staring at her own knee-slung knickers when the woman says, 'Complete waste of time, security people just confirmed she's here, you know what he's like.'

The voice is unmistakable, breathy and curt, but it cannot be.

'PhD in panicking, that man, I'd forgotten. Apparently she's being made up to partner, which I suppose was inevitable.'

Her sister.

'I'd think it was some kind of elaborate ruse' – yes, 'ruse' is one of those words she fits into every conversation – 'to get the two of us in the same room, but the police are here and everything. Did you take the dog out yet?'

Joy hovers her palm over the sensor flush, smooths her skirt. She swallows, thinks, opens the cubicle door.

Annie is the first to speak. 'My God,' she says. She repeats those same two words several times, as if they contain a secret that would unlock itself if only she could get the pronunciation right. Leaning back into the phone she whispers, 'I'll call you later.'

The two sisters assess one another. Annie has lost weight. Some of her thirty-eight years are etched in fine lines around the eyes but otherwise she looks taut, slim, nicely dressed in figure-hugging jeans.

'You look great,' Joy tells her.

Annie says 'You look . . .' and her sentence falls to the fiercely mopped floor.

'This is . . .'

'Yes, a surprise, think how I feel.'

'How come you're –'

'More to the point, you. Dennis said you'd had an accident, the police have been round –'

'Oh no.'

'Why do you say oh no?'

'I don't know.'

'You don't know why you said oh no?'

'I don't know, Annie, I just . . . consequences are sinking in, that's all.'

'Finally,' she says, dropping her phone into her bag.

'What does that mean?' Joy says. 'Finally?'

The lost boy is there in every conversation, a residue of blame at the bottom of each word.

In the silence Annie walks over to the full-length mirror and applies some lip gloss. A PR trick, perhaps, for gathering up her thoughts. Her movements show a slow caution, limbs going through their motions in a kind of disinterested drift, and only towards the end of her routine – jerking the bag zip, shaking out her hair – does her manner fall back into the youthful snatchy self Joy remembers. Even when you grow up, she's noticed, muscles recall the way you once were. It's the same with voices: even now Annie's accent has the slightly chafing texture of two continents rubbed up within it, North America not quite ready to relent. And she is here. Her sister. Here.

'Anyway, I'd better be getting back,' Annie says. 'A little girl and a dachshund to look after. Jamie's home today but trying to work.'

'Dachshund?'

'Yes.'

'You have a dachshund?'

'That's what I said.'

'You probably have another dog too, do you?'

'Is that a burn on your hand?'

'It's fine.'

'And grazes?'

'They're fine, Annie.'

'I live in Finchley with a little girl, one sausage dog and a management consultant called Jamie. Why the inquisition?'

'Finchley?'

'We moved.'

'Not Hampstead?'

'Correct, Joy. Finchley is not in Hampstead. All that hunting for child-snatchers clearly improved your sense of geography.'

Joy dissects this comment in her mind and finds what she needs in it. 'You moved out of Hampstead,' she says.

'Jesus wept we moved from Hampstead to Finchley, is that so hard to understand?'

Her brain feels so crowded it hurts, too many thoughts competing for space.

'It was Dad's house,' she says.

'Joy, I bought out your share when Daddy died, you know that very well. You're really something, aren't you? I'd forgotten that my little sister really is –'

'I wasn't saying.'

'Is it so strange, after what's happened, that we might want to change our surroundings in some small way? Does that offend you, have I offended you in some way?'

'Sorry. No. It's just.'

'Just?'

'I was passing by a while back,' Joy says. 'The Hampstead house. Saw a motorbike in the garden.'

'We sold the house to one of Jamie's biking buddies. Probably his. Passing by?'

'Walking. On the Heath.'

'So you still do that.'

'Less than before.'

'Yes, well. Less is more these days, I'm told.'

Joy has a sudden lurching pain behind her ear, the room in momentary blackout.

'What was that?'

'Nothing,' Joy says, blinking.

'Your head jerked.'

'It was nothing. When did you move from Hampstead? Have you been getting my letters? I mean, I know you got the first letter, I mean the one after, after. Wimbledon. Maybe a letter wasn't the right way but I thought you deserved the truth of what happened that day and . . . I'm just sorry I didn't tell you straight away face to face when the police, at the time . . . really, God, ashamed, sick, every day sick, but I didn't think when you got the letter you'd just cut me off and not that it isn't fine if that's what but –'

'Dennis knows all of it too, does he?'

Silence.

'Listen, Joy, I'm glad you're obviously fine. I am, J, I am. Clearly it was just a prang or whatever but you must be shaken up and your hand looks sore so I'm glad you're fine but really I must be heading off.'

'Your little girl, what's her name?'

'Grace.'

'Grace. What a beautiful name.'

'Thought Dad would have liked it. You got Joy. I got Liberty chucked in the middle of mine, which I still think is fucking ridiculous, but there you go. I should be going.'

'Please, sis, Joy says – too desperate, too needy, even to her own ears – 'please, Annie, stay a while. I've got to give a two-minute speech and then we can chat, not chat but talk, a coffee only how about that, I'd be really grateful to talk?'

'Look, J, the thing is I . . .' There's that cautious grace again: the hand floating slowly to her face, the fingers half-heartedly massaging her temple. 'I didn't mean for it to become like this. But, also, I'm just not sure I have the energy, you know?'

'If you could wait a few minutes,' Joy says. 'That's all. I've got to run up to the second floor. There's a platform and I'll be undressing' – did she say *undressing*? – 'the little crowd gathering out there by the lifts.'

Annie's brow folds and unfolds. Joy has a faint sense of closing in on her goal, and her only hesitation is the prickle of suspicion she feels at any prospect of pleasure. 'Please say yes,' she eventually adds, feeling the air tremble on her lips.

'A few minutes. That's all. If it's longer than that I'll have to head off. There's two officers in reception waiting to speak with you; that'll take time too.'

'Two officers?'

'That's what I said.'

'Waiting to see me?'

'Correct. Let's not get into another Hampstead-Finchley-Hampstead-Finchley farce, OK?'

Samir

It has been decided what I will wear for the marathon. Who I will be.

Please guess.

No.

Please guess once more?

No.

David Cameron!

No no. Not him. Mrs Hasan's cat. She assists at a refuge for cats missing owners. They have a suitable tabby-cat costume left over from last year. It is the refuge I am running for you see. She said she would be very honoured if I could wear it. She offered to dry-clean it in advance.

She also said . . .

Well she also thought I should not worry too much. About setting the lizard free.

Yes. She said that too. Yes.

And I discovered it is what Peter was wearing in the towel room that Friday. Not cat fancy dress but lizard fancy dress.

Yes! It is why he had the weird green Lycra on. Lawyers can be strange.

That Friday afternoon when I returned from releasing

the lizard Jack was in a far from brilliant mood. He had arrived early for his four thirty to eight shift and found the desk unmanned. I entered the gym and began to explain that I had been extremely delayed in the towel room but he interrupted me. Sam mate listen up he said. Sometimes you're dumb as a box of rocks. He told me manning the desk has priority over the towels. He was unusually pink and creased in the face. Perhaps it was the effort of contemplating a box of rocks and its purpose. I asked him if some additional bad event had occurred to affect his mood and eventually he explained. A fee-earner had been awkward with him perhaps twenty minutes before. Came into the gym stepping on a sit-up mat with non-protocol shoes and said his suit was very expensive and he did not want to leave it in the changing room. He was doing something for the Make Law Fun Day. He wished to leave his suit in the back office where it was safe. And you see it turns out the fee-earner is Peter. Jack told Peter clothing in the back office is unfortunately not allowed. But Peter said Do you not know who I am? and Jack took the suit but was left feeling small. Which I suppose is why he took it out on me a little bit. Because I was there. Same reason Father says he got annoyed with me that day in Sylhet. Because I was there. Why did you get in the river? he said. Why did you get in the Kushiara if you cannot bloody swim?

It was the hour before the speeches and the ambulance that took Miss Stephens away. The hour before I glimpsed blood in her hair before people knocked me out of the way before I saw how even lying there she could draw people towards her. I had nearly finished my shift and Jack had nearly started his. He decided to do some exercise to relieve the tension Peter had put in him. Exercise is brilliant for this. He peeled off his joggers wearing shorts underneath of course and he scratched his stubble. He said to me not really looking Sam Man if you want to start your run now you can there's no legal bumtouchers here. And I said But then the desk will be unmanned. And he said Jesus Christ Samir the point is we are both here. Then he began stretching and stepped onto the treadmill.

With another scratch of stubble he started running. I wiped down the treadmill next to him with the blue spray. I did some neck exercises while counting the number of balls of varying weights on the triangular medicine ball stand behind the treadmills (seven minus two). Next I went through my hamstring stretches my quadriceps warmer and my heel-to-buttock leans.

Running next to Jack created strange sensations. I have never done it before or since but there I was right next to him trying to look straight ahead at myself but seeing him in the mirror too. Looking at people in mirrors is always very strange I think.

Because it is them but not them. That is the brilliant trick of the mirror!

They make me think of working in the toilets of the Raj. Mirrors do. English stomachs in curry houses. Spice in the diet. You had to clean every two hours. Father's boss the overall manager was very strict about it. He wanted corporate customers. The table was set with wine glasses. But despite the need to clean every two hours the big rule was if the customer comes in to do his business stop what you are doing and do not meet his eye. At most in the mirror. Never look direct. Father said the customer is a man of delicate tastes who does not wish to connect with the cleaner. Be see-through. Be silent. Because if you are really there you make the man of delicate tastes think he is a man of belches and splats. No one wants to be a man of belches and splats. But I made a mistake . . . I spoke to the customer . . . Just a piece of advice when I saw he had forgotten to wash his hands . . . Which is a breach of the rules. So I was asked to leave. Father covered my shifts until they found my replacement. And it is like he is in the Raj bathroom all the time now. He used to have his confident teacher posture. Shoulders back. Meeting your eye. But now even when he is trying to make small talk with Mrs Hasan or is in his favourite chair he has a different posture. Hunched and small. There but not there. See-through. Nose close to the television. When I pull my chair alongside his chair the tiny static tickles.

And that Friday it is Jack in the mirror. Him on one treadmill. Me on the next. The handles of mine are still damp with blue spray. The motion of him sends air my way. Very smooth movement. A natural athlete.

The motion of air like the first time I ran for fun back in Bangladesh. In Sylhet everything that is running is running to get somewhere whether it is the rickshaws baby taxis or children rushing to Friday prayer. There is street football street cricket and so on but no one is going to put on special shoes and jog through traffic and horns past stray goats and cows you see. But then there was this one occasion when I was fourteen before I came to England. This one occasion after my mother died when I received the most brilliant treat. I got to go and visit my best friend who had moved to Dhaka. We were walking along holding hands which back home is nothing strange and he tells me about this brilliant club. This running club in Dhaka for the ones no good at other sport. And the next day we wear very bad old plimsolls and go to the club. A nice lady draws us a route. We take the route. We run side by side like this time I am telling you about. This Friday in the gym with Jack. Running. Picking up pace. Getting into the flow so we look as effortless as Mrs Hasan's cat chasing leaves. Nothing to beat the feeling. A brilliant feeling when you switch off on the road or on the treadmill. Switch off in the manner Miss Stephens switched off that last run she did. You go inside your lungs. Running up Begam Rokeya Sarani. Left before those Commission buildings. Route I did with my best friend that day. Running past the crescent lake. Up onto the Mirpur road. Running uphill. Past the row of little homes. Endless modern windows on the right and on the left people living in careful mounds of mud. Down past the graveyard and the next marker as your lungs warm up is the Kalatan. You probably have not been but it is the Kalatan. You hug the bank of the brilliant lake its colourful water inviting you to swim and past the whatever it is called hospital I want to say kidney hospital you see? All along the lake. And I must tell you. I must tell you even with your lungs on fire it is magic there.

You sigh when you hear the horns and get back onto the very big roads and run and run back through to where you began. In this little world inside my lungs I am seeing the trees and the university and the Jagannath Hall Pukur but I look up and I see Jack running there with me. And it is very very strange he is there but like the lizard he looks in a way pretend. Like a cut-out. Smooth and flat in the brilliant light of the glass. There but not there. Raintrees eucalyptus and akashmoni all around him. Lake shining even though I know it is just the mirror in the gym making things shine. And the T-shirt is tight against his arms his biceps triceps just catching the light here and there and he really is such a brilliantly nice man. And suddenly I do not really know where I am. I am running in the gym on the treadmill next to Jack and it is Friday afternoon before Miss Stephens gets hurt before the legs that Jack loves get broken but I do not really know you know. And I try to stop thinking about my mother and the cut on her foot just a very little cut and the infection that got in when she waded into the river back in Sylhet to help me because I yes I cannot like a rock I cannot swim and I focus straight ahead feeling off balance and when I look up again he is gone. Vanished. I mean the trees of course are gone and I know now I am back in the gym but Jack is gone too. And I cannot quite believe Jack is no longer there. And that is when it happens. The realisation comes too late. I feel this irresistible force. Like a very bad hand dragging me back. My footing all wrong. And I try to correct with the longer stride. But once you lose your natural rhythm you are finished. I was finished. I was flying backwards. This non-existent hand dragged me back very very fast. Very fast it dragged me until my feet were in the air. Nothing solid under me. Just air. And it was long enough I could reach four or five before I hit. Counting as I am pulled back through the air with this strange light feeling. Almost into the ergos but back straight back into the medicine-ball stand. Crunch. I am twisted in a heap across the floor and just as my brain is catching up there comes down from the brilliant space between me and the ceiling these balls. A green ball first. Falling. Coming from the medicine-ball stand I have knocked. Lands on my chest. Winds me. Then a smaller one. In my private parts. Twists everything up inside so I feel I need the bathroom. And I shield my face while the metal medicine-ball stand itself topples and luckily it lands to my side and the other balls roll away. They roll away. And lying there I feel this warm blood trickle down my neck. Things start to hurt very badly but they take a moment have you noticed? Does that make sense? And without thinking as pain surges in I see what is it what is the name for it the little glass fire box on the wall above me just within reach and I think without thinking yes I am here I am panicked I might even die and I stick my fingers right through the glass and only then do I understand what will happen next. I see among everything in the wrong place in the room that the breaking of the glass will start the alarm. I see that the alarm will start the sprinklers revolving. I see that this is how it is set up in here the great logic of the system and that water will shower down on the treadmill and ergos and climber and chest press. For a few seconds I understood all of this brilliantly and then it came. The watery wrecking of the place. The most brilliant kind of alarm scream. Two sprinklers on the ceiling. Then three. Then all of them. All revolving. The quick sizzle of the blood-pressure monitor screens and items of that nature. And I was afraid. I was afraid but I realised I was not going to die today. This would take some explaining but for a moment I was lying there in pain with the water messing up the whole world and I was not dead. My testicles like mushy dahl my stomach sick wrist now feeling stranger and this blood on my neck that would normally make me faint. And among this mess I see Jack. I see Jack coming out of the office and standing T-shirt wet holding something. Laughing. Not even trying to shield himself from the pretend rain but just laughing and staring straight at me looking only at me. And right there in the rain he points to the long dark shape hanging from his hand which I now see is Peter's suit. The one he wanted us to monitor while he wore his costume. And it is absolutely soaked and ruined. Very very bad. And I start to smile still lying down. Does that make sense? A very big smile. And for those moments lying there, the moments before we stopped the sprinklers and went to see Miss Stephens do her speech, for those soggy moments, the room in disarray, for those moments Jack standing there laughing, the equipment in bad condition but me laughing too, for those moments I did not feel so alone.

Does that make sense? Does that make any sense?

4.58 p.m.

In some pockets of the office it's as hot as Bangkok. The glass-walled building seems to have slid beyond the Square Mile, down the frozen banks of the Thames, through ice-shard shingle, under bridges and a restless sky, over fish and mud and the deliberate dead, out and out into the cleaner ocean, still and blue, where the equator waits with outstretched arms . . .

'On top of establishing a taller railing,' Charles says, causing a kink in Joy's daydream, 'they need to find a less aggressive way of heating these platforms. That vent's like a blowtorch.' He rises from the bank of chairs he demanded a moment ago.

'Blowtorch,' says Brian, repeating for the rest of the row. Beside him Joy nods, mimicking the colleagues seated to her left. She alone unfurls her legs and thinks how, under the fluorescent ceiling panels, they are all ghosts, casting no shadow.

'Did you burn your hand?' someone says.

She blinks as Charles moves closer to the ledge. He begins to hush the rising chime of voices, plates and glass, mingled sounds you only really hear up high, and she imagines him on the edge of a bridge. 'Quiet please, thank you, thank you.' She feels hot, a little afraid, that gaseous weight in her brain is back, the pain expanding, but now her sister is downstairs waiting all the disappointments of the day seem to have a purpose and a shape. Those piecemeal grazes on her knuckles have acquired the significance of survival scars. The fingers of suicides fished from the Thames are often shredded, she's read; too late they tried to cling to things, groping at the river's piers and props.

'Ladies, gentlemen and yet-to-be-defined species of this firm. Most of you will know that I am Charles Jestingford, a partner in the Dispute Resolution team.'

He holds the microphone gingerly, as if scared the mesh ball will come loose, plummet forty feet, leave him with a trickless stick. The tips of his oxfords are shiny and black, snug against the base of the railings. Each iron bar tapers and twists as it reaches his knees – a candle, Joy thinks, becoming its flame.

'I had a strange incident this morning which I thought I might share with you by way of introduction. I have, of late, been spending quite a lot of time visiting a client's offices in Swindon. Now, hang on' – he shades his eyes – 'is my lady-killing Swindon-born Senior Associate down there? Ah yes, there you are, Peter, how could I miss you? Now, good people of Hanger's, I must say that having visited Peter's home town – really is your home town, is it, Peter? – it is much easier to see why he works so bloody hard here, pro bono for our charity panel all day and billable all night. It came to me during rush hour as I was crossing the third bleak roundabout in as many minutes, listening to the incessant West Country whinge of the radio disc jockey, the ghastly monotony of his voice: Peter's terrified we'll send him back!'

One thing about Charles: he won't play to a particular audience. You'd get the same speech at weddings, funerals, gates of hell. Over the weak crackle of laughter from below, the M&A lawyer to Joy's left says into her ear, 'Got to make a call; back in two; very quick call,' and scuttles away. She is tired of scuttling. She is tired of making calls.

'And of course we wouldn't dream of sending Peter back. Swindon's bowel-looseningly banal business parks would certainly not know what to do with his talents. In the headquarters I was visiting, talent was a scarcity. Indeed, mere attendance at work was a scarcity. The employees were clearly unhappy. Never was an organisation so in need of a workplace counsellor to improve productivity and protect itself against the risk of getting . . . Anyway, over there the average number of sick days per employee per year is somewhere over the twenty mark, which is worse even than the public sector, on which don't get me started. It seems only the CEO is happy to attend to the nine to five, and he has the consolation of – every Friday – heading to the BVI in a private jet.'

The word 'jet' flies like one, quick and crafty, a reminder of why all those people down there work so hard: the yearly promise of more money, more treats, more *stuff*. Up here in this stark box of light, on a level with Charles, her headache brings a resharpening of the senses. As he turns to look full-faced at her, she can see inside his complex smile, can unpack the many compressed longings in his lips: to apologise for this inane corporate banter (we'd both rather dispense with the formalities); to nevertheless soak up her gratitude

(I am up here doing this for you, delaying getting blotto in Private Liaisons); and to indulge his own lawyerly need to assess a thing from every angle (the crowd down there are warming up, are you on board too?). The process of decoding his expression makes her remember what she felt looking at that poor cabbie's slumped posture, his body despondent at its own dying. She could not have helped him, probably couldn't have helped anyone at that time, sleepy-weak as she was. She saved herself. Head pain, tingly limbs, dots in eyes, but she has saved herself and sabotaged a client's feathery poisonous plans. On this accident-strewn day she has improvised and survived. What more can you do?

'So I said to the CEO, a terribly nice chap, I said, What do you do when a repeat offender phones in sick? And he said – how's this for hands-on management? – that this very week he'd been faced with just such a problem, and decided to phone up the employee personally. The phone rang. Eventually the employee picked up. He sounded tired but basically fine. The CEO explained who he was and felt a satisfying ripple of fear pass down the line. So, the CEO said into the phone, I'd like to hear exactly why you can't come in to work today. And the employee, sounding grave, hesitated. Come on, the CEO said, out with it. At which point the employee, apologising with some sincerity, said, Look, I'm terribly sorry, I really am, but I've been in bed all morning, and I'm simply too sick to come in to work today. For God's sake, man, the CEO shouted, I've never had a sick day in my whole life, just how sick can you possibly be? Well, the employee sighed, if you really want to know, I've just had a double blow job from my brother and his dog.'

The silence gives way to three or four inert laughs, a dozen bewildered claps, a hundred muted expressions of derision or disbelief, and the needless repetition of 'brother and dog' by Brian. Joy herself joins the ranks of the clappers, but as she starts a slow show of approval, the motions that politeness require, she notices something strange about herself: her hands will not join up. Once, then twice, a cupped palm misses its target, succeeds only in slapping the shapely base of the other hand's thumb. Even on the third attempt she fails to find the sweet spot that amplifies sound. Her own fingers look Martian in the synthetic light, gadgets of creaseless pink. Her arms seem limp and inhumanly thin. The floor tiles are made of a substance she can't name and the air around her contains a chemical tang, an alien influence.

'Without further ado, please give a warm round of applause for our star litigator and brand-new partner, Joy Stephens!'

Must have missed some words somewhere, but she sees now that Charles has put the mike back on its stand, that she's expected to get up, and on high heels that are as much a part of her as teeth, as lungs, as her healthy British heart, she floats dreamily to her feet and detects the silky tickle of Charles's mouth touching, not her lips exactly, the soft skin to the side, his warmth, his breath, intimate enough, it turns out, to make her wonder, as she reaches the railings, how she has felt so removed from life these last few years.

Dennis

HAS SHE been behaving normally? the louder of the two officers said, one thumb on the steering wheel and the other up his nose.

What's normal? I said, staring out of the window at the fuzzy pedestrians we passed. A few of them flicked furtive sideways glances at our car, perhaps remembering past crimes they'd committed: jumping Tube barriers; stealing penny sweets.

Then he asked, with a slight smirk jerking the corners of his mouth,[19] whether I could think of anything which might explain, in the absence of concussion, why she hadn't reported to a police station.

Concussion? I said. (Nobody had mentioned concussion, or the possibility of concussion, or intimated towards any head injury whatsoever, until this point.)

We can't rule anything out, he responded. Even a small blow to the head can induce temporary memory loss.

[19] For I think when I'd said *What's normal?* he had taken it as a dry aside on the mercurial nature of my wife's moods, rather than in the intended spirit of broad philosophical enquiry.

And that's the moment, Counsellor, at the mention of the phrase *memory loss*, that I began to think about dates. Dates are just dates, little boxes on a calendar that you squeeze your life into, but to forget an important date – an anniversary of a life event – is a kind of suicide, the death of past and present. This was the overwrought thought that came to me as we raced through London streets, and I took out my expensive phone, the one Joy-Joy made me buy, and I saw in the flawless screen that today really was the twenty-first of January, and I shuddered.

The quiet officer in the back leant forward, head sandwiched between seats. Have you recalled something? he whispered.

Nothing much, I replied. It's just today is exactly five years since that whale got dragged from the Thames.

They both shared a look, a look which delivered a cascade of mute announcements: one, I had now crossed the infinitesimal boundary between Normal and Abnormal; two, they hated their jobs; three, that was an end to the questioning.

And do you know what I did next? Looking down at my phone, at the date and the time, I pressed a button to take me to the SMS menu, and I sent myself a text message, a text message which read To forget a date is a kind of suicide. I had a thought which I sensed might look pretty in my book, a thought about dates and suicide, something to tie in with the ahistorical theme of suicide in Shakespeare's work and its links with the temporal matrix in which that theme, all of Shakespeare's themes, are (for some scholars) enclosed, and I sent it to myself, lest I forget it. I think it's important for you to remember that I did that, Counsellor, particularly if you've made a value judgement so far, an assessment on the nature of my personality. Perhaps you've decided that, of all the patients who walk through that door, I stand as one of the harmless people, the conceited but well-meaning, the pretentious but pleasant, a benevolent irritant, the extra post-meal Jaffa you neither desire nor despise?

Well that's nice, that's nice of you to say, it really is, it's very generous, but would any *good* man, travelling along in a police vehicle, aware that his wife is very possibly brain-dead and lying against a lamp post, no one stopping to check if she's OK – because people *don't* stop, do they, not in this Britain that is always changing its voice and values; they keep walking when they see someone slumped and in need, not in case the slumped, needy person is drunk, or else in case they (the slumped person) cannot be dismissed as drunk, and will instead require some kind of more serious assistance, disrupting the smooth flow of the passing stranger's day – would any good man, knowing this, stop to text himself a pretentious little thought, stop worrying about his wife and instead text himself an empty little riff, just because the texted riff might add something, a small flavour of calm philosophy, to his otherwise paranoid prose?

This isn't the way to her office, I said. I reminded them what we'd agreed when they turned up at my door and perched on my sofa – that instead of messing about on the phone and continuing to wait for news we should *do* something straight away, go to her office straight away, see if she was there, see if anyone had heard anything from her since the crash.

They shared another look.

There's a lot of traffic on the normal route, the loud one

said, becoming quiet, quiet like the quiet one, but more eerie in his quietness, because it was not his usual style. Vehicles obstructing the road.

I decided I needed to phone Annie. Having realised the date it seemed to me that Joy-Joy might have disappeared to Hampstead, to try and make peace with her (Annie). I googled her PR agency on my phone, found a number, called it. I told the receptionist I was a potential client, found myself – who knows why! – using an improvised Welsh accent in my verbal tussles with her, an accent which I suspect further reduced my standing among the two aforementioned members of the Metropolitan Police Service present to hear it. Eventually I was put through to Annie's mobile number. We spoke awkwardly, hesitantly, but as the conversation evolved it dawned on me that my wife's sister was concerned by my news – upset, even, to hear of the taxi accident – which perhaps shouldn't have surprised me, but surprise me it did. She offered to meet me at the offices of Hanger, Slyde & Stein, and the next time someone spoke it was the Formerly Loud Officer, addressing the security guard at the reception desk of the very building you (Counsellor) and I (Dennis) are sitting in now.

Various dark-suited people arrived, all acting like I wasn't there at all, the Silly Eccentric Invisible Dennis.

I interrupted their discussion. It's ten minutes to five, I said.

So? they all said.

So, I explained,[20] if she's here, if she's all right, then she'll

[20] (Wanting in my heart of hearts to take a machete to their bovine skulls.)

be about to start her speech, her pleased-to-be-partner speech, that may be why she's not answering her desk phone.

They went back into their huddle and after a while the Always Quiet Officer broke out of it (the huddle) and said, Seems you may be right, sir, one of the guards says he lent her a temporary pass a couple of hours ago. You can relax while we go upstairs, to this viewing platform she's due to speak from, and talk to her.

So she's here, I said.

It seems so, he said.

Then please, I said, please couldn't it wait till after her speech? She's done nothing wrong, there's no need to make a scene.

The Always Quiet Officer consulted the Formerly Loud Officer and the latter said, after a pregnant pause, Very well then, if it's brief.

Annie marched in at that moment. I'd met her only a couple of times in my life, years ago, but since then she'd become so familiar from the television and newspapers and my wife's constantly consulted photo albums that I recognised her straight away. The denim of her jeans was an apparent blue which, in the bloodless glare of the reception area, moved through a subtle spectrum of other colours: greens, purples, silvers. She seemed almost annoyed that the drama had been resolved in her absence, whereas my mood was bright and buoyant, my sense of luck and light and life inflated by the assurance that Joy-Joy was not slumped against a lamp post, that she had been spotted coming back to work (so like her to come back to work!).

Aren't you relieved? I said.

Of course I am, Annie said.

Yes.

Yes, Counsellor, I don't doubt the sincerity, although in the course of our discussions that day – in the lobby, in the ambulance – it became clear to me that Annie is one of those people who instead of exhaling say *I'm very relieved*, or instead of laughing say *That's funny*, or instead of loving say *I love you*. She had become one who did not see or feel, who instead merely played at seeing or feeling. This was my impression.

Annie went to the toilets and, by the time she had re-emerged, a man called Charles Jestingford was telling leaden jokes and it was almost time for Joy-Joy.

I was thinking about the speeches today, actually, as I sat in the hospital. I was feeling, yes, I must admit, a little low. And then I went outside to get some air, switched on my phone, and saw – ha! – that I'd received an email from Beverley Badger's agent. Amazing, is it not, how a sense of abnormal dismalness can so quickly be transformed into one of abnormal joy? Below zero to beyond boiling; beyond boiling to below zero. Two opposite states which are nonetheless equally effective, I suppose, in shattering your average thermometer.

5.09 p.m.

THE RAILINGS are the kind good parents like Annie put at the top of stairs, a gate to keep their children safe, so low for a five-foot-nine adult that Joy's hands can only reach the cool metal when she curves her back, spine tight against skin. Each fingernail holds a perfect pastel moon. Beyond these moons the function space – big, square and stylish – meets a reception desk, two sofas, and pink newspaper splayed on glass.

All this is clear, but maybe only in her memory. The furniture and the *Financial Times* are always there, whereas the impermanent parts of the picture – the slowly shifting bodies and faces below – resist clarity, form a smudged alphabet she can't translate. The cloudiness in her vision is alarming. She's always been a noticer, twenty-twenty eyes that thrive on small truths, the way in iced lemonade the smallest bubbles cling to the cubes. Dad said with her attentive eyes she'd be a pilot or a painter, had a gift of seeing through facades to the deeper details others miss, and although she's a grown professional now and the fizz is from champagne not R Whites and her dad no longer emerges in striped pyjamas on the stairs to sing, deep and silly, like the ad, that he's a secret lemonade drinker, Joy reflects on the last few hours and concludes it is still true. The realisation sweeps through her, thinning her fear, leaving a peculiar composure: she is still a noticer, she still has that, regardless of this temporary failing of sight. The squirrel padding its face; the leggy crow stepping over twigs; the complex tickle of Charlie's lips. She has felt these details today. She has been alive to them.

Secrets, secrets, secrets. If you knew the stuff that people hide you'd run a bloody mile. She adjusts the mike on its stand with a clammy drowned hand. She starts to talk. *Thank you all for coming; so many friends down there.* How odd is it that among this lot only she knows where she was this afternoon, trying to take her life on the Heath, God the wilful fucker unzipping His thing and pissing down on her parade, angel-sent squirrels scuppering the plan. If it really was her plan. If she was ever really serious. Another thing her dad said: Tell God your five-year plan, He'll wet Himself laughing. The more serious the thing you do, the more you are alone. Nobody has a clue that she was on the verge of death. Inches from death, maybe, all about the exact tilt of the bottle that toppled, the pills that spilled, but it's a world where inches matter: heels, bullets, lovers. She is talking, but her faltering voice is an impersonator's and her spine arcs more, microphone catching less sound as its stand drops down a notch, head full of tingle and throb, it is so very hot. *Really is a pleasure to become part of.* She is stuffed, on a baking tray, glazed and seasoned, skin crisping up. *Charles is too canned, toucan, too kind.* Leaning further, seeing more of reception, she makes out a policeman's helmet cradled in thick arms, and Samir waving cheerfully, his skin inexplicably glistening, oily-wet like he's just been born. Her mouth is full of clumsy bubbles that shouldn't be there, secret lemonade spittle, popping plastic, the stuff fresh furnishings arrived in when she and Dennis did the house, cellophane sadness rolled around her tongue. Something is wrong. Something is really wrong. *Been here for tame years.* She cannot speak. She cannot think. Her brain has become a place of mischievous play, disobedient in its every direction, and she's standing here, dumbstruck, with more and more coloured dots in her vision, blurry blobs of paint from every shop under the sun, realising that if she had her time again she'd pause things after the car crash, see if anyone needed help, give the police their report, go to hospital and get her selfish head checked.

Main thing? Get through this, downstairs, speak to sister.

People below grow impatient with her stuttering and so must Charles Jestingford because through a lucid coiling wave of pain – up her neck, around her ear – she senses him moving towards her back, a man's bulk slinking through a dream, and her knees seem to be going soft, so it is good that he is coming for her, he can catch her if she sinks back into the sing-song of whispers from the row of chairs behind. But in her eerie suspended state, having nothing more to say, she cannot stand still and wait, cannot hear him calling, can only hear her own breathing, a distant sorry sea, kissing coast and retreating, kissing coast and retreating, amplified by the mike, made more total and consoling, the deep rhythm of her being. Rocking back and forth on fragile heels she thinks not of boats but of cars, the Ford Sierra in which Dad drove them to Worthing every August, Mum asking if her hair looked dislodged by the draught, little carsick Joy needing air back there, Annie blank and pretty with her Walkman on, and him saying Looks good, knowing that in unmanly matters brevity is his best defence, knowing the route so well that he leans before the bend is there, and the four of them travel pristinely past Cissbury Ring, around Highdown Hill, sunglasses hiding the eyes of passers-by, the sun sliding shadows into their laps, Dad asking What do you want to do today?, the question making whole worlds spin on her lashes – ice-cream parlours, pebble piles, games arcades, the doll's-house shop with the funny-faced lady, the mini-golf man with a cabin full of lollies, always lollies if you ask, Dad argues with Mum about whether it's rude to ask.

She feels herself falling backwards. Charles's shadow expanding at her side. She's heard six feet is the width, fingertip to fingertip, of a pair of outstretched arms. He feels nearer than six feet when her body overcompensates. Jolts her forward. Fights against the sense of sinking back. Jolts her forward by inches, surely, only inches, but enough to see her sister beyond the ledge, seeming to cry, and Joy knows all control over her own senses has – must have – disappeared, for her sister never cries, is not the crying type.

Metal spikes her legs. Seems to be – is – toppling over. Charles, his fingertips, missing her sleeve.

The sensation, going down, doesn't feel like falling. Her hair hangs below, but that is all: it hangs. One shoe comes off and the other stays on. It is the floor below that is moving, semi-liquid, coming back to her with its steady greedy glare. Her head is full of such pulsing pressure, a magnet tearing up the bright tangle of champagne flutes and eyes. As the floor with all its luminous things moves closer she feels she remains suspended, dilated, high. This feeling: it's grotesquely agreeable for the swollen moment it lasts; the heady clarity of your first line of coke, cutting it with plastic money, breathing it with paper money. The floor comes up and up, but slowly. People make no sound. Funny how free she feels, surrendering to gravity and luck, falling through holes in her own control. The final swivelling sight is dark cape-shapes and a canapé tray. One of Dennis's tricks is to wander through the house reciting lines from *Lear*, leaving cups, saucers, wine glasses on whatever surfaces occur to him – windowsills, bookcases, speaker system – and hanging here she feels a hitherto hidden rush of love at that frustrating habit, a sense that this is what love is, that one of you grows sarcastic and the other leaves cups on the sill, and now the tiles bobbing up contain her own face, closer, closer still, the air singing many different songs, Joy's reflected features getting bigger as, impatient, rising, rising, the floor finally attacks.

Barbara

LIFE. *LIFE*. Everyone's got their own slant on it, haven't they? Whichever angle makes them happy. Whichever throws light on their favoured side. Would you care for a Hobnob?

One of the hazards of your occupation, I suppose. To work out when people are telling you lies about things. To see through their disguises.

Give it some more volume. The whistling from your nostrils – everyone's got something, haven't they, this time of year? – it's drowning you out.

Well, how can it not matter? What kind of profession puts no emphasis on whether a thing's true or not?

If you say so.

Anyway.

It's none of my concern.

Hey not wishing to stop you in full flow but who's in therapy here, you or me?

Alfredo? Oh, fine, I expect. He'll be covering for me while I'm away. Might even send him a postcard if he's lucky. Empire State, probably. Best building they have left.

Did you hear that? It's mine, hold on, I've got a thing, a textual message.

Ah! Here we are! It's Jackie. Look at this message here, lean a little, it's my cousin Jackie telling me she's going round with a duster, see that – she's still the same, Jackie – in preparation for my visit. But, to answer your question honestly, I really think sometimes you wilfully whatschacall, *misinterpret*. I've never had anything against Alfredo. *Against* is not in my nature. I mean, he could do with pulling his finger out once in a while, but everyone's different, aren't they? He's Italian. There's no cure for that.

My gift presentation went ahead on Monday as planned. But it was all a touch overshadowed. Monday morning was when we finally heard about Christine, you see. By then everyone knew something must have happened. Surprising, very surprising. I hardly knew her, she sat in the Employment team, but she came round regularly to see Joy. Became part of the scenery. The Half . . . her husband, Peter, he's not dealing with it so well. That Monday, some of the partners were in a meeting discussing what to do about him. So attendance at the bath-oil-gift debacle – is that how you say it? – was confined mostly to the girls in my section.

Come again?

Well it's none of my concern. I try not to intrude. But – are you going to eat that? – it seems there was a series of strange events. That's all a life is anyway, I've had my fair share, but this series starts with Christine and Peter having some big argument, maybe on the Thursday night before Joy's fall – personally I could not live with that man, he's lewd, aggressive, insulting – and Christine says she's going to stay with her parents. That's just what I've heard. Needs some space to think or whatnot and calls the office to arrange days off at short notice. So Peter goes to work the next day, leaving her there in the apartment, packing. He gets back from work. He sees her suitcase has gone. He assumes she's travelled to her parents as promised. But, of course, she hasn't gone to her parents.

Well, I despise gossiping, so let's leave it there. Let's leave it there except to say that it turns out Peter wasn't the only one in that marriage who liked a flirtation. If you want more than that you'll have to ask the one with the big tie knots they call Tiny Tony. Because he likes a flirtation too. Which is all I'm saying. I'm just reporting facts. The fact Tony comes up to me on the Monday morning of my presentation and gives me Joy's tennis racket with the fluorescent grip, the one she took to play with Christine every Friday. The fact everything in their lives needs a meeting request, even tennis. The fact if it's not in the Outlook Calendar, if I don't put it in their calendar, it doesn't exist. I know Joy cancelled her match that Friday because she'd lost her racket. I remember her getting me to book a gym session in lieu – she used these kinds of terms, *debacle*, *in lieu* – of the tennis. And now, after all this time, hours before my gift presentation, her racket turns up in Tony Oakley's hands. Explain that! Some things are forever mysteries, you can't explain them. And Tony says to me, he says, Christine asked me to give you this for safe keeping, and quick as anything Peter charges out of his office, his fist in the air, and he snatches the racket just as I'm taking it, and he breaks Tony's nose with a forehand whatschacall, *smash*. Blood all over Janey's glare-free screen! Tony's nose swollen bigger than yours.

Anyway, you'll have to make your own enquiries, but it seems Christine's had a clear-out – got rid of both Peter and her job. Monica, her PA, got a call. Resigned. Not so much as a leaving drink or a thank-you for Mon's help over the years! And Peter, after the tennis attack and an earlier incident involving bananas, hasn't been in the office much either.

For a while, before the truth came to light, we feared Christine might have got caught up in that taxi accident on New Change. Unidentifiable state, the papers say. The driver, I mean. All burnt up. Took dental records before they could tell his wife and little ones for sure, tell them it was him. Information from teeth! The world we live in! Police are investigating the car crash but not the fall Joy had. The car crash they're investigating, but as for what happened in this very building on that Friday they're not treating the incident as suspicious. The paper had those actual words! Not suspicious. Like TV. Just like TV.

Hmm?

It is, of course, it is. It's always sad when someone nice leaves. Though most of us don't go round breaking noses with sports equipment.

After all that drama my little forty years at the firm presentation was a little subdued, is the point. But it goes ahead. The odd surprise attendee. That Samir turned up. Muttering about cat costumes and the fact his father has a date with Mrs Hasan. I don't even know a Mrs Hasan! There's applause. Big card full of messages. You give people complete freedom and they all write the same thing. Everyone wrote Congratulations! or Can It Really Be Forty Years? or Here's To Another Forty. I open the card and pretend to read all the messages, even though I don't have my glasses or an inclination. And then – look! – surprise!

– the bath oils come out. Scallop-and-strawberry flavour, something like that. Might give them to Jackie's little grandson at bathtime. Make the little bugger smell like a fancy milkshake. Forget your newfangled medicines; children are the best antidepressants. And I accept the oils and the applause and don't give them any of the sarcastic lines I've got stored up. I'm still thinking this is a big disgrace, to give someone bath oils after forty years of uncomplaining service, but I hold my sarcastic lines back because it would seem like bad taste – you know, with everyone shocked about seeing Tony's nose smashed in, and Joy still near enough dead. I have an acute sensitivity to what might be bad taste. I just take the oils and tell them all thank you, it's been a long four decades but I'm still just about breathing.

Well, this is the thing. After most of them trundle off, and I'm about to go up to my team supervisor Debs to discuss a work matter with her, give her some papers I've pulled together from Alfredo's workspace, which I won't trouble you with –

Really? Did we? Did we discuss those?

Showed them to you? Well, that I don't recall . . . That I do not recall.

Memory, eh? It's like Jackie's George after a couple of drinks: unpredictable.

But anyway I'm at Debs's elbow about to have a word in private but then I notice that the girls in my section, plus Alfredo, are loitering and looking at me with these funny smiles. So I say, What's with you lot, you look like you've just discovered Christmas. And they say, We've got an extra little something for you, Barbara, just from us. And Liz comes up and gives me an envelope that sparkles like a glitterwhatsit. Ball. So I take it and say all the usual banalities about Oh you shouldn't have et cetera and But you bought me the lovely bath oils and How exciting what is it. But you can tell what I'm thinking. If oils is all I get for the main prize, this is a slither of soap for the hard-to-reach places.

I don't mind admitting I was wrong. With good cause, but I was wrong. Because when I open the envelope there's not soap, there's just paper. And when I unfold the paper it's not a voucher for a scrub-down, or anything like that. It's what they call an e-ticket. Have you heard of those? And, though it takes me a minute, I see after some staring that it's an e-ticket to New York. To travel what they call first class.

It was Alfredo's idea, Liz said. He had all these air miles saved up, and Joy put in the money to upgrade you. We emailed your cousin Jackie to check the dates worked.

You went into my contacts folder? I said.

Sorry, they said.

And I looked at it, this ticket in my hands, this ticket that otherwise I would have been saving up for, saving up to buy, for a long time. And despite the intrusion into my privacy I was pleased.

Kind? Yes. It was kind.

Now don't get carried away. I mean, the timing could have been better. It's cold in February, really it is. But the last thing I am is ungrateful, so I'll probably only mention how cold New York winters are once or twice – little asides in the postcards, so they know for next time.

You're grinning.

Why are you grinning?

Well of course *I*'m grinning! I'm going to New York!

I gave that young joker Alfredo a bit of a hug. He hugged me back. In fact he really went for it, so I said Next on your list am I, Alfredo? And because they find me funny all the girls laughed. And the Italian laughed too. And eventually I thought why not, and joined them in the laughing. And I'm really looking forward to seeing Jackie and the family, I have to say. Excited about getting in a plane again. I fly next week. Excited about wandering around the city, ice permitting. But I'm glad it's only a five-day trip. More than five days would have been too much. Because I'll need to get back. Not just for work reasons but because I do like it here, I have to say. Holiday's a holiday, but London's where I live. There's kind people here, in London. Kind in their own weird little ways.

5.12 p.m.

THEY APPROACH Joy from different directions: Dennis, Peter, Barbara, Samir. Something unexpected about the way the four of them move and breathe. Harsh little stops in the flow of their limbs and lungs. Heads down or nearly down, pushing through colleagues to get close.

Joy does not see this. She has no sense of how, rushing towards her at varying angles, these four people seem linked. As they draw closer to the centre of the event, their faces begin to exchange expressions. For several seconds at a time Dennis wears Peter's anger, or Barbara wears Samir's panic, or Samir wears Dennis's fear. It's like some weird law of physics: feelings flow between them until the maximum level of emotional chaos has been reached. And only at that tipping point do the outsiders arranged around and between these four linked souls come to life. Someone says 'Dead' and another says 'Dead!' and the word keeps coming in great spurts, effortful bursts, as if the crowd has overcome a collective stutter.

Joy can absorb none of this. Even her sister, standing still in the corner, fingers wrapped around her own throat, goes unnoticed.

Champagne glasses shatter. Associates gasp. Trainees squeal. They spend half their days wishing upon their bosses nasty unnatural deaths involving exotic stationery products found in the fifth-floor reprographics room, and now here is one such boss – Hanger's star litigator – in a staple-free version of their ugliest visions. They barge forward. They take a better look. Dozens, hundreds, too many to count. Grouped in twos and threes, a mass of fluttering ties and reeling legs and handbags spilling secret things. No one wants to miss the moment.

Anger, panic, fear.

Joy feels none of it, lying here, all the rigidity blown out of her body.

Before order is established by the police, the police who have been here all along, the four linked witnesses see Joy's left ear. They see the whorl is plugged with blood.

Probably. This is probably what they see. These four were the first to move towards her, we can be sure of that, and a glass of some kind shattered, we know that much. But it is just possible that none of them got close enough to see something like blood in the ear.

And if Joy perceives anything at all, unconscious on the floor, forced inwards by the impact, it is some runny-coloured scene from the past.

The time on the first Tube of a Tuesday, maybe, when a shambling bald man in a comedy coat looked at her, a look too long and eager. When she realised he was wanking (wanking!) her shocked hand threw coffee on his crotch and caused the tramp to recoil with a whimper-sob which, as it expanded in the otherwise empty carriage, made her feel like the worst kind of woman in the world.

Or Wimbledon. She may see that. The scene she's edited and improved in the cutting room of her mind so many times but which now and then, like a botched punchline, comes out its own way, refusing to be shaped.

There is a long queue for the ladies' lavatory. She has to take him to the ladies' lavatory. Too small to go to the men's on his own.

In the line there are sun hats. Flip-flops. The occasional cagoule.

Joy is holding him in her arms. Smell of sugar, wet wipes, factor 50. Getting heavy to carry so she sets him down.

The stretch of queue behind them becomes longer and thinner. The tract in front becomes short and fat. Someone sighs. A woman looks at her watch. People take sidesteps and discuss the weather. It is raining but they are sheltered. They discuss rain. A radio clears its throat.

At first she ignores him, the stranger who has appeared at her side. He is standing too close. It is irritating. But if you mention these things you can create a scene. She shuffles to her left, holding her nephew's hand.

The stranger leans into her ear. 'Gimme your money or the kid gets it.'

Back straightens. Grip on child tightens. But when she swivels she sees, not a stranger, but Peter.

'Sorry,' he says, 'just a little joke.'

'What the fuck are you doing here?'

'Client do. Did I not mention?'

'You know very well you didn't mention.'

'You're here with . . .'

'Yes, your wife.'

'Well I *definitely* mentioned it to one of you.'

She looks down and sees the child jigging his leg. Sure sign he can't hold on much longer. Red light on her BlackBerry pulsing.

'Don't mind me, I'm in no hurry to get back to those Big Four fuckers.'

She strokes the rollerball. Sighs. Needed in the office tonight.

'Gorgeous, you need to relax,' he says, shouldering his way into the queue, hugging her from behind. She feels his hot breath in her ear.

'Stop, he might mention to you-know-who.'

Lets go of her nephew's hand now. Now or later. Lets go.

'A spy in our midst? Poor little tyke looks more concerned with pissing himself.'

Only seven or eight people ahead of them now. Only seven or eight as he slips his hand inside her summer jacket. Six or seven as under cover of cotton he feeds his fingers, cold at first, past her belt buckle and into her knickers, all these oblivious people huddled around them, wide-rimmed hats shading his movements from view.

'Cut it out,' she says, 'Christine could walk past.'

The boy touching a dent in the wall. Hint of sister's disapproving curl in his lip. Should stop him playing with chocolate wrappers by the wall.

She can feel her knickers soaking through and his stubble on her neck and people's shadows dappling the ground around them and his fingertip in the right place.

Feels something brushing her ankle. Ignores it. Nephew within reach, looks and sees him distracted with the wrappers, within reach, and she is losing herself in pleasure.

Body beginning to tense, anticipating orgasm. Would only take a few minutes more. Has to concentrate with all the concentration she's got not to sigh and submit. Enough, this is silly, enough, stop it. Pulls Peter's hand out into the open.

Then she looks to her left, and her right, and swallows, and repeats the movements, and the child is gone.

But first she looked and saw him playing with the wrappers and thought a good auntie wouldn't let him touch litter and sensed Peter's hand slipping down there.

Then she felt a shiver building and looked left and he wasn't there.

And the way she swallowed and did a pirouette and couldn't see him.

But before all that she let go of the boy's hand and told Peter Stop It.

She said Stop It and ended the pleasure even though she'd been babysitting for the last two days and having sometimes dull dates with Dennis and deserved a second's release.

But first the child was jigging his leg and the BlackBerry was flashing and she checked an email.

Then she looked to the wall and thought of how he'd inherited that curl in his lip.

Looked to the wall and he wasn't there and she was left with the weak feeling Peter was playing a joke.

But first Peter was pressed into her back with his fingers in her knickers and why would she let him do that when the boy was near?

And as she runs up and down the line moving in an abstract unstructured way breathing with awful desperate effort she goes through each link in the chain of events but cannot make them properly cohere.

Peter making her pause for a second says, 'It'll get out we were cosy, say I just arrived, saw you running.'

He gets her to repeat it, like she's the child, like it's the important lesson of the day: 'Say you just arrived, saw me running.'

'It will be OK,' he says, 'you go there, me here, bugger won't have tottered far.'

Just arrived, saw me running. Just arrived, saw me running. A statement strung into the chain of events, becoming fact. He just arrived and saw me running.

Some of the words she might or might not hear, lying in this building, face down on the stone.

Dennis

I HAVEN'T seen you for a while, Counsellor, but actually it has been rather a good few weeks, both on the university front and the cerebral-but-nonetheless-highly-commercial book front, yes, really rather a good few weeks on both fronts, I was thinking that in the hospital today, sitting in her new room, really quite positive, things as they say coming together, and in truth, though I shouldn't admit it, just being in the hospital day after day, seeing Joy-Joy lying there with the tube for fluids and nutrients, and the ventilator machine wheezing, the tube in the windpipe lifting the lungs, the contortionately polite professionals pricking her skin, moving her minutely to avoid bed sores, checking Do I need tea, asking Do I want a custard cream (no Jaffas, Counsellor, sadly no no no), just all of that makes me pleased with my own body's elastic power, its stubborn self-sufficiency, the obstinate miracle of its *working*.

The blankness in her face is the only upsetting thing. Awful and vacant, like a tragedy mask. But I am feeling positive. The people with printouts and clipboards say fifty–fifty. When is any chance better than fifty–fifty?

Yes. Exactly. Yes.

Her face is like a mask now, but even giving the speech it seemed somehow alien. The microphone came alive in a hailstorm of spittle. She squinted down at us, stammering as she spoke, imprecise with her words, more like me than her. Something in her eyes looked surprised by the nonsensical story coming from her lips, and I'd only seen her like that once before, only once before had I seen her features hold that unleashed look you get when the cupboard is being cleared, the cupboard in the back of your brain, the one full of secrets and corpses.[21] Her make-up looked thick and strange, a Tim Burton version of her everyday self. Yet she was Joy-Joy. She was my wife. Five foot nine, long slim limbs, a careful smoothness to her neck and chest, quick to smile but slow to laugh, keener on a good chicken sandwich than a Michelin-starred supper, beautiful, faithful, unfaithful, kind, cruel, a secret reader of trashy magazines, an unashamed follower of Fashion. A person who became depressed.

The new room? Oh, very nice, yes, thank you, and I fought hard to get her moved to that room, it's one of the reasons I'm so upbeat. A good view from the window. I'm often looking out of that window. Sky moves through a tree. Clouds pucker here and there. The ventilator hisses and her stretched chest lifts. When I think of my mother, long dead now, it is in a room like this, sleepy and clean, lying still, wearing blue. If someone vanishes you dress your memory of them, don't you? Imagine where they'd be, construct details to fill the

[21] (The time I checked her phone – in the twenty-first century a person's phone is the clearest window onto their soul, don't you think, their messages, their pet names, their pictures, the SIM card that is a deeper form of truth – and asked her if she was sleeping with Peter.)

gaps, make the image less abstract. Sometimes I wander away from her, from Joy-Joy, into another wing of the hospital, to give others a chance to visit, and I pace around, texting myself thoughts. There's a noticeboard under a skylight in one corridor, and it's headed 'Have You Seen Any of These People?', and beneath that question is a confused reverie of faces, patchworked photographs of people who, by virtue of some illness, accident or escape, have been reported lost; so many of the pictures blurry or faded beyond their age. Impossible not to look at that noticeboard. It fixes you to the floor. The sheer variety of faces and trivia. All the ways you can be missing and missed.

Beg your pardon?

Probably. Probably Joy-Joy is peaceful, comfortable. She looks peaceful but you cannot really tell. It never was easy to reach the reality of my wife. Things you thought you knew about her would vanish in an instant, as if never really there. Her perceptions of herself and others were always (I'd say) in flight, in flux, and it was true even of her father, the man she loved most in the world, she would constantly reinvent him, scrub him out and start again, long after he was dead. He worked in bars, first in America and then in England – a sarcastic old chap, by all accounts, funny but not friendly, a terrible gambler, wooed Joy's rich mother with a brand of cool, almost cold, charisma. Joy-Joy herself spoke of him this way for a while, but as time gave her distance from his death she made him a minor god, forgot his gambling debts, described him as warm and welcoming, a tragic figure who would never have killed himself but for the cancer. She liked to recreate people according to some private ambition of her own, and as her ambition changed, as her standards shifted, so did that person. But it was all down to the pursuit of perfection, you understand. A restlessness with the plain grey truth: that was her only flaw.

There's a man down the corridor who sobs and gurgles a lot. Sometimes when the nurse goes in she wakes him (I think) from a vast dream, because he doesn't seem to know what's going on, or where he is, and cries out What The Fuck?, or on occasion, when confusion puts a pause in his thoughts, What The Fu—? But it's better to listen to his swearing than his sobbing. Better his life be an interrupted obscenity than one long sob.

In the months after Wimbledon she seemed to be growing stronger, more determined to find the boy than ever. She said she could hear his voice in her head, urging her on. Of course she would get upset if we spent a weekend pursuing a tip-off that came to nothing, wandering through a Gypsy camp in Cyprus and realising this woman wanted to sell us her baby, of course she would cry then, but in general she was continuing with the search, following up on sightings and leads, staying in hotels all over Europe, searching sometimes with me, sometimes with journalists, never with her sister, often alone. She got pregnant, we got married, she looked set to get stronger and stronger, and then a week or two after the ceremony, only a week or two, she decided she could not bear to have a child after all, for what if she proved careless again, and I tried to persuade her, tried to tell her it was my last chance at fatherhood, and her doctor convinced her to think it over for a while, suspected she might merely have been going through a phase (for you medical types everything's a phase, is it not, ha ha, you've seen so much of life), but her mind was made up, and I realised I'd never be what I thought I'd always be, which is a – please don't laugh – a family man.

I prefer to be alone with Joy-Joy, but often Annie arrives. It is good that she comes but suddenly I feel the need to, yes, to perform a little. I realise it is not enough to sit there slumped, considering the sky and the tree. The room is so clean and pristine, has such a finished feel, that it seems rude not to act dead in it, but with Annie there everything acquires the air of some auspicious entertainment, and I must haul myself out of nothingness and partake in the show. She wants to look at photographs, for example, and discuss them, which is sweet. I can show you pictures of her with my son, Annie said this morning. Pictures of the two of them together before he went missing. You probably don't want to see the pictures but they are here, Dennis, photos of Joy and my son, if you'd like to see.

They found a note, you know. From the pocket of her favourite skirt, bundled into a plastic bag in her office, inexplicably muddied, and the police have shared it with me (the note) for it is addressed to me, it is a note for me, it is mine, one of the things that has been left behind, and her colleagues visit, and my cousins visit, and they all tell me that it will be fine, and they are so quick to say this, to deliver elegantly choreographed little lectures on life, and I wonder, why didn't anyone say, on my wedding day, why didn't anyone say to me, Dennis, old Dennis, Dennis old boy, there's a problem here, a real problem, and the problem is this: she doesn't love you, it's plain she doesn't love you. She. Does not. Love you. If I say the words out loud they arrive like that, not long but short, and it feels just right, it feels just about right, just about true, and it must be true, mustn't it? Because you can cheat on a person but still love them, maybe, possibly, perhaps, but you can't love them and want to take your life, wreck their life, can you? I consider these questions as part of the constant background battle of whose fault is it and why has this happened. The days fade down to a drowsy flicker behind my eyes.

Annie was right. I did not want to see her fucking pictures.

Sorry.

Sorry?

Oh do not misunderstand me Counsellor! I am feeling positive. I am content. I have friends. And I got that literary agent I always wanted.

The so-called Abby Aardvark! Indeed. Yes, yes.

She says the market is . . . I believe the word she used was *terrible* . . . but that if I make a few small changes (like taking the whole thing out of iambic pentameter, and applying a scalpel to the overwritten bits[22]), that if I make these changes the book could be a reasonable prospect for some small imprint trying to prove there is more to books than ghostwritten memoirs of gravity-defying surgery on bottoms or breasts.

Well, yes. The book may bring in some money but actually all that (the financial side of my life) is, ha, less pressing now. The student who filed a complaint against me is currently in the midst of her own disciplinary process. It seems that in pursuit of the not-all-that-objectionable aim of ending factory farming she joined an objectionably aggressive march through London, a march partly inspired by the poultry

[22] Even though I can't help thinking *all* writing is overwriting, Counsellor, for it's hardly as if any book *needs* to be written, is *required* by the world.

revelations in the press these last few weeks, a march which appears to have ended abruptly on the outskirts of Peckham when she paused to assault a surprisingly thin kebab-shop owner. She denied all involvement when the police came calling, but CCTV footage clearly shows her and a more muscular acquaintance jumping over napkin holders and trays of soggy salad, approaching the vertical spinning griller on which a glossy grey leg of sweating doner rotated, freeing a great flap of rubbery meat from said sweaty leg with a machete-like instrument, and beating the poor floored Turk around the cheeks with it (facial cheeks, initially). When that event came to light she became rather less crazed in her pursuit of my career, and her father coincidentally – ha ha – declared his intention to stand down from the Board of Governors. Too busy with his charity commitments, he said. The committee has cleared me of all charges. I start back on, yes, on Monday. Ha ha ha. You have to laugh, don't you, when people get their comeuppance?

Don't you agree, though?

Don't you like to see the *sinners punished*, the *righteous saved*?

I do not believe you. Ha! I simply do not, Counsellor. Because for all of us that's the most grimly satisfying thing, I think, in any story, ha, it really is, it makes us who we are, yes, sorry, did you say something?

Oh forgive me, ha, I was chuckling so hard, I thought you said something. I feel you have seen the best and worst of me and yet, and yet, you remain so opaque . . . But then does *anyone* really know all that much about you, do *you* even know that much about you? I wonder whether you spend so much time in other people's heads you lose, from time to time, a sense of who you are?

Really?

Oh good.

That is good, and I thank you, I *will* have some water, water would be lovely, that is better, that is better, I thank you kindly for your concern. And I should make sure I enjoy these refreshments, actually, because this will be the last time I come here.

At your clinic? Ha ha, no no, that will not be necessary, thank you. I think I now know as much about my feelings, my internal workings, as I want to know, yes, and obviously there are still things I don't understand, for example, for example, I'm not sure I'll ever understand – ha ha, you have to laugh, it's so slapstick, the whole thing – why she did it there, in front of so many people. Without the note I would not believe it, the note and the pile of papers on the dresser, the columns and rows of facts, sort codes and phone numbers that go on and on and on without pause, would not believe she'd thrown herself off there deliberately, would not wonder why I stayed silent that Friday morning when I sensed something strange, ha, why I did not get out of bed but instead lay there, on my side, facing the wall, ha, why I didn't run downstairs after her but instead lay listening to the footsteps, loud then quiet down the stairs, ha ha, the key-jangle and the zipping sound from her bag and the nothing which followed as her body blended with the city, the bedroom . . . the whole house we shared . . . shaking with cars heading to Upper Street and Essex Road. Do you know why I didn't say anything to stop her? You'll tell me, Counsellor, won't you, if you find out? A bad time for me to have been lost for words, no? Ha ha ha. Ha ha ha ha ha. Ha ha ha ha ha ha ha ha ha ha ha ha ha ha ha ha ha ha ha ha ha ha ha ha ha ha ha ha ha ha ha ha ha ha ha ha ha ha ha ha ha ha ha ha ha ha ha.

Untimed Fragment

IN THE room people come and go, talking of television. Down the hall a person is practising the discrete arts of sighing and sobbing, slowly finding perfect pitch. The light soaking through Joy's eyelids is a bulging blue. She feels a flannel on her face. She wants to open her eyes. She wants to keep them closed. Dad's voice echoes in some lit bit of her brain: *Go easy on yourself*. Never good at taking his own advice, her dad. The great parental prerogative. Someone says *urinalysis*. Someone else says *Narcan*. Both young feminine voices, but croaky at the edges, a hint of the weary women they mustn't become. There is the soft slosh of liquid in bags. The voices exchange views on whether the girl group that are still in the competition are a bunch of chavvy tramps with shit hair or whether in fact the black one can sing and it's just bad luck that they've got the worst mentor. Her neck feels wrapped in another neck. She senses the ceiling is sinking. A machine beeps. Means she is alive. Never one for reality TV, but had a brief thing for hospital dramas. Fictions of disaster. Carefully crafted loss. Every day we invent the stories of our lives. Another machine noise, like a *woo-wooh*, a half-forgotten song stuck in her head. Feeling disembodied, her body a puppet for which she can't quite reach the strings, but if she concentrates hard and harder still on lifting her lids the bulging blue takes on a green underglow, becomes a deep complex sea. Her sister had a favourite dolly she took everywhere. To the shops. To the beach. White hair. Unnatural tan. Sea-green eyes. She hears feet departing, then heavier steps coming close. A man's breath, full of chewing gum and burnt toast, turns her forehead firm. The sensation tingles and mingles with the feeling of warm torchlight on her lids. Every other feeling bombed away. She imagines her own eyelashes, great lunar crescents, flitting open to give this guy the fright of his life, but the machine beep stays steady and the thought slithers away like a . . . no, nothing like a snake at all.

Last week, you left your phone at home.

And?

Nothing.

Frankly, Dennis, I'd prefer to talk about *something*, or else smoke in silence.

You think they like me, your work colleagues?

You were invited, you're my husband, they like you.

What about Peter?

I'm going back in.

Wait and I'll go back in with you. Assuming you'd, yes, like me to.

It's not a question of what *I'd* like. Come back in if *you'd* like.

Well, I'd like to if you'd like me to.

Make your own decision, Dennis. You'll find it refreshing.

Is it just me or would you rather I went home?

It's completely your choice! Come back in if you think you've got more to say to the boring lawyers.

You want me to leave.

Come on.

I'll leave.

Dennis, come on, that's not what I'm saying.

But it never *is* what you're saying, is it? It's the things you don't say.

In this room the air is thick like overstewed tea. Definitive moments swim through dreams and you lie here being tended to, shuffling through a pack of memories in your mind, a fat deck of days. And, if you realise anything at all, it's that they can be dealt in any order; it makes no difference which order, or which voice; Lemme shuffle them this way; You may be the one to, yes, do the proverbial shuffling; Hi Miss Stephens no your shuffling is brilliant. The Sigh Sobber down the hall experiments with more bass and the odd gargled noun like *Jesus* or *Essex*. She misses his swearing days, where he'd shout *Fuck!* in surprise now and then. Once last spring she played Scrabble with Christine on a little travel set at the City Tennis Club, too tired to hit more balls. Christine tiled out a proper noun, a brand name, something like Pepsi, and Joy reminded her that only limited proper nouns are allowed, those determined by a limited word list drawing on the Collins dictionary, and Christine replied, a rare smug plumpness in her voice, that new rules actually came in three days ago, that the manufacturer is now allowing place names people names company names and brands, has actually rewritten the rule book to allow an element of popular culture into the game, and Joy, thinking of her childhood Scrabble battles, complete with cool milk and custard creams, of the way her mother would check the dictionary in cases of irrevocable family dispute, said out loud in a way that caused Christine to twitch: *Fucking hell, people can't keep changing the rules!* The Sigh Sobber is no longer sighing or sobbing, certainly not swearing, just weeping with such a hushed sadness that . . . One of the female voices from before is back. Her perfume is overcooked. She says *Doctor Chapman is there anything I can do to help*, which, depending on the precise shape of her body language, could mean *Doctor Chapman is there anything I can do to help* and/or, concurrently or in the alternative, *Doctor Chapman let's have babies*. In the silence Joy fancies she can sense the good doctor weighing this up, probably taking from the breast pocket of his white coat a rather expensive pen, giving the nurse the look of deep highly controlled concern all doctors come to master, glancing down at his clipboard while slowly introducing a tremor of disinterested thoughtfulness into his features (an equally important doctorly expression, adaptable to both patients and subordinates). No thank you, Nurse, nothing to do right now. *What's your view, Doctor?* Hard to say. A three on the GCS. If she comes out of it, probably some damage. Visitors still waiting? *Yes, Doctor, shall I bring them in?*

It's over.

I love you.

You're married.

I love you.

You're married to Christine.

And you, soon, to Dennis.

It's over.
Is it mine?
It's his.
Are you sure?
It's his.
I love you.
You love *you*.
Yes, well, that's true too.

She can picture the room clearly now, can see it through the prison bars her own lashes make. The ceiling lowering slowly, as if this is the sea and she – bottom-dwelling in a place of great pressure – is gradually beginning to surface. Always wanted to be a mother. But what if she lost another young life? Maybe her dad thought she'd be OK without him. Maybe he had his own unknowable reasons. Maybe she can forgive him for going. Maybe maybe maybe. Her sister was out with Dad in the rain one Sunday. Didn't take the favourite dolly. Worried it would get wet. Should have outgrown it by now, surely, but still worried it would get wet! Mum downstairs doing a roast, plates clinking in the kitchen. Joy hated the dolly because Annie loved it so much. Did not realise this then, that you can despise something just because another person loves it. Scent of roast chicken wafted up the stairs. Joy sneaked into her sister's room. Took the dolly out of its box. Snapped one leg clean off. Sister, later, enraged, crying in the car, Mum wailing too, and after that the sad sound windscreen wipers make, rain stealing outlines from things. Annie wanted to know who had done it. But no one had done it. One of those things. And her shame for that mean deed has not lessened in the years since. It has grown deeper, cutting a groove within which her wider need for forgiveness sits.

Auntie Joy, why is Cretine with us?

*Chris*tine!

Why is she with us?

She's my friend, sweetie.

Why?

Because she is, she's my friend.

Why?

She does nice things, like giving us these strawberries.

You're my friend, Auntie Joy.

Don't eat the green bit.

Why are you smiling, Auntie Joy?

Because I'm happy.

Why?

Because I love you.

Why?

Nothing to do right now. Listen, just listen. She listens for the Sigh Sobber Turned Weeper, but there is no fresh sound coming from him, only the afterhum of the noise he once made, and other voices stirring within that hum, shapeless and strange. Perhaps there are always gaps in the way we feel. Perhaps happiness is best kept as a side effect. Perhaps people swallow fictions quicker than facts. Perhaps perhaps perhaps perhaps. The ceiling like a bright hydraulic stage comes lower, lower still. Lies catch a current, find a life of their own. She is floating upwards, feels her lashes getting loose with stinging salt. Her limbs twitch. Machine beeps cluster. Feeling light, lighter, like a bag catching a current, plastic but alive, floating to meet the stage halfway. In heavy supportive water with the surface coming soon she is not sure if her body struggles to get out or to stay in. Part of her, dead tired, wants to disappear down here, find Ben – there, done, she has named him, *Ben* – and all the other vanished children here and there, sinking or floating in the gossamer light, waving or drowning, happy or sad, find them drifting in timeless places, dark spaces deeper than death. Through walls come the words *What the fuck?* – the Sigh Sobber lives! – and she tries to summon some of his energy, energy and imagination, qualities which save few lives but on which she relies, for they bring something of the world's colour into being, a consolation prize of a kind, and she must not fall asleep, not now, just must not sleep.

Peter

Dear Doctor Odd,

It has been several months since we discussed the side benefits of elastic bands. Months in which you seem to have lost interest in the City's occupational health. But, if my sources are correct, you still deal in paper, so I've enclosed a little gift with this note.

That's the last of my stash of Hanger-branded office supplies. As you probably guessed when I stopped turning up for our little chats, I am no longer in active employment there. Bananagate, I must report, did not go down well. And although I despise half the people I worked with, I miss the firm a little more than I thought I would. In this flat the days are grey. Cloud grey. Whale grey. Dirty tea towel. Aged paper. In France, to be 'grey' (*être gris*) means to be drunk. And to be extremely drunk? That's to be 'black' (*être noir*). Did you know that, at all?

I am a little drunk, writing this. I have found it helpful of late to be a little drunk at all times.

We get used to repetition, don't we? It provides a framework. The documents I'd draft when a company had gone into admin, the witness statements and the notices, they'd all be adaptations of something done before. I'd find pro forma templates wherever I turned. There were times when I felt all of us at the firm existed in a kind of template. The things we said and did had a recycled quality to them. We said them and did them in a dead, duplicated way. Unique things were welcomed at Hanger's, but they had to be uniformly unique – I'd wear turquoise cufflinks every second Friday, but never more turquoise than the ones the others wore. And with all this there was the feeling that one day some crazy motherfucker would hack into the know-how systems, erase every precedent, and leave us all lost.

At 8.30 a.m. on Friday 20 January 2006 a commuter passing over one of London's bridges looked out of a train window. What he saw made him call the police. He told them he feared he was hallucinating. But he was not hallucinating. By lunchtime Sky News had set up an uninterrupted live feed. Tens of thousands of Londoners flocked to the banks of the Thames.

The River Thames Whale. I have just looked him up on my ultra-fast broadband, to better remind myself of the details. And it turns out that, despite the resemblance to my father-in-law, the bottlenose that got lost in London that January was in fact a *she*. Did you know that? Strange, actually, because for two days in January 2006 the news contained nothing but information about the whale, and I followed the rescue attempts closely, yet at no time did I realise it was a female bottlenose I was looking at. Somewhere in the cross-current of perceptions I lost a salient fact. I now know how Tiny Tony O felt all those years ago, when he had that unfortunate mix-up with the Thai bar worker. Back in the days when he had trouble getting women. The days when women liked men to be taller than them.

Everything would have felt foreign to her: the sandy banks, the five-foot depth, the dinosaur rumble of helicopters, loudspeakers, trains on tracks. All these noises reverberating in the whale's exquisite ear bones, hard and dense, pitchfork-fine. Onlookers waded in, trying to guide her back into the deep. An environmental-science student going by the unimprovable name of Edwin Timewell whispered messages of support into the shallows.

I've developed a purely ironic attachment to daytime TV. Unlike evening TV, there is no sense of shared vision. If you're floating in the higher channels before dark it's probably just you and some chronic old grandma watching, observing the can-opener that is also a cat flap, navigating ingenious products that are always in stock. Sometimes when I go to bed I leave it on low, buzzing through the wall. A TV playing to an empty room: the only thing spookier is no sound at all. And the next morning I'll pick up the remote, start the process again, catch the chatter of property shows on 124. I barely feel alone. Loneliness is the half-second wait while the screen sputters to life, a tiny dot becoming planet-sized.

Around every fact there are a thousand theories. Why was she there? Disease, parasite infection, pollution? Any one of these could disorientate a whale. Submarines, ships, military sonar? NATO preparing messages of war, sending Nature's signalling off track? That or the simple hunt for food, the old primeval fear of not having enough to eat, a wrong turn on the way to the North Atlantic, swimming too far south in the search for squid. I can see why you'd go searching for squid. Thai Chilli Squid was my favourite dish at the Icarus.

A few days after Christine confirmed she wasn't coming back, I bumped into Dennis at the hospital. During Joy's time there our visiting schedules clashed once or twice. We were silent at her bedside, but on the asphalt, two men moving on, we discussed going for a beer. He was busy, and I needed to get back to the flat, so we left it. Probably best to avoid a drink with that misery guts anyway. Joy was beginning to improve, he was back in proper employment, some pretentious publisher had bought his book – he had everything he wanted, in short, and yet he seemed to have become broken in the getting of it. All his fizzy enthusiasm had gone flat, become a sort of sour hysteria. I explained as much to Nurse Covas Callas, a kind and moderately alluring girl who I subsequently invited to share coffee with me. She smiled and said she wasn't attracted to 'conventionally handsome' men. That made me laugh for a long hard time. Interesting how some girls think flaws add colour: a stammer, a scar, terrible teeth. They think it amounts to 'character', that elusive magnetic thing. Their world is not ours, Doctor Odd. We are tuned to different channels.

The beast showed signs of flexion when briefly stranded and the next morning, 21 January, a vet in the marine rescue team expressed concerns that it was not swimming in a determined manner. I loved that choice of words: 'determined manner'. It's the kind of thing you'd say in your clever nasal way.

I have been meaning to get round to Mum and Dad's, to replace that light bulb. But I get distracted watching DVDs and arranging their boxes on the shelves. I make little lists for myself these days: take out bins, change light bulb, rearrange DVDs. During office days I never thought about my parents much. But now I do. As I wander through London alone I see planes waiting to touch down at City Airport, flickering in the fog, and I think about my childhood a lot. Would it make a difference to your analysis, out of interest, if I told you I had a tricky time at school? My memories of happy childhood times shame me with their thinness. The lack of nostalgia they gather. One C Team football game here. One split knee there. I can only hope that by the time I've finished this letter they will feel different, somehow, my memories. Less flimsily fake. More like holy wishful things that transcend the walls, the walls which are cloud grey, whale grey, dirty tea towel, aged paper.

By the time Christine and I got to Battersea Bridge the banks were five-deep with bodies. The London Eye downstream stood still. Christine said this was the sort of sight Joy wouldn't want to miss so we tried, with no success, to phone her. We elbowed our way through the soft jostle of coats and scarves and found ourselves at the water's edge. The air smelt of damp clothes and fast-food farts. We were cold and miserable. Vets had decided to deliberately beach the bottlenose at low tide, then winch her onto a rescue barge. It sounded exciting, but the operation was taking shape under tarpaulin – slowly, and in silence.

And then it happened. After what felt like hours, we finally got the glimpse we wanted. A seven-tonne beast hoisted high in the air.

'Wow,' Christine said.

'Wow,' I said.

It was a sight so strange it made us small again, instilled in us that toddler trait of wide-eyed awe, faithfully repeating the already said. Wow. Wow. From our vantage point she looked like a sleek black bomb, an effete missile waiting to be loaded onto a plane destined for Iraq or Afghanistan, somewhere we'd never been but had seen on screen. There was an odd kind of truth to the moment, a whale hanging in the sky. It contained an unleashing from our daily lives.

She had many identities, some betraying the same gender mistake I made. Wally in the *Sun*. Whaley in the *Mirror*. The *Daily Mail* called her Willy and in *The*

Times she was Wilma the Whale and/or the Prince or Princess of Whales. The *Sun* got bored of Wally and rechristened her Celebrity Big Blubber for a TV tie-in. The barge swept her away to Margate, a place called Shivering Sands.

Do you know what I miss? I miss the hidden energies you get in air-conditioned air. The electrical currents of whispered secrets. Friday flirtations at departmental functions. The way you could meet your best friend's girlfriend and steal from her a glance or smile, no more, just enough to feel alive. There was no intention to harm. Eye contact over crisp cold wine. The pout of a mouth as smoke's blown out. You would shore up such moments against your weekend, keeping them charged in your mind until the tranquil melancholy of Sunday evening, when the dishwasher had finished its cycle, and the unread newspapers nagged, and shirts hung creased in the withering light. Monday's alarm always had a panicked, risky ring that Tuesday's could only echo. I'd wake to the faint scent of Christine's clammy-sweet skin as she stretched to hit Snooze. We would spend ten minutes huddled and quiet, feeling our way back into the world. And after brushing fuzzed teeth, eating dry toast, journeying underground with millions of other Londoners, our office seemed luminous and fecund. Every phone call after nine could bring a glamorous case, or a pay raise, or the offer of some fantastic new role we'd never known was there. It didn't matter that the phone calls never did bring these things. The possibility kept us content.

Shivering Sands. The Internet says that as night fell on the barge the medics monitored her breathing for signs of stress. I imagine this whole circus of survival taking place in space, somehow, on some faraway planet, but it was Margate, just Margate, England. It must have been quite something, though, don't you think, to see the dreamy sway of torch beams criss-crossing in the dark, catching patches of water, sky, or the whale's scarred skin? They had the barge floodlights on low. Just enough glow for the helicopters overhead to keep the live feed going. She was at eight breaths a minute. Eight breaths a minute seemed encouraging. She'd been taking oxygen at that rate in the river. Barge travel did not disagree with her, or rather was only as disagreeable as the river itself – narrow, noisy, shallow.

Sometimes something happens which seems to rewrite the rules of what is thinkable. It was like that on the search through Wimbledon the previous summer, me and Christine and forty-odd officers and locals in streets and fields, our flashlights finding insects and dust, all of us silent in a long shining line, our sense of purpose dwindling with each baby step we took. And I felt an odd distant grief, didn't I, wandering through the night, a sorrow shaded with relief that the affair had stayed secret, and only later could I think myself into the marrow of that small boy's bones.

Just before 7 p.m. the breathing went to eight,

ten, twelve breaths a minute. The veterinary pathologist on board the barge produced a bottle of Large Animal Immobilon. Fourteen, sixteen, eighteen. Euthanasia seemed the kindest way. Twenty. Twenty-two. With this strong delicate creature convulsing he loaded the syringe, tried to navigate the wounds on the underbelly – the rub of the riverbed, the bruise of passing boats, the gashes in the grey flesh that looked (did they?) like a split in the Great British sky. Finally the needle pierced her thick skin. Dehydration, muscle damage, failing kidneys. The autopsy showed a wet plastic bag in her stomach, along with algae and a single potato. Sea-glimpsed things, swallowed half hopeful from the river's floor. The twistedly perfect details that stay lodged in your soul. Long after the lights have gone off, long after the live feed has stopped.

I bet you like it, don't you, me talking about souls the way you used to talk about souls, you putting hope in my mouth? Does it make you smile that at this point I want to believe, to believe that the boredom and betrayals of those years, the sex and con calls and aimless dogshit days, had some sort of form and coherence?

The charity shop has done well out of my shattered marriage. Christine decided she didn't want most of her old stuff, preferred to start afresh with Tiny Tony O. Tiny Tony! What a humiliating choice! I went round there, to his nasty little maisonette, shouting a bit, boozed up, aiming the occasional fist at his already-injured nose. And when things calmed down, and I asked her to come back, asked her in as many different voices as I could muster, all she said was 'Take my things to the charity shop'. I started to explain about my trainee – I'm sure now, almost sure, it's the trainee she knows about; not Joy, not the others, just that meaningless fling with Jess – and she stood there without a blink or a tear. It took an age for her to speak again, and when the words came I barely heard them over my own heartbeat. 'I wanted you to love me,' she whispered. 'I wanted you to love *me*.'

There was a squat freckled man behind the counter. If he was a toadstool you'd avoid him. Avoid him as a man, too, as a rule. And it took some time to untangle Christine's things from mine, to get them organised, but now it's done, almost done, it's as if she was never here, and it makes me a little sick to think it is that simple, that the sky changes one day, a cloud spreads itself out, and someone you love in your own imperfect way disappears into the grey. They disappear, but your failures stay. They remain undiminished. You squirm and plead with yourself but the same base shadow remains, a dark limbless thing, the shape of the things you've done, the shape – you eventually realise – of *you*, you are the monster, you do not see it at first but then you do, that this shadow trailing behind is yours, no outlined horns or extra eyes, no brutal despicable fangs, just you, pinstriped and pleading, wishing you could be better. I was a monster but I loved her and sometimes I tried to be better.

It didn't make the televised news until later, but we saw it that night, Christine and I, a thin column of text huddled between Eriksson's Football Corruption Claims and an ad for a high-impact bra, and we knew. *Remains of Child Found in Thames*. We read all the pages about the whale, about how a team from the National History Museum travelled to Gravesend to bag up her bones, and then the pieces about how the divers helping in the rescue bid had found old boots, drowned cats, passports, remote controls, condoms, relics of sex and death and truth and television, and then we read that spindly story and we knew, the way you know something without thought, like when you're sorry or sad.

The police said the remains would have been washed out with only two further turns of the tide. They said there were signs of recent struggle. So his body, such as it was, had not been waiting in the water since summer. After Wimbledon, Ben went somewhere with someone. I do not know who, or why, though I think about it every day. He was killed, and bagged, and dropped in the Thames. And you come to realise, don't you, that the facts just show you gaps. Even the scientific details, the most miraculous facts, the way everything a person eats bears the trace of the soil in which it was grown or reared, the way you can look in someone's bones and find the hint of a strawberry seed, can compare soil samples around the world until you're sure the fruit came from some unceasingly still place far from car horns and headlights that supplies fruit to the world's greatest tennis tournament. Even hearing this, finding out what science can do, feeling the immensity of design, something humbling shaping the century, even in the midst of this grim epiphany you sense the facts just show you gaps. And once they've finished with the bones and have given up on catching the killer the family can burn them up, of course, the bones and other remains, and scatter the ashes on the Heath. Ash being blown every which way, mixing with air. A kind of closure, I suppose.

I rearrange the DVDs on the shelves, ordering them by Director or UK release date, and make myself a sandwich. I listen for the soft suck of the fridge door closing, as if Christine is there to close it. I consider a trip to the shops. There's always more action lists to make: phone parents, take out bins, pay water bill. I wander around London, watching planes circling the city, saintly sun-streaked things hoping to land, and increasingly where there are passenger jets I see nearby the malevolent gleam of a green-grey Chinook, a great urban insect made to keep the sky safe.

Today is my birthday. I bought a new suit on Upper Street and caught a film at the Screen on the Green. Afterwards I went walking through supermarket aisles but struggled in my search for the intended purchase, taking the wrong routes, peering through cracks in arousing packaging. And then straight ahead, in Poultry no less, I saw Joy. Still in the wheelchair, one leg in plaster, thumbing the buttons of a phone. Not a BlackBerry, she no longer works in the City, just a clumsy antique thing. So pale, so thin, but laughing. I heard the musical laugh, the one that filled the hours we stole together, and I looked up, saw it really was her. She was with Annie, her sister. Annie's body was arranged in a boxer's crouch and she was shuffling through cellophane trays of chicken breasts, sniffing them in a way that would make old Dennis proud. And there was a child there too, a pretty little girl with a deep stare, keen to carry the basket. With resolve Joy's sister turned the wheelchair in my direction – the wheels didn't seem to be moving, but I suppose they must have been – and I hurried away. I bought my knife from a different shop. For some jobs you need a brand-new thing, don't you? Wrapped and clean. Without history.

I've tried to call Christine, write to her, send gifts to her parents. I've done everything I possibly could. We can do what we can but there are things which flee or get lost or are just beyond our reach. I've decided some people are beyond our reach, Doctor Odd, blown too far by the years to hear us calling. We try to call out but the air gathers up our voice and there's no way we can reach them, not there, in that place, there's nothing we can do. There is only in the end the calling, the fact someone was trying to call, and I do not think anyone will call for me. I hear nothing but the shushing of the taps and the staticky cackle of the TV but the DVDs are all nicely arranged and the planes are still sinking into London and I spot the odd Chinook. I have not got all the way through my action list but the weatherman with his deeply flawed face says summer is coming. In summer Mum's defective light bulbs will be less of an issue. And it's not my birthday – I lied, I'm sorry – but I hope this gets to you, I hope you can read it despite the smudged full stops and shaky lines, because you seemed the best person to send my note to, the one most likely to understand. Everyone else has vanished. They have vanished, they have gone missing, and it seems I have waited until this moment to love them fully – waited until the moment they are no longer in my life. And when I climb into the bath with the knife, fully clothed in a fine new suit, this letter written, my brogues getting heavy, I'll try not to think of whatever awaits, whatever darkness, whatever nuance of night. I'll try to focus on the early-evening light slanting through the bathroom window, flirting with the surface of the water, and the colour it will catch when the blood blooms from my veins. I'll try to focus on that, in a determined manner, for as long as I can hold my breath

ACKNOWLEDGEMENTS

Thank you to everyone who gave me encouragement and advice as this book took shape. Skilled counsellors on whom I've relied include Clare Alexander, Jason Arthur, Anna Stein, Stephanie Sweeney, Emma Finnigan, Laurie Ip Fung Chun, Sally Riley, Suzanne Dean, Ed Caruana, Rebecca Lenkiewicz, Jennie Rooney, Ben Johnson, Robert and Elizabeth Lee, Peter and Pat Norman, and Amy. Thank you to all at William Heinemann, and thank you to all at Aitken Alexander Associates.